Washed Up

AMELIA J. RIVERS

To all those who followed their own path

One

JASPER WASHED up on my shore just like the rest of the ocean's garbage.

On moonless nights the Sirens went silent, resting their song. This one night a moon cycle, the silence permitted large debris to breach the Sirens' barriers. The morning after, our beaches were covered in artifacts and people. Like Jasper.

Salty brine tickled my nose as my eyes adjusted to the darkness. A mosaic of stars swept across the sky, but the thin thread from the flame in my lantern reflected orange on the rocky shore, just enough for me to see my next step. The gentle gurgle of the waves left foamy white across the sands, dotted with the sea's prizes and garbage. Sand slid beneath my boots on my slow trek.

It was on these moonless nights that people were most likely to wash up. Anomalies of another world, a slip into a crack that shouldn't have been. Despite the circumstances, they usually washed up alive. Some of the islanders felt it was a gift from the Sirens, not an absence of their duty; treasures to select from and new blood to add to our family lines.

For me, the Washed Up were something to leave for other Scavengers. They required care and resources, and my mother vehemently opposed bringing them into our house. But tonight was different.

I heard someone call *"Rainey,"* in the distance, but I ignored the other Scavenger as I pressed towards the rocky shore where treasures were more likely to get caught.

I crept along the coastline, tucked against the stony perimeter that trapped trinkets from the generous waves. The normal twist of hope curled in my veins. As a Scavenger, I picked through the treasures strewn on the beach and resold them to the island. The work was grueling and dangerous; without the aid of the moon, it was easy to misstep or trip. But with other Scavengers out on the beach, the last thing I wanted was a bright torch to show them the treasures I'd found. It was first come, first serve, and I wouldn't earn my land by giving my stuff to others.

Unlike most Scavengers, I'd stuck with it after multiple years instead of moving on to village life as either a merchant, farmer, fisherperson, or artisan. Without a natural talent for working with crafts and with thumbs that killed plants, fishing or cooking was the only option. I was more likely to tip a boat in the deep waters trying to remain still all day than I was to catch a fish, though, and after I almost burned my grandparents' house down following in my family's tradition of baking bread, I'd stuck with Scavenging. Besides, it was the fastest way to make trades to own my land. And I was good at it.

My expertise, so to say, was in mechanical objects. Even though our island didn't create metal items, enough people had washed up to show us how to use them. We'd learned quickly how to maintain and mold them with forging and metalwork. I could fix most of them and made good trades.

As the warm breeze carrying the promise of sun washed across my cheeks and my eyes drooped, I'd about given up my search. The disappointment of waiting for another moon cycle to own my land settling heavily in my heart, I noticed an unusual shape in the sparse light. Unlike the rigid edges of human creations, it was organic and uneven.

Instinct told me to move on, but my breath hitched at the possibilities of the Sirens' gift and final approval to own my land. As I edged closer, my heart slammed in my chest and my toes curled.

Finally. A Washed Up.

His clothes hung off him, waterlogged and drooping. Unlike some others, he didn't wear breeches, tie-based shirts, vests, or jackets. He didn't wear military gear from any land era, or scuba gear. He washed up in jeans, a t-shirt, and a flannel shirt. The stench of his world had washed away, leaving a white layer of salt crusting on his flesh and the sharp smell of the sea in his hair.

His still form sprawled on the beach. My throat tightened at not seeing the rise and fall of breath. Was he already dead? Had the Sirens sent me my last piece only to shatter my dreams? I bit my lip and moved closer.

With my boot, I toed a rounded object that made a metallic rattle as I watched him. Inching closer, I caught sight of his face: warm brown, with a square jaw, thick eyelashes, and dark tresses. His face wasn't marred by the rocks or nibbled by the creatures slithering beneath the dark waters. I blinked and cursed as an unnecessary blush stole across my face. Many in the village would be interested in him, though, if he was alive. Pushing my silly nerves down, I nudged his shoulder.

A gasp escaped my lips seeing his chest rise and fall as wheezy sounds escaped his lips. He was alive. *The Sirens had finally blessed me.*

My hands trembled as I knelt beside him, the crunch of shells beneath my boots breaking the still of the ocean air. I skimmed my hand over his drenched shirt.

His warmth soaked through, and my fingers lingered too long on his torso, confirming no serious injuries. Chiding myself, I moved to his sleeves. A watch on his right wrist glistened gold in the light of my lantern. I moved my fingers along his pockets, catching on a rectangular shape. He'd call it a phone, but it wouldn't work here.

Careful to not touch more than his sides, I lifted his hips from the ground: left side first, then right to expose his pockets. Sadly for him, they appeared empty aside from the phone. He wouldn't have much to trade for his care. But it was to my benefit that night. I rested him back on the ground and dusted my hands over my pants.

A brisk wind swirled from the waters, catching my attention. The horizon glowed in light blue as the sun readied to crest the border and start the new day, and later, the return of the moon. The other Scavengers, a dozen or so, were darkened forms that danced in shadows on the lightening beach, creeping slowly back home as they looked for final bits to gather. I should have been with them.

My eyes tracked back to him. No one else had noticed him. I'd have to deal with my mom, but I needed to harbor a Washed Up if I wanted my land. Even if she didn't like it.

The first rays of the sun pierced the horizon, and around his neck, the glint of gold reflected. I moved his collar, biting my lip as he grunted in his sleep. My fingers brushed against his warm skin, sending unwanted heat curling down my chilled arms and into my stomach. If I was going to harbor him, I'd need to reign in my foolish reactions. The thick chain of braided gold dipped below his white t-shirt. A place I wouldn't venture into.

Even if it was jewelry, something unhelpful to island life, it could catch a hefty trade value—especially with the elders who liked status symbols. Most would offer him the monthly harbor in exchange.

But that wasn't his lot. He was mine.

Even if he was my Washed Up, his jewelry belonged to him. Scavengers didn't steal; only claimed what was abandoned on the beach. And he was.

He was the final piece I needed to secure my land contract. I'd made trades, and had items ready to go, but until I cared for a Washed Up, I couldn't own the land I'd cared for and developed for years.

It was a tradition as old as our village. Land in our village was almost always inherited or cleared, not sold, so the traditions for sales were hazy. But when a plot was cleared, the landowners harbored the next Washed Up—a gift from the Sirens. Most of our village believed it was meant to bring continuing luck and fortune. We honored the Sirens by tending to their gifts.

Although the plot I wanted was not newly cleared, Molly, the landowner, was as superstitious as many who lived on the sea. She claimed the gesture of harboring a Washed Up was symbolic to our Siren foremothers. It wasn't. She just never believed I'd take a Washed Up. As my history had shown, I preferred inanimate gifts and left Washed Up on the beach to walk up to the village. She believed that I'd take her other offer—marry her son, Owen, and be gifted the land as a wedding present.

I wasn't going to marry her son. I'd rather live with my grandparents again and burn bread. But I also couldn't challenge her or the island's superstition or I'd be blamed for the storms, bad harvests, and bad catches.

To deny the tradition of the Sirens would bring their wrath.

My land would be cursed.

So Molly said.

With this Washed Up now an integral part to owning my uncursed land, I found myself hauling him up under his arms into my cart. He wasn't as heavy as some of the metal objects I hauled in, but he was dead weight and his body fought to stay down. He let out a groan as I accidently hit his arm against the metal bar of my cart. He'd certainly have a bruise, but not as many as the ones that were forming on my arms. With his torso in the cart from the waist up, I let his legs dangle in the air.

My eyes tracked home. Dark trees masked the house, but I knew the fight that waited with my mom. I needed the Washed Up for my land.

And it was just one cycle I had to care for him.

We made it back to my home, a simple but sturdy structure made of scraped-together pieces like the others on the island. Mine was made of mostly metal from vessels. We had natural trees on the island, but most of our homes were made of driftwood, boat pieces, and metallic siding from newer vessels. The created items protected our natural resources and required less work and waste.

The cooking fire was smoldering in the stone hearth, and faint hints of bacon and eggs lingered, meaning my mother had thankfully already headed to her shop. I wouldn't have to face her yet.

My stomach rumbled in anticipation, but I couldn't lose time. I'd only have a few hours of reprieve to sort through my finds and figure out a plan for him before my mom came back.

Even with the thick air and rising heat, I didn't open the window. I didn't want others to know I'd found a Washed Up and tell Molly before I did.

Unloading the cart took longer than loading it. I took out each piece, assessing it for its value to be repaired or for use in repairs of other items.

A few pounds of treasures I'd found on the trek back sat nestled on Jasper's flat torso, his slow breathing causing them to rise and fall and sometimes clink together.

He took in a few snorts of breath, his face twitching, and his toned body jerked.

I quickly removed the items so they wouldn't become a casualty to his waking up.

After a flinch, his eyes fluttered open. His long eyelashes framed dark brown eyes. Dark locks fell across his face. A slight stubble darkened his strong jawline. His face froze but his eyes darted around the room.

My muscles twitched and I bit my lip.

We'd reached the tricky part. He was young and muscled. I was also young and muscled, but I didn't have fear fueling me. My fingers wrapped around a crowbar as I stepped a few paces back. I tested the weight in case I needed to use it.

I was uncertain which language he spoke. It wouldn't be our island's, but with his clothing style and grooming, I tried Italian, Spanish, Portuguese, and then finally a variant of English. "You washed up on the beach."

When understanding hit him, his head whipped around to face me as the rest of his body jerked away defensively. His brown eyes scanned over me, assessing. He mistook me for a non-lethal threat as his eyes drifted to survey the rest of the room while he remained rigid and alert, taking in the hanging planters with herbs and the sundry of items strewn about.

With a lick of his lips, his cautious gaze found mine again.

"What beach?" he croaked, his voice dried from the salt water.

I smiled and he eased back. "Our beach doesn't have a name, but you've reached our island."

"Island?" he asked as his eyes widened. His voice sent tingles through me, and I scowled.

I nodded. I didn't bother to tell him the name. We had our own name, Siren Island, but those who washed up often tried calling it the Bermuda Triangle or Atlantis or something else from their world.

"Which island?" His face scrunched. Then he flinched and groaned, "My boat. Where is it?"

"You didn't wash up with one."

"Dammit," he growled. "It was a rental."

He rubbed his forehead, then patted his pockets, likely for the black rectangle. He pulled it out and cursed seeing the reflective face give him nothing.

"Do you have a phone I can borrow?"

I shook my head. We didn't have those, and we didn't need to deal with this diversion.

"No cell service? Landline then?" He lifted his hands out from his sides in a questioning fashion.

My eyes flicked to his frame and corded arms before I averted my gaze. I needed to stay focused. He was a Washed Up. An increasingly agitated one.

Although the terms didn't mean anything to us, I knew they dealt with his time. His term "cell service" helped narrow down his window.

"What's your name?" I asked.

"Jasper," he answered automatically.

"Jasper, when are you from?" I prodded as I took a tentative step forward but kept out of his reach. His phone meant he was from a two thousand-something.

His brows furrowed, and his eyes darted around as he tried to process my question.

"I'm from Florida," he said and ran his fingers through his salt-crusted hair. They stuck and he grunted.

I sighed. "I asked *when*."

"When?" he parroted, staring at me. His warm eyes hardened and narrowed. His jaw ticked.

I nodded and rolled my hand in the air to encourage his answer.

"I think it was April seventh," he said and shrugged. "Does it matter? I just need a phone. I need to let my friends know I'm okay. Shit, I hope I didn't miss my final."

I let out a longer sigh. People came from different decades and centuries to our home. Depending on how early of a century, it limited how much of our washed-up technology they could handle. Based on the black rectangle, he could handle all of it, but it also meant he'd most likely be more resistant to accepting that he'd washed up on an island with Sirens.

I smiled.

He flinched in response.

Why couldn't they just answer simple questions? Washed Up always had to be argumentative and resistant.

Cell service overlapped with other technologies.

"Do you use Wi-Fi or dial-up?" I asked. The words sounded natural on my tongue despite the fact that I didn't know what they meant.

"Dial-up?" he choked. "We're not in the stone age."

"Your clothes definitely confirm that, as does your use of English."

He narrowed his eyes at me, his hands fisting as he said, "Where am I and who are you? Is this a prank?"

"Prank? No. You're on our island, and I'm Rainey."

He rolled his tongue against his teeth and nodded as he rolled his eyes.

"Am I your prisoner?" he asked, once again assessing me before moving his gaze to the shadows. I assumed to check for hidden people or torture instruments or a prank.

I shook my head. "No, you're not a prisoner."

"Then why am I here? Wherever *here* is."

"As I said, you washed up."

He moved so his legs dangled off the edge of the cart. With a quick thrust he jumped to the floor and brushed his pants off. He shot me a dark look and then took a sweeping glance around the room. His frown deepened. "I'll be going, then."

"Okay," I said and nodded towards the door. My heart pounded in my chest but I stopped the growl in my throat. He'd be back before long. I just needed to be patient.

"You're not going to try and stop me, right?" he asked, taking a step towards the door.

I shook my head. "Nope."

I picked up the bicycle frame I'd found the previous night and pumped it against the floor to test the tires.

It'd need a patch job and the tubes inflated, but the frame was pretty solid, and the tires matched. I could probably trade it to a merchant for a month's worth of meat.

Light spilled across the entrance as he opened the door. A waft of salty sea air whirled in, stirring the few bits of dust in the house and teasing the fire.

I watched as he stepped outside but hid my grin when he froze half in the doorway, an odd pang twisting in my heart. His fingers lingered on the door handle as only his eyes moved, taking in the scenery.

"Either in or out," I said. "I don't want a bird flying in here."

He swallowed before turning back to me.

"Where exactly is *here*?"

Two

"So, you're telling me I fell into the Bermuda Triangle or found Atlantis?" Jasper paced the floor, his rubber-soled shoes squeaking as he pivoted for the umpteenth time. He ran a hand through his dark hair, leaving his fingers buried. His eyes darted around, unseeing.

"No," I said, leaning against my workbench with my arms folded over my chest.

"Right... I got past these 'guardians?'" he said with air quotes.

"Sirens," I repeated, again, for the umpteenth time.

"But they don't work... or sing... on a moonless night?" he asked, stopping to stare at me, his eyebrows arched and chin dipped.

My gaze fell to his lips and lingered too long before I met his eyes. I ran a hand over my cheek to hide the burning heat. I sighed and half-heartedly nodded.

"How did you get here, then?" His face scrunched as his eyes tracked around the room, focusing on the windows.

"I was born here," I said and rubbed my forehead. This was why I didn't bring people up from the beach. It was always the same questions. Same disbelief. Same blabbering. Their knowledge, though valuable, wasn't worth the time. If it wasn't for the land contract, he could be someone else's problem. My throat tightened unexpectedly at the thought.

"How did your family get here?"

I shrugged my shoulders and averted my eyes. Another pointless question.

"Did they get past the keepers, too?"

Sirens, but I didn't correct him. Again.

"My family was born here," I half-lied. Only the family I knew was born here. My dad had washed up and left when my mom was younger than me now. At some point, all my mom's ancestors had probably washed up or had been on the island before the Sirens built their magical barrier around us. None of it really mattered, as I'd been born and raised here and would die here.

Jasper rolled his eyes and threw his hands in the air. "So, what you're saying is... I went for a boat ride, got caught in a freak storm, passed over your keepers'—er, Sirens'—barrier because for you it was a moonless night, even though it was a sunny afternoon for me, and washed up on your shore. You found me while scavenging."

"Pretty much," I said with a nod.

Those who washed up often said it'd been midday or a moon-filled night when they'd crossed into our waters, but our waters didn't follow their timeline. They'd crossed into our realm on a day the moon was hidden, and our Sirens were quiet.

"That's... crazy." He blew out a breath and shook his head. "This is ridiculous. Can I go home?" His dark eyes cut back to me. His jaw ticked as he assessed me.

Something warm twisted in my stomach and I licked my lips. Uncomfortable with my reaction, I curled my fists and anchored my feet to my floor. My gaze fell to his lips again before I realized it. Blinking, I blew out a breath. I needed to focus. It was one moon cycle, and he wanted to go home. I wanted him to go. I didn't even want him now, but I needed him for the land.

"Yes." I bobbed my head. "You can go home. The next moonless night."

"What?" he barked. "No! Now! I have exams, work. What about a boat or plane?" He moved to the window and pushed the curtains to the side.

I forced a smile while shaking my head. "You can't get past the Sirens until the next moonless night."

"Right," he drawled. He shot me a glance as he moved to the next window, which provided the same view. "So how do I get off the island, then, on the next moonless night?"

"Well, we have some rules..." I said, forcing a grave expression.

He stopped pacing to stare at me, his eyes wide. "Okay?"

"First, you must pay a passage fee to leave."

"Passage fee?"

"Don't interrupt me," I said, and pushed myself off the bench to take a step closer. I held a finger in the air. "You must pay the passage for a Ferrier to risk the waters to get you past the Sirens."

I cocked my head to the side as I took another step towards him and lifted a second finger. He flinched, eyes dancing between my finger and my eyes. I stalled when we locked eyes. After blinking slowly, I continued, "Second, you must wait until the next moonless night."

He opened his mouth to speak, but stopped when I sent him a withering look.

"Third," I said, biting my cheek to stifle laughter. I lifted a third finger. "Third, you must never lay with a person here, or you'll forever be bound to the island. As legend has it, we are the land descendants of the Sirens."

"Land Sirens? Lay with a... Oh geez!" He flinched, his cheeks reddening.

A chuckle rippled out of me before I could stop it. Deciding not to fight it, I doubled over, clutching my side as I laughed.

"What's really rule three?" he growled, fisting his hands and glaring down at me.

I gasped to catch my breath and finally stood up meeting his intense gaze. My eyes shined with merriment. "There isn't one. It was a joke. You have to pay the passage for a Ferrier to take you on a moonless night. You also have to carry your weight until then if you expect to receive food or shelter."

"What about..."

I shook my head, stopping him. "We have laws like most places. Don't steal. Don't kill."

"And don't lay with a person," he mumbled and rolled his eyes.

"Oh, you can," I said. When his eyes, glossy with concern, shot up to meet mine, I added with a grin, "It just means you can't leave."

His face fell as his color drained, and his eyes took on a distant look, but he said nothing. Likely the reality of how long he had to stay settling in.

"Joking, I'm joking. There isn't a rule against it as long as it is consensual." My cheeks burned when his eyes sharpened on me. An image flashed through my thoughts: us, together. Heat flooded my veins, settling in my center, and I blew out a breath to focus. He was a Washed Up. I had no intention of becoming my mother.

"What skills do you have?" I asked, averting my eyes to clear the thoughts.

Jasper smirked. "Besides laying with people?"

"Hey, if it's your skill," I said, lifting my shoulders, the tendrils of heat tightening again. "I'm sure we can find takers. Many villagers like Washed Up. We call them the Sirens' Daughters."

"What?" he stammered, his face flooding with color. "I wasn't serious."

"You have twenty-eight days. No one will let you freeload for that long."

"I didn't ask to freeload. I didn't ask to be here." His nose flared and he pressed his lips into a thin line. "I just want a phone."

"Well, we don't have those," I said, "and we didn't ask for you to be here, either, but you're here. We're used to Washed Up. We understand it's no more your choice than ours. It's the Sirens' gift on their songless night. You can wait on the beach, if you want." I gave him two days at most to live on the beach before he was back.

Jasper stared at me, his expression unreadable.

"What skills are helpful?" he finally asked, dragging a hand through his hair.

I cocked an eyebrow. "Tell me what you can do."

He shrugged. "I don't know. I can fix a computer."

"Not helpful here," I said, and gestured towards my work area. "We don't have electricity."

"You don't have it, but know what it is?"

"We've had people wash up from the nineteen-hundreds and twenty-hundreds."

He groaned. "What does that mean?"

"Your years."

"My years?"

I nodded. This was another baffling situation for them. I picked up a rag and began cleaning the bike's frame. The acidic smell of the cleanser burned my nose. It was going to take a long time to explain, but the work wouldn't wait. "You know about cell phones, landlines, and the difference between dial-up and Wi-Fi. You're from the twenty-hundreds."

"Well, it *is* the two-thousands right now," he muttered, stepping closer to watch me. The briny smell of the ocean still clung to him. An unwelcome shiver stole through me. "Twenty twenty-one, to be exact."

"Ah, see, you're wrong there," I said, blinking away the thoughts of him. I nodded towards a bucket of rags and then pointed to the cart still housing my treasures. "That is when *you're* from. We don't have the same timeline. Your timeline exists outside of ours. Last new moon before you, we had someone wash up from the year twenty-twenty and the cycle before was a man from fifteen-twenty, both talking about plagues, but different plagues. Their clothes and languages were different, as was their knowledge of the world. We've been called many names, including Atlantis and the Bermuda Triangle. Those from later times seem to know about us as an island but struggle more to believe. Others believe we're Sirens or curses or answered prayers. They accept our existence more readily."

"Hey, I have heard of the islands you mention, but they're sea myths. Urban—er—sea legends."

I cocked an eyebrow at him without lifting my head.

"I'm not wrong." He folded his arms over his chest. My gaze hovered on his hard torso before returning to my bike frame. "I don't believe anything you're saying. This is all bullshit."

He was wrong. Eventually, he'd learn I was right or try swimming back early and become prey for the Sirens.

"Tell me how you got here, then," I said instead of arguing.

He absentmindedly ran a hand through his thick hair, his squinted eyes distant as he thought about it. "It was Saturday. Instead of hanging out in my apartment with the guys to play video games like we normally do, I rented a boat..." Pausing, he licked his lips, as if choosing his next words. "I went to some favorite family spots to think. Monday... I have my history final. Tuesday, I have my processes final, which is going to be a bitch. I really need to study for it."

"You're in college?"

He nodded, his eyes following my hands as I grabbed and started to clean a rusted shovel. With a grunt, he grabbed a rag and dug through the pile. A frown darkened his face as he perused the odd treasures, pushing aside a cracked green plastic watering can, some glass jars, and a damp red jacket. He pulled up a chipped blue side panel of a car door, rusted from the ocean. After staring at it for a moment, he leaned it against the cart and started wiping it down. His muscles flexed as he worked, snagging my attention for a few moments.

"Yeah, finishing my senior year. I have some job offers, but I'm not sure what I want to do," he said, pulling my attention to his face.

"What's your major?"

"Cyber Security."

It meant nothing to me, but I nodded anyway. "Do you have a job while in school?"

"Yeah, I work at a shop part time fixing up computers."

"What is the last thing you remember?"

He stilled. His eyes unfocused as he stared at the scarred tabletop. "My friends kept blowing up our group chat about my roommate's new car, so I turned notifications off. I was idling the boat in calm waters." He paused, his face scrunching. "The sun was really bright. Like blinding and all around. I..."

Silence hung between us.

"Then all I remember is waking up here."

Jasper went quiet for a few beats. He rubbed a hand over his forehead, smearing dark grease across it. After swallowing, he said, "Okay, now tell me the truth... where are we and how do I get back home?"

"Today, you'll learn I'm serious. Help me get the salt off the parts in the cart and I'll provide you with food for today and a trip to Old Man Willis."

"Old Man Willis?"

"He washed up before my birth. He'll help answer your questions."

"Can he help me get home?"

"No, he can't. He's not a Ferrier, but he'll tell you about the island and answer your questions."

We finished washing the items as the sun arched in the sky. The full intensity beat down on the house, but the crisp breeze of the sea kept the air cool and spiced with hibiscus and mint.

I stamped out the fire after boiling water to clean up after lunch. The kettle swayed on the post as it cooled, sending ghostly tendrils into the air. I pulled out the loaf of bread my mom had made that morning and cut a couple slices. The rich, thick, yeasty aroma made my mouth water.

Then I took a few dried pieces of meat from a glass container. I gave half to Jasper. With my half, I sank into a cushioned seat and let my body rest. The long night on the beach and day hunched over my table was catching up with my back.

"How do you have bread?" Jasper asked, picking up the corner of a slice and examining underneath it. He took his flannel off and draped it over his chair, leaving his wet t-shirt stuck against his chest.

Averting my eyes, I blew out a sigh. "Just eat it."

"How big is the island that you can grow wheat?" He dropped the bread and turned his gaze to the window.

"We have farms. Most are on the other side of the island. Trade across the island is huge."

"How big is the island?" he prodded, shifting his attention back to me. His dark eyes were cautious but curious.

A growl rolled in my throat. Twenty-eight days of endless questions and I may want to push him into the ocean for the Sirens. If it wasn't for my land, I'd do it now and avoid the complications of a Washed Up.

After swallowing a bite, I shrugged. "Our units of measurement aren't the same, but the Washed Up who traveled the island said it was fifty to sixty miles, or eighty to a hundred kilometers across, not including the hills."

"Huh. You'd think that size would show up on a map."

I flashed a patronizing smile at him. Our Sirens kept things out and us hidden. We weren't meant to be on a map.

His stomach rumbled.

I nodded towards the food. "Twenty-eight days is a long time to not eat."

His lips curled into a frown as he stared at the bread, emotions warring on his face. With a sigh, he lifted it to his lips. He sniffed it.

"How many people live on the island?" he asked, then took a big bite. He stilled, staring down at the bread. Around his food, he said, "This is really good."

"Several thousand people." Nodding towards the bread, I added, "My mom makes the best bread."

"Your mom?" His eyes bounced around the house.

"Yeah." Heaviness weighed on my veins. I'd have to face her soon about Jasper. My mouth dried and I swallowed.

"Where is she?" he asked around another bite of food.

"Probably trading bread," I said, pushing down the thoughts of what was likely to come later. "Her skill is baking."

"What's your skill?" He inclined his chin towards me.

"I find and fix things."

"Does it pay well?"

I rocked my head. "I make good trades for items I need. I can trade for better cuts of meat and can keep our house up. I used trades to build the house."

I'd always wanted to be a Scavenger. When I outgrew my grandparents' house with my stuff and required space, I wanted my own shop.

My own land where no one could tell me what I could do with it. Instead of going to a different village, and away from those I loved, Molly had offered to let me rent a section of her land. Now I had a chance to buy it, and truly make it my own. If I met all her requirements.

His eyes tracked around the room. "You built this place?"

"Yeah, took me a couple weeks. I have my workshop." I waved my hand to the open space. "The big, open grand room is where we mostly work and live. My mom bakes her breads in the hearth."

"You don't have a construction business here?"

"You mean trading someone to build your house?"

He nodded.

"I guess, but that'd be a lot of trading for something you can do yourself. I traded for help with the foundation and stuff, but not the actual building of it."

"You own this land?" he asked.

I sighed and shook my head. A curl of excitement slid through me. Soon, though, thanks to him. "Not yet. I'm renting it. The house is mine, so if I leave, I'll take what I can. I'm working towards owning the land. Land is rarely traded, but this is a small part of a larger lot."

"What's the cost?" he asked, his eyes bright with interest.

I snorted. "She wants to build a small farm on her property to offset the costs of trading. I have to provide the needed trades for twelve chickens, four pigs, four cows, and two goats." He didn't need to know I needed to harbor a Washed Up yet. If he did, he could use it against me in our agreement.

"That's—" His voice trailed off. His brows scrunched together. "—something."

We stared at each other for a beat.

"So, animals wash up too, then?"

I nodded. "They're the rarest of all and the most sought after. They usually find their ways to the other similar animals, though."

"So how will you get them?"

"I have the animals secured with trades. The night of the festival, the people I'm trading with will be here. I finally have the last piece, and I want to make sure we're still in agreement. It should just be a formality.

I need to finish the fencing on Molly's property. I already built the barn. Then I'll schedule deliveries with them before next cycle."

He eased back in his chair. His warm eyes focused on me. When heat curled in my cheeks, I stood and busied myself cleaning up our lunch.

"Ready to meet Old Man Willis?" I asked, wiping my mouth of crumbs and shaking my tunic.

"You said he washed up, but stayed?"

I nodded.

"So, outsiders can be a part of the community?"

Something twisted inside of me at his question. Although the village welcomed Washed Up, and I enjoyed the trinkets of their world, I avoided them. Too many brought pain and heartache to the island, leaving behind Sea Widows.

"We don't choose if you land here anymore than you do. If you want to stay and carry your share, you're welcome to. If you don't, then you can leave willingly or by our choice."

"How many wash up? How many choose to stay?"

"Depends. Some new moons have none and others have several. Washed Up from the earlier centuries usually stay. The later centuries, it depends on what's going on."

"So, if I'm to believe this is real, you're okay with a world out there beyond your... Sirens?" He tossed his hand towards the window, his eyebrow cocked.

"Why wouldn't I be? It is what's there."

"Don't you want to see it? See where all this stuff comes from?"

His world existed out there. One ripe with its own issues. Their world, visited in glimpses through their treasures on our shores.

I wondered about what we hadn't seen. The buildings and machines only known through books and Washed-Up stories. But being out of reach and mysterious didn't make it better.

"Why would I? My life and world are here."

Three

AFTER USING the heated water to wash up, I looked at his ratty clothes clinging to his damp skin, stiff with dried water and starting to grow the gamey smell of dead bacteria. We'd have to locate him something else to wear. We still had my dad's old clothes tucked away, my mom's last grasp on him, but I wasn't sure if they'd fit.

If she was even willing to let me have them. I could already see her enraged eyes and hear the hiss in her voice.

Otherwise, we'd have to trade for more clothes or hope some washed up. Just another reminder of how transitory Washed Up could be. At least it was just one cycle.

Outside the house, the air hung damp around us, frizzing the ends of my hair and coating my skin in a sheen. I led the way through the rock-laden path. Trees drooped over our heads, protecting us from the sun's rays and blocking the ocean breeze. Birds sang in the canopy and insects droned around us.

"Does it look like Florida?" I asked after a few minutes of our silent trek.

"We have palm trees, too, but this looks like a different variant. We also have oaks," Jasper said, nodding towards a behemoth oak that stretched across the path and choked out vegetation. "But we have light posts, not lampposts with flames. We have wires and paved roads."

"I'm told it looks different, but we have paved roads in town, too. Those of us who live closer to the sea don't bother. The sand is easier to pack down than pave over."

"So, is it just you and your mom out here?" he murmured, swatting at a bug circling him.

I turned to look at him over my shoulder, his brown eyes watchful and guarded as he met my gaze.

An unwelcome and unwanted curl of heat wove in my stomach and lower. My neck warmed. I needed to get a grip. Yes, he was incredibly attractive, but he was a Washed Up. I needed him for a moon cycle to own my land. Anything else was a distraction.

"My dad's no longer with us," I said. It was the truth, even if I didn't know whether or not he was alive. Though I never met him, I was told I looked just like him other than my auburn hair, which matched my mom's. I had his hazel brown eyes, pointed chin, high cheekbones, and button nose. I was a constant reminder of him and his absence.

"Oh, I'm sorry." He grimaced and rubbed a hand over his neck.

I waved off his concern and continued forward. "If my mom still has some of his clothes, they may fit you." I frowned. I still had to face my mom about scavenging Jasper. She was one of the few on the island who wasn't welcoming of the Washed Up. At least, not anymore. She also thought I should partner with Owen, Molly's son, to have the land gifted to me instead of buying it. Buying it seemed a waste of resources to her.

Jasper's steps hesitated, and I risked a glance back to see him regarding his clothing.

"I guess they're going to smell after a bit." A faint smile danced on his lips when he pulled his shirt forward.

"Going to?" I chuckled.

The look he shot me was dark, reigniting the earlier sensation within me, but a grin tugged on his lips as he started walking again. I swallowed down my reaction and forced my eyes and feet forward.

"I am sorry for your loss," he said, clearing his throat and spiking his fingers through his dark hair.

"I never met him," I dismissed. "From what I was told, a partnering wouldn't have worked long for them, anyway." My mom only used bitter words for my father, which I assumed were born from him impregnating her and leaving. My grandparents didn't speak of him often, preferring to spare my feelings despite my lack of emotional connection to him.

The village, though, didn't mince words. He'd been an attractive man who'd laid with several people. My mom had been naïve enough to offer him a space to stay, including her bed. When the third moonless night returned, he disappeared in the night. No Ferrier would admit to taking him, but I'd always wondered if my grandfather had paid a Ferrier or been the one to take him, either willingly or by force, after he found out about their pairing. Or if my grandfather had sent him to sea for the Sirens to deal justice. He just hadn't known at the time I had already been conceived.

"You have divorce here?"

"Divorce?" My mind reeled, and then the meaning hit me. "We can break a partnering if we want. From what I understand, it's not as big of a deal as in your world."

"The village doesn't have to weigh in?"

"No," I chuckled. "Why would they? They aren't part of the relationship."

"I guess.... You have any siblings?" he asked, glancing back towards the house.

I shook my head.

He gave me a sympathetic smile. "Your mom must have been heartbroken from the loss."

"Something like that," I said noncommittally. Mom was bitter at best, hateful more often. "How about you? Any siblings?"

His smile dimmed and he shook his head. "My mom died giving birth to me and my dad never had any interest in another woman. He passed a couple years ago in a car accident."

"I'm sorry—"

"Rainey," a familiar voice called out.

My step faltered. I sighed and rolled my eyes. Owen. Molly's son. He had once been my childhood best friend, like a sibling. Then his mom had her visions, and everything changed.

Jasper flanked my side, eyes searching the foliage, his body heat warm against my back. A weird curl twisted in my stomach, and I tightened my muscles to stop myself from leaning into him.

He whispered, "Who is that?"

"A really annoying person."

"Rainey!" the voice called again, closer this time. His steps sliding on the sand scratched at the air.

"Just ignore whatever he says," I gritted out and balled my fists. He was going to tattle to his mom that I'd found a Washed Up. I didn't need him spilling it to Jasper yet why I was taking him in.

The bushes rustled as he drew near, and the air thickened. A chilly sliver raced down my back and my skin prickled, ready for the fight as I squared my shoulders.

"Hello, gorgeous," Owen said, stopping on the path. Sun-bleached, sandy blond hair hung in wind-swept curls around his face. He wore only shorts, his chest bare. His bronze skin was dusted over with salt, and his blue eyes locked onto me.

As kids, we'd spent hours in the thicket of trees on his property looking for signs of his ancestors that had farmed the area centuries ago. The tale had various renditions, but they all agreed that the ancestors had angered the Sirens by not repeatedly offering gifts on the Full Moon. The day after the anniversary of the first missed ceremony, the last known cyclone to come ashore had destroyed the crops, making the land unusable for years. Our Sirens protected us, but they also demanded respect.

Back then, he'd been shorter than me. Now, Owen was a good foot taller than me, his muscular frame almost double my width. His lips curled into a smile as he took me in.

"I was looking for you this morning." He spoke in English, which meant he'd heard some of what we said.

I shrugged, suppressing the repulsive gag in my throat.

"Make some good finds last night or did you strike out?" He rested his hands on his hips and cocked his head to the side.

His gaze never jumped to Jasper, but it was still an insult.

"I never share information about my finds," I said, and let out a long breath, anchoring my feet to the ground and accidently pushing into Jasper's side with my hip. I gulped but didn't pull away despite the enticing jolt that shot through me. Desire to rub against him again teased through me, but I ignored it and watched Owen.

"How about a fish fry over a campfire tonight on the beach?" His eyes flashed with delight and his smile grew while he continued to ignore Jasper's presence. "And then we can take my boat out to watch the sunset."

He always preferred the water to the land.

I forced a bright smile. His grew in response to mine.

"That's a great idea," I said cheerily, turning towards Jasper. His lips were pressed in a straight line as he glared at Owen. I slapped his arm, causing him to flinch and his confused eyes to jump to me. I stared a moment too long before focusing.

"How about that? You can catch the fish tonight for our—" I said 'our' while moving a finger back and forth in between just Jasper and me, "—dinner. I fed you for helping me clean stuff. You'll feed me for a change of clothes."

My stomach twisted at the possibility of it. The images of sand, fire, and our bodies flickered through my mind and a tingle shot through my veins, thumping in my heart.

Jasper's eyes narrowed as he considered me and they flickered momentarily to Owen. He returned his gaze to me and a warm smile spread across his face, causing the weird flutter in my core to return. "Sounds like a great plan."

Owen's face darkened and a sneer replaced his smile as he finally moved his gaze to Jasper. "Taking in strays now, are you? You don't normally offer pity to those that Wash Up. You finally get enough to make the trades and need—"

"Well," I cut him off, swinging an arm around Jasper's shoulders. I was pretty sure it was instinctual, but his arm wrapped around my waist and his hand rested on my hip. I swallowed to hide my surprise and the small flush of pleasure that raced along my spine. "There was something about him."

Unfortunately, it wasn't a lie. I needed to keep my senses clear.

Owen's eyes darted between the two of us, snagging on Jasper's fingers curled around me. He took a step towards me, his fingers furling.

"Dude," Jasper said. "She's clearly not interested in you. Why don't you back off?"

I stilled. My gaze unfocused. Everyone knew about Molly's visions. They also knew my aversion to them and that I could handle Owen's advances, even as annoying as they were. But something odd flickered in me at having someone say something to him instead of chuckling to themselves.

Owen sputtered, fire burning behind his blue eyes.

"You think she's interested in you?" he snorted, his shoulders shaking. "You are a fool, a distraction, and the Sirens are going to destroy you."

"If she is or isn't, it's not your business," Jasper countered. He sucked in a breath, expanding his chest. Slowly, he released it through his flared nostrils.

A wicked smile cut across Owen's face. He thought it was his business.

"I've told Owen *no* enough times that he more than knows," I gritted out, heat clawing at my face that Jasper was witnessing one of my and Owen's perpetual fights. He'd never physically pushed the line. I would never tolerate such an act, nor would the village or his mom, and it wasn't in his nature. But he was still possessive about our future. One he felt promised to him by his mother. If he thought Jasper was an obstacle to it, I wouldn't put it past him to have the Sirens weigh in.

Owen's gaze snapped to mine. "Land isn't enough? Going to turn into another island Sea Widow?"

My body tensed but I forced my smile to remain. Jasper shifted as my muscles tightened, but he didn't say anything.

"I don't plan to be like your mom," I shot back.

Owen's face pinched in rage, and he growled.

"I wonder if my mom waited long enough for the trade to move on, or if she'll raise the price," Owen shot back.

I sucked in a breath and bit my tongue to stay my response. Heat clawed at my face, and I twisted my fingers together to not lash out at him. His mom wouldn't, but she had a right to.

"Raise what?" Jasper asked, his thumb rubbing small circles on my hip.

The comfort distracted me, ebbing my anger, and I found myself leaning into his touch.

Owen noticed, too, and his eyes burned. His nostrils flared and he curled his fingers into fists.

"The price of the lot Rainey wants to buy. One she's willing to go against her long-held habits on," Owen said. His face darkened and eyes narrowed. He folded his arms over his chest, leveling his glare at me. "She seems set on that option instead of the better one."

"Better one?" Jasper asked. I felt his eyes move to me, but I didn't take my glare from Owen.

"Maybe Mom will get a better offer." Owen's lips twisted into a snarl.

Jasper made a throaty noise but didn't ask again.

"I'd rather lose the land by not being able to afford it than getting it by partnering with you."

Owen's eyes widened. Red clawed at his cheeks and his body tightened.

"Whoa," Jasper breathed, his grasp momentarily tightening. "I can see your point."

Owen's glare darted to Jasper and I chuckled, breaking his trance.

"You know Mom's a stickler for tradition, and the tradition says the full cycle," Owen said. A dark, triumphant smile cut across his face.

We both knew it was true.

"When Rainey's done with you and the moon cycle," Owen said, tearing his eyes from me to glare at Jasper, "I'm a Ferrier."

"Ferrier?" Jasper parroted. Alarmed eyes tracked back to me.

"There are other Ferriers," I said, tightening my hand on Jasper's shoulder to usher him forward. "He won't need your help. If you'll excuse us."

"I'd say nice to meet you, but I won't lie," Jasper said with a forced smile and a nod as we passed Owen.

When we were a good distance away and out of earshot, I reluctantly let go of Jasper's shoulders and threw my head back. I scrubbed my face with my hands and let out an exasperated sigh. "Sorry about that back there. I really invaded your personal space."

He shrugged.

"No big deal," he said with a smile. His face softened. "Are you okay?"

"Yeah, I'm fine. He always does this. He's just annoying."

"He can't take the hint?"

I shook my head. "I've told him for years I'm not interested. He makes it a point to talk to me and ask me to go on boat rides."

"You ever take him up on it?" Jasper's jaw ticked as he watched me.

"Uh, no," I snorted.

He swallowed, his gaze bouncing down the trail before he returned it to me.

"What's a Sea Widow?" he asked, leaning against a tree across the path from me. He folded his arm over his chest and crossed his legs. His head tilted to the side.

"A person who laid or had a relationship with a Washed Up who went back to their time, but the Sea Widow didn't want them to."

"I thought you said there was a rule against it?"

I waved away his question with my hand. "I told you I was joking with you. I just think they shouldn't. It's just horrible to watch an islander get attached to someone who chooses to leave."

"Do islanders ever leave with them?"

I stalled. My eyes darted around, unseeing, as I thought about it. Finally, I shook my head. "Not that I am aware of. I don't think we can get past the Sirens."

"Even on a moonless night?"

"Even then. I think their magic keeps us bound here, but I don't know. I don't know of anyone ever trying."

He quietly assessed me before saying, "That's unfortunate."

I shrugged and looked away, trying to swallow the lump in my throat.

"What's the difference between a Sea Widow and a Sirens' Daughter?" he asked.

"The emotional toll. A Sea Widow didn't want their partner to go back. A Sirens' Daughter purposely laid with a Washed Up to have fun or conceive knowing they'd likely go back."

"His mom is a Sea Widow... like your mom?" His brows furrowed together as he considered the terms.

"A Sea Widow has no interest in partnering with anyone else. They're lonely and unhappy. Owen's mom... she was sad, I guess, but she didn't really show it, that I remember. She didn't partner with anyone or seem interested in anyone until a recent Washed Up. But she was happy. I was concerned he'd break her heart again. I still am. But he's been here for several moonless cycles, almost a year. He participates in the village. He plans to stay and he's really nice. They're expecting a child in a month or two. They're both very excited."

"He's planning on staying?"

"He says he is," I said, and shrugged. "Molly was willing to sell me the land once she met her partner. I'd asked for years while renting it. I think he helped convince her."

"So, were you serious that you could get the land by being Owen's *partner*? Does he have a business, or did you mean...?" His voice trailed off and he cleared his throat.

I snorted a laugh. "Yeah, meant it like partnering. Like your marriage. I won't partner with him to get the land. I can earn it myself with trades."

"But his mother is trying to bribe you to marry him?"

"No. Yes. I don't know. She always says I'll be the mother of her grandchildren, but I don't see a future where I'll partner with Owen, and I'm way too old for her second child, who isn't born yet." Her visions had started when we were children. Certain she was right, it became all Owen focused on. He talked of our marriage, the children his mom saw, and the unbridled happiness we'd live in. Unable to see the same future or believe I could ever feel that way about him, I stopped hanging out with him. Stopped going to the cove with him and took to avoiding him altogether.

"So, you just need to settle the trades for the animals, finish the fencing, and transport the goods? So that you don't have to partner with Owen for it?"

I nodded, omitting that I had to harbor a Washed Up.

"I'm here until the next moonless night," Jasper said measuredly.

My stomach tightened and I swallowed. That was certainly my plan.

A small chuckle fell from his lips as he shook his head. "This just doesn't feel real. Like some dream."

"It's real to me." I wouldn't argue with him about his own feelings. He'd either accept it or live in denial until he left.

He nodded. "Then let's make sure you have everything prepared. I can help with the fencing and transport."

It was a sweet offer, but he was only staying for one cycle and would need to make his own trades for a Ferrier. I didn't need his help. I just needed to harbor him for one month. And not become a Sea Widow.

Four

WILLIS' place sat tucked back by the forest's line. The flat plot was sectioned off into different garden zones, with neat little lines marked by sticks and twine. A straight path made of white shells dotted with pinks, oranges, and yellows led to his door. Two of their sons still lived at home but worked in town during the day. Their third married a man in a village that was a day's walk to the west.

Willis' house was similar in size to mine but was made completely of lumber that had been scrapped together over time. He'd done construction work before coming to our island. He'd answer questions and, for the right trade, would help out if you needed it.

I'd traded him some silverware that I'd found to help me with the foundation of our house, especially since our plot was towards the sea and the sand caused me some difficulties.

"This looks nice," Jasper said, scanning the area. His white t-shirt already clung to his damp torso. "It looks like a log cabin."

I tore my eyes from him and rapped my knuckles on the door.

Tillie opened the door. Streaks of gray wove through her auburn hair wrapped tightly on her head. She wore a patched apron over her yellow linen dress. White flour dusted her warm brown skin. She was the person everyone came to talk about their issues—mental, emotional, or spiritual. Often paid with plants for her help, her garden was one of the best.

"Rainey?" Her brown eyes jumped to Jasper. "I didn't know you took in Washed Up."

Jasper's eyes cut to mine, but he didn't say anything.

"It isn't a big deal," I said, dismissing her narrowed eyes. "Is Willis available?"

Tillie's attention bounced back to Jasper before she pursed her lips and nodded. She leaned back into the house and called, "Willis, visitors. Rainey is here."

A deep voice called back indistinguishable words and stomping feet pounded towards the door.

Willis was a broad man and stood several inches over six feet. Weathered lines decorated his face, but his eyes shone with a youthful brilliance.

"Rainey," he said, smiling. He turned to face Jasper. His smile dimmed slightly as he took him in. Finally, he extended his hand towards Jasper. "Another Washed Up. You have a familiarness about you. Welcome."

Jasper smiled tightly while he took the offered hand and shook it. His eyes scanned over Willis, narrowing in contemplation.

"Wait..." Jasper said. "Aren't you Captain Willis Jenkins?"

"I am," Willis said with a bob of his head and a wink towards me.

"You know him?" I asked.

"My final on Monday is for US History 400. I'm minoring in it. We read about him in the European Theatre—you were a flying ace! His disappearance sent shockwaves."

I quirked my brows. His words meant little to me.

"United States of America history," Willis filled in. His lips pressed into a thin line and his face slackened. Sadness darkened his eyes as he watched Jasper recite his history.

"Ah," I said. Few who washed up from his time would speak of it.

"But your plane went down in World War II..." Jasper murmured, staring at the relic before him.

"Aye, we did go down," he said, waving towards the rear of the house and the wreckage that decorated his yard. He and his plane had washed up together. It would never fly again, but he'd left it intact. The metal and interior could have made many trades, but he said it would have been like dismembering a friend. It was his, and so was the choice of what to do with it.

"But... you should be like a hundred years old," Jasper stammered. "You're, like, fifty at most."

Willis chuckled, the deep bass-like sound carrying across the yard. "In your world, I would be. Here, I landed a little over twenty years ago."

Jasper stared between the two of us. His gaze kept snagging on mine until he said, "He's a legend. He shot down so many enemy planes."

"Willis washed up in his plane," I said, smiling at his giddiness.

"And you stayed?" Jasper asked.

"Son, the world was on fire. We were winning the war. I was injured, and by the time I healed, I didn't have the fight in me. I found where I belonged."

"But you're a hero..."

"My legend is a hero. Here, I'm a man."

"I don't understand," Jasper said, shaking his head.

"You may never understand," Willis said and turned his attention to me. Dipping his chin, he said, "I take it you want a Ferrier?"

"I figured Grandpa could help connect him with a Ferrier," I said, averting my eyes and ignoring the unpleasant twist in my stomach.

"Ah, I see." His eyes were sympathetic for some reason. "He can help connect you. What can I do for you, then?"

"He has questions," I said, jerking a thumb towards Jasper.

"I bet he does. Well, come on in." Willis gestured towards the door. "Tillie made some fruit cookies this morning and we have some herb brew. It's like tea, but not quite."

The inside of their home was inviting, and the sweet yet tart aroma of cherry cookies greeted us. My stomach rumbled in anticipation.

A large desk made of driftwood sat tucked into a corner with books and papers spread out on it. The few books that washed up on the islands were coveted by the Washed Up. They'd trade handsomely for them regardless of condition. The loose papers were old maps and notes and such that had washed up with different vessels over the years.

Next to the office space, the room opened into a gathering room with furniture covered in different wool blankets made from the islands' sheep. The kitchen area butted up to the other wall, a hearth at the center.

A matching door to the one in my house flanked the wall on the side of the kitchen that led towards the bedrooms and outhouse. His outhouse was attached to the house through the bedrooms, which became a new feature for homes built after his. He'd built a pipe system with washed-up pieces that directed the waste away. My layout was almost an exact match, but I had two bedrooms instead of three.

Jasper's focus darted around the room until he found me.

Meeting his gaze, I involuntarily caught my bottom lip between my teeth.

His eyes darkened as they momentarily dipped to look at my lips before returning to mine. "This looks like your house."

"He helped me with the foundation and drainage system," I said. "His is larger, but it's the same design." I sat down on one of the chairs, sinking into the plush furniture.

"What did you trade for it?" Jasper took the chair next to mine. His rigid form twitched as he glanced at Willis.

"A silverware set," Willis said, grabbing a tray of cookies before he took his seat. "A complete eight-person setting." He took a couple and passed the tray to Jasper. "Came in the box. I broke the box up for paper scraps, the silverware replaced our older set that we traded, and the plastic liner is used as an organizer."

"I didn't think one set offered so much," Jasper said. He stared at the cookies a bit before taking one.

"We have what we need. You have real questions? I can answer the common ones from modern times right away. Yes, you're on an island locked from time. You must wait until the next moonless night to leave. No, we aren't interested in bringing electricity here. We don't have the normal power sources to generate power. Now ask your other ones."

Jasper's jaw ticked and he looked to me.

I took the cookie tray, snagging three. Keeping his gaze, I nodded towards Willis and said to Jasper, "He'll answer any questions. You likely won't ask anything others haven't already."

Jasper nodded, gulped, and turned to Willis. "I get it's an island, but where are we?"

Willis smiled patiently, a twinkle in his eye as he leaned back. "I assume Rainey told you we're on an island in what some call the Bermuda Triangle, Atlantis, and some other names?"

Jasper nodded.

"She's correct," Willis said, staring directly at him.

Jasper's eyes darted to me before returning to Willis. Red splotches danced up his neck and cheeks.

"Is the island magical?" he stammered.

"Magical?" Willis repeated, running his hands over his knees.

"You know, people wielding magic, magical plants, creatures." Jasper's words trailed off almost to a whisper as he looked to the floor.

"No, not in that sense." Willis chuckled.

"But there are Sirens...? What do the Sirens really do?"

Willis made a throaty sound as he contemplated the question. "They protect us from invasion or getting discovered. We're of a time that doesn't exist. They keep us separate. I haven't seen one. Some Ferriers say they lay on the rocks dotting the blue beyond, but I don't have a need to leave the terraform."

"But on moonless nights..." Jasper said, his palms up in the air.

"It's not that they sleep or are incapable, it's just that stuff can get past them. Their song doesn't lure sailors or others to them on that one night. We were fortunate."

"Fortunate?" Jasper parroted. He looked at me and swallowed.

His time didn't understand the true nature of the Sirens. They'd allowed the warnings to slip into lore, myth, and fairytales when the Sirens sealed us away. Those before his time knew their song meant burial beneath the waves.

After clearing his throat, he asked, "But why are they all here?"

Willis smiled and shrugged. "We all have our own theories, but mine is that they are remnants from a time when the world had magic."

Jasper stared incredulously at him.

"Rainey, you're a born islander," Willis said. "A daughter of a Sirens' Daughter. What are your beliefs?"

Both of them stared at me. Willis had a mischievous smirk on his face as he leaned back. Jasper shifted so his frame faced me. His dark eyes searched me for truths. A flutter danced in my stomach.

Leaning back, I closed my eyes, blocking the distraction. I ran a hand through my brown hair and finally met his gaze. "The truth...the truth is, we don't know. Some believe we were an island like all the rest until the Sirens built their protective net around us, sequestering us from the rest of the world. Others say we've always been an island of the Sirens. In the beginning, we were a land where the Sirens saved their favorite catches until they grew bored with us and stayed out at sea. Some say we really are born of the Sirens but are their landlocked daughters, unable to join them in the seas. Others believe we are all from Washed Up who stayed as refugees and built settlements. It doesn't matter, though. We're here. Like all areas, we have our origin stories, and like all, we can't prove them, so we embellish."

"So, the Sirens are real?" Jasper asked.

"Did you think I was lying?"

"No... it's just... they aren't real, you know?" he said, flopping backwards and rubbing his forehead.

"I don't know, but I do know it's hard for Washed Up to grasp."

He lolled his head towards me, his expression dark.

"All right, I'll go with they're real," Jasper said, thrusting a hand towards Willis. "He's not supposed to be alive. But I know who he is. And he's real. I'm here, and *here* isn't supposed to exist. And I'm not dreaming."

"That's logical," I chuckled.

"Do they ever come ashore?"

"Not in my lifetime, nor any islander that I know of for centuries," I said.

"Then how do you know?" he asked, throwing his palms in the air.

One of the most common Washed-Up questions. Ferriers claimed they saw them on the rocks every moon cycle, even my grandfather. But you don't have to see something to know it exists. To know you're connected. To know you belong.

I stared at him. The wind rustled the window's cotton curtains, the only sound until a bird cawed. I licked my lips, the salty residue ever-present.

Willis' voice broke the seaside silence. "Before you arrived here, did you think the Bermuda Triangle or Atlantis was just a sea tale to keep sailors alert?"

Jasper half-heartedly shrugged. "I never really thought about it."

"Think about it now," Willis encouraged.

Jasper leaned back, staring at the scraped wood ceiling.

"I guess they saw something, real or imaginary. Long stretches at sea, away from loved ones, not knowing what will happen but knowing danger lurks everywhere. Magical places seem like a dream and magical creatures seem like an easy excuse for bad fortune."

"Or maybe what they saw was real," Willis said.

Jasper rolled his head towards Willis.

"You've been landlocked with your head stuck in books and movies and desensitized to the world. You may be able to travel the earth easier than even in my day, but you see less. You lump the unknown with things slightly similar so you can make sense of it. You strip things of their originality so it all fits nicely together. I don't fault you for it. It's a nice existence to be ignorant of the terrors of the world, but you miss out on the fantastical, too."

Jasper sighed but didn't say anything.

Willis' speech was one he gave to some Washed Up. He reserved it for those who seemed genuinely curious, but more so to the ones he liked and wanted to stay.

Jasper just wasn't going to stay.

I looked away and swallowed, a heaviness settling over me.

He was my last key for the land. The Sirens had gifted me what I needed. It would be uncomplicated. I would make sure of it, no matter how I reacted to him. I wouldn't be a Sea Widow.

"What are your thoughts, son?" Willis asked, his voice gentle.

Jasper paused a beat. I felt his eyes on me but didn't look back around as I picked at another cookie on the tray despite not being hungry. Finally, he asked, "Can people really leave?"

"Ah, the heart of the intent. Yes, people are allowed to leave. Ferriers can get you past the Sirens on moonless nights. It'll cost you, though."

"Even those born here can leave?" Jasper's voice sounded hopeful but small.

I looked to Willis. I'd never wondered before, so I didn't know the answer.

Willis grimaced and shook his head. "I don't know. None have tried since I arrived. I don't know of any stories, either."

"Haven't people wanted to?"

"Did you want to get sucked into the Bermuda Triangle?"

Jasper opened his mouth but didn't respond.

"Exactly. You've heard the mystical tales of this place. Based on accounts from those claiming to have gone to the triangle or such, they returned to their approximate time. Our understanding is that Washed Up rejoin the timeline they left very close to when they crossed over—as if they never left. That is based on those of us who have washed up and heard the tales of magical islands. If an islander exited, when would they be delivered? What is their time in our timeline? Who knows what the world will look like?

"We have knowledge of much of the world at large here but experience with little. Even me, who lived out there. I know so little of the other times other than books and Washed-Up narratives. The Washed Up keep our knowledge growing, but it's like living in the pages of a book."

A skeptical look darkened Jasper's face. His unreadable gaze found me. Disappointment wormed in my chest. Jasper, like many, may not understand or appreciate our island, but in a moon cycle, he'd get to go home. Not seeing the beauty of my island. However, I would harbor him and finally own my land. Then, Jasper and I would move on with our separate lives. And we'd both get what we wanted.

Five

As we weaved through town on the way back home, the smells of spiced meat and baked breads wafted our way. The town was built on a crooked grid. The cobbled stone dipped and buckled on the sandy dirt. Built hundreds of years ago under the guidance of several Washed Up, the streets required constant tending. In areas where bricks had buckled too much, they'd been dug out and a tree planted.

The shops sat snugly, with enough space for a person or two to walk between. Each was about ten feet by ten feet unless the artisan used it as a workspace. Those tended to be double or triple in size. The blacksmith had a thirty-by-thirty shop with a dirt floor and two mules to help turn the tools.

Mom had a small front which she shared with Owen's mom, who mended clothes. Mom often wandered the shops for trades while Owen's mom stayed in the space with her work. My ancestors were all bakers and had built the shop space centuries ago. I was the first to break the tradition.

My eyes darted around the venue. Thankfully, I didn't see Mom. I didn't want our confrontation to take place in public. Granted, everyone would know it happened, but they didn't need to witness it.

At this time of day, she was likely already home, baking more for dinner after selling out.

"I didn't realize the town was so big," Jasper said, his steps trailing behind mine.

"We live throughout the island; this provides us an easy gathering place. Our harbor is through the thicket of trees." I pointed to an outcrop of palms blocking the view of the ocean.

"Do you have a shop?" Jasper asked as a bicyclist whizzed past us on a red bike I'd traded for nails he'd scavenged. The chain sang as he rode on.

"No, I'd need a bigger plot for mine and those are all taken. I could trade with Gerald, the blacksmith, and share his space, but I don't like to share my tools. When I built our house, in addition to my forge, I built a space for me to work and a storage shed."

"Rainey," Beatrice, a local baker, called out. Plump pastries sat displayed in a glass case. The golden-brown confections were drizzled in fruit puree and nuts, running off in pools of sweet goodness.

I smiled and waved back, pulling Jasper to her shop. His warm forearm sent odd shivers up my fingers. The wooden structure was built from local trees over a hundred years ago when they cleared the last plot. Display cases lined the walls with spaced-out delights beckoning patrons in.

Stopping beside me, Jasper sniffed the air and narrowed in on a strawberry pie.

"You have a sweet tooth, huh?" Beatrice asked with a wink.

Jasper blushed and nodded. His dark trusses brushed his forehead.

I forced my eyes to take in the treats instead of Jasper and I finally let his arm go.

"There's nothing wrong with that," Beatrice said, smacking his hand playfully. Deep dimples highlighted her large, toothy smile.

My teeth clenched. Jasper shifted closer to me and his fingers brushed mine, the jolt it shot through me pulling my focus. Despite wanting to reach out to him, I ran my hands against my trousers.

"Now, Marianna may make the best bread, but my pastries have no rival," Beatrice boasted.

A shudder stole through me at the mention of my mom.

Jasper smiled back and slipped his hands into his pockets in polite refusal. An odd, excited curl pulsed in my heart at his rebuff.

"You're the newly Washed Up, aren't you?" Beatrice cocked an eyebrow and fisted her hands on her hips.

Jasper's gaze darted to mine before he nodded.

Beatrice tsked, her dark brown eyes finding me. "And you, Rainey... you brought him up?"

A growl escaped my throat. Jasper turned his gaze to me and a flush bloomed on my cheeks.

"There must be something special about you," Beatrice said, tilting her chin down and giving him a knowing look. She winked at me. My toes curled and I willed her to shut up, but of course she didn't. "Rainey doesn't ever bring in Washed Up. Even when a whole boatload shows up."

"Thanks, Beatrice," I gritted out as I looped my hand around Jasper's elbow and tugged. His steps fell in pace with mine, but he didn't try to reclaim his arm.

"Wait!" Beatrice called out, waving her hand at me.

I paused and glanced back to her without turning around.

"Wait, wait, wait," Beatrice sang, scurrying around the small shop. She put a thick slice of pie on a porcelain plate with tiny blue flowers scattered around the edge and grabbed a silver fork. She shoved them at Jasper and nodded her head in encouragement for him to take it.

He looked to me and I shrugged.

"What do you want for the pie?" I finally asked, staring at the thick slice, filling oozing out the sides.

"It's on the house," she said, her eyes glinting at Jasper. "Once he has a piece, he'll be back for more."

I stared expectantly at her.

She sighed, throwing her arms out and staring up at the ceiling.

"And?"

"And... when you return my plate and fork, you can bring this back, fixed up." Beatrice dropped a pendant in my hand. "The toggle broke."

"Ah," I said bitterly. Releasing his arm, I inclined my chin towards the pie. "Take it, Jasper. I have to fix this, regardless."

After a long pause, he took the plate.

Beatrice waited for him to take a bite.

Jasper hesitantly broke off a small piece and popped it into his mouth. His eyes widened and he smiled. "This is delicious."

Beatrice beamed and patted his arm. As she turned back to her shop, she called out, "He's a keeper, Rainey. Don't toss him back or I may snag him."

A blush clawed at my neck. Without looking at Jasper, I continued down the street.

We passed a few other stores: a cobbler, a whittler, a place specializing in cleaning driftwood, and, as we neared the street's end, a butcher.

"Where's the police station, the prison?" he asked around a bite of pie.

"Police? Prison?"

"Are you telling me you don't have crimes?" he said, offering me a bite.

I shook my head at the plate. "Theft isn't a huge issue on the island. We have nowhere to run from each other. Even if we are one village of ten, we don't harbor other villages' criminals. Murder is usually only an issue with Washed Up. If that's the case, they're dealt with."

"Dealt with?"

"We won't wait until the next moonless night. Our justice is simple. If you're caught stealing, you're cast towards the Sirens in a vessel. If you come back, your crimes are forgiven. If not, the ocean was justice. We don't have the means or desire to tolerate theft. Harboring another village's criminal only causes a rift and we rely on each other for survival."

"So Washed Up who murder are killed?"

I shrugged.

"That's up to the Sirens and the ocean."

A gust of wind brought with it the smell of heat and salt. The sun stretched above us, basking the island in light and bleaching the darkness. It'd only get hotter.

"The people have been welcoming so far." Jasper swallowed hard. His full fork clattered back onto the plate.

"So far, and they likely will be. I'm the one responsible for you and your choices." All a small price to own the land.

"Oh," he sputtered. "Well, I'm responsible for my share and helping you with the fence and transport."

My heart tightened at his remembrance.

"The animal set up is my business. You just need to make sure you support your needs."

"Helping you secure the trades is my offer to cover my room and board. But I owe you for food, the pie, and clothes."

"Your food was covered helping me clean the finds. As for the rest, it's time for you to catch dinner."

Six

JASPER STOOD in the shallow banks, scowling down at the fish. The pole I'd loaned him rested against his shoulder.

His pants were rolled to his knees and he'd ditched his flannel, leaving him in a t-shirt. The surf rolled over him, dampening his clothes. His muscles tightened as he readied the pole to cast. I normally did our fishing and hunting, so it was nice watching someone else try to catch our meal. And the show was quite attractive and entertaining. My hand shaded my eyes from the sun and from being caught ogling him as he fished.

"The water's clear," I called, lying back on the sand. I'd built a small campfire in a shallow pit with rocks encircling it. The warm flames licked the air, ready to cook dinner.

His scowl turned towards me and he huffed.

"Wade out farther if you need to," I encouraged, and moved my hands in a swooshing gesture towards the depths.

"Don't you have a boat?" he called over his shoulder. He tiptoed into the deeper waters.

"I do," I said with a nod.

"Then why am I wading out here scaring fish instead of in the boat?" he gritted out, his eyes dark as they met mine.

"Water's clear there, too. You'll scare them anyway. Do you need help?"

"No," he barked as he flicked the line out again.

I watched for another ten minutes before finally standing up and dusting the sand from my legs. I grabbed my spear resting in the sand.

His gaze flicked back to me as I waded into the water, splashing through the current and startling the fish as I trekked. The cool water washed the sand from my skin.

"I said I didn't need help," he seethed. Jasper flicked his line again. Ripples rolled around his legs.

I waved away his words. Standing a few feet away from him, I watched the water and the fish as they weaved through the current. Catching sight of a large bass, I jabbed the spear forward. It pierced the fish, causing it to lurch.

With a quick yank, I pulled the spear back with the fish on the head. The fish was plenty big for two people.

"Let's eat," I cheered, turning around and sloshing through the clear water. The setting sun cast flickered light through the water ripples.

"I still owe you dinner," he whined. He cast his line once again.

"We have dinner." I waved the spear. "You can cook it."

"That wasn't the agreement," Jasper argued. After a moment, he trudged behind me, splashing loudly.

"Well, you can fish tomorrow, but I want to eat tonight, and it wasn't going to happen with what you were doing."

He mumbled under his breath.

"You can use the spear tomorrow, if you want," I offered as I trudged up to the firepit and basket with our dinner supplies. The warm flames were welcoming against my damp skin.

"I haven't done that type of fishing," he admitted. He took the fish from the spear and used my machete and tools to clean and filet it. I watched his muscles as he swiftly made work of the fish. His pants clung to his legs and his damp shirt emphasized his chest.

"Doesn't look like you've done the other fishing, either."

I smiled when he shot a dark look at me, but he didn't say anything.

"You can practice tomorrow with the spear. You have four weeks here. I assume you want to eat most days. Or I can teach you to hunt."

"You have guns?"

"No. Well, yes, some have washed up, but we don't use them to hunt. Most don't really work by the time they reach the shore. To hunt, I use a bow and arrows."

"You have deer?" he asked.

"A few herds," I said. "Some wild sheep, fowl, and hogs. I suggest going in teams for hogs, though. I usually go for deer or fowl."

"I thought your mom did the cooking," he said, laying the fileted pieces in the pan. He then settled the pan on the fire.

"She does. I do the hunting, and she cleans and cooks it. Otherwise, we trade for meat in town."

"Will she miss you tonight for dinner?"

I chuckled. "No. We're on different schedules. We rarely eat together."

He sat on the sand a few feet away, leaning back on his sand-coated elbows. His head bobbed as he soaked in my words. A lock of dark hair swept across his forehead and he pushed it back, dusting sea salt through it. My mouth dried as I watched him. Images danced in my thoughts of us together, and I was thankful that the firelight hid my flush.

A companionable silence fell between us, the fish sizzling in the pan. A gust of salty-sweet air tickled through the flames, sending them higher towards the encroaching dusk.

"It is really beautiful here," he said, watching the waves roll against the sand. The setting sun shimmered on the waves, rippling in pops of yellows, oranges, and whites.

I nodded.

"You probably get tired of looking at it. It's just common to you." He cast a curious look my way.

"The ocean is always changing. The colors, temperament. Storms roll in. It is always doing something. It is alive and a constant in our lives. You can never ignore it."

"Have you ever thought about leaving the island?" he asked.

"I leave the island to fish."

"I mean, try to get past the Sirens?"

I shook my head and rolled my eyes. He was only focused on getting off. Leaving. Trying to encourage us to leave something he didn't understand or appreciate. Something I didn't want.

My heart tightened at the thought of leaving. This was my home, and I loved it. It would never be my choice to leave. But I knew he wanted to. Had known from the second I saw his watch and clothes. It was one of the reasons I'd pulled him up. He'd want to go back. His eagerness to leave was common enough, but I bristled at the thought of not giving the island a try. Washed Up were so quick to dismiss it, escape it, all without understanding it. Though I didn't want to leave my island, I embraced their world that barraged our shores. Learned it. Appreciated it. Respected it.

"No, I like my life here," I finally said. "I've heard enough about the world out there. The wars. The struggles. We have struggles here, too, but it just sounds like your solutions to those struggles create new and deeper issues."

His eyes shot open in surprise and his gaze unfocused as he considered my words. "That's pretty accurate."

"Why don't you like the island?" I challenged. I settled into the sand and bent my knees so the fire could dry my legs.

A breeze rustled in Jasper's hair as he glanced at me. His warm brown eyes shone brightly with the campfire, darkening into liquid pools the longer he looked at me, warming my insides. "I guess it's like why you don't want to leave. It's not home. I have school and a future there."

"You're married?" I asked, using his term for a partnering, my stomach knotting at the idea.

"What?" he stuttered. "No." His gaze fell to the fire.

"You're of age." I dipped my head to maintain eye contact.

"Sure, I guess," he said, meeting my gaze from the corner of his eyes. He swallowed hard. "But I have school. I'm close to a degree. I have time."

"Does your family like your partner or partners?" My throat thickened waiting for the answer.

"My partner?" he said, his face screwing up in confusion.

I chewed my lip thinking of his term for it. "I think you use something like fiancé, girlfriend or boyfriend."

"I know what you meant. I don't have one. My family passed away. I broke up with my girlfriend a few months ago." He picked at something in the sand.

A pang jabbed at my heart and I nearly flinched at the unexpectant reaction. It was ridiculous to be jealous. He was a Washed Up, with whom I had no history, and he was leaving. I wouldn't have a future with him, either.

"Why'd you break up?" I choked out.

A long sigh escaped his lips. "She was talking about marriage."

"Ah," I said, a firm understanding setting into my stomach. He'd leave anyone on the island as a Sea Widow unless they sought to be a Sirens' Daughter. My mom's many warnings spun in my brain. I glanced towards our house, where my mom might have been by now. I'd have to face her soon enough about Jasper. At least I wasn't bringing him home as a partner—temporary or foolishly thinking permanent. "You don't want commitment."

"That's rich coming from you," he said, smiling. His eyes shone brightly as he met my gaze.

"What do you mean?"

"You have Owen, who is obviously interested in you," he said, sitting up and giving me a mockingly stern look. "If you were involved with someone, I don't think he'd be so bold, or he'd be putting them down in front of you. Or he'd threaten to tattle to them about me. I highly doubt he'd ask you out on a date, especially in front of someone, if you were already seriously involved with someone else."

Heat clawed at my face, but I refused to look away. I swallowed the lump lodged in my throat and licked my lips.

I wasn't against love. I wasn't against partnering for benefits or comfort or even love, despite my mom's insistence it was all foolish. She believed that if I couldn't find a partnership that provided an advantage, I should only rely on myself. I'd done that. I built up our rented land, almost had the payment secured to buy the land, built our house, and helped provide for our daily needs. Sharing that load seemed impossible.

When the fish started to crackle, Jasper moved to plate it up. He scooted around the fire to grab the plates and serving utensils.

I hid my smile as he handed me the plate with a larger portion.

Instead of returning to his spot across the fire, he plopped down next to me. I suppressed a delightful shiver. He poured water from a canteen into two glasses, handing me one.

"Cheers." He lifted his glass and bowed his head.

I chuckled at the gesture but mimicked it.

He clinked our glasses together, his dark eyes watching me over the rim. My mouth dried and I guzzled the water to satiate the new sensation.

We ate in comfortable silence. His warmth soaked through the short distance. The delicious fish was seasoned with salt and some herbs. Even after we were done, we sat as night bled across the sky, soaking up the sun's light and providing its own spectacular show of colorful, dusty swirls and stars.

Our quiet revelry was interrupted by someone clearing their throat. I suppressed a cringe at the familiar sound.

Jasper swiveled around, his arm brushing mine.

"Owen," he drawled and shifted to block me from view. It was cute and completely unnecessary.

"Well, well, you two seem to be cozy," Owen said, his voice saccharine.

"What are you doing here?" I asked.

"It's the beach, I was taking a nightly stroll."

"That's new," I deadpanned. Every night, he sailed out into the deeper currents. As kids, Molly hadn't let us go out beyond the riptide. A few years after her vision, when I started looking for land Owen started going further into the inky blackness. "You normally prefer to sail."

"Watching my activities, are you? That's flattering."

I rolled my eyes.

Jasper rolled his shoulders and neck, and repositioned himself so his arm was draped behind me. His fire-heated skin was warm on my bare arm, sending tingles up my back.

"Most people don't come to the beach at night," I snapped. "I know because I'm always here." I shifted to take advantage of Jasper's new position. I aligned with him so our hips and upper arms touched, and the warmth of his skin seeped into mine. "Why are you here?"

Jasper wrapped his arm around my shoulders, cupping my shoulder and pulling me closer so we were flushed against each other as a united front. A strange tingle twisted through me.

A growl escaped Owen as he stopped in front of us. His darkened blue eyes glowered at us from where he towered, tracing our linked arms.

"What's wrong with me being here?" he asked, his gaze burrowing into me. "Am I interrupting something?"

"Yes," Jasper replied immediately.

I choked a laugh.

Owen's ferocity turned towards Jasper. His lips curled into a snarl and his hands furled into fists.

"I doubt I'm interrupting anything important," Owen said. "We all know Rainey's family's aversion to the Washed Up. I wonder why she'd be willing to take you in. What does she get from it? It goes against her nature."

I saw red and my lips twisted into a scowl. If Jasper hadn't been sitting next to me with his arm wrapped around my side, I'd kick Owen's knee and slap his face with a stick from the fire.

Owen must have sensed my intention because he braced himself. He continued, "There are only a few reasons why she'd do it, or you must be paying handsomely for her to take you in. What, do you have knowledge on how to get us that ever-popular electricity?"

"I'm paying her the price she requested," Jasper said. His grip tightened on my shoulder as he tried to keep his temper reigned in. "But you obviously have a problem with me."

"I have a problem with Washed Up."

"Really? As a Ferrier?" Jasper tensed next to me. "You have a problem with your livelihood?"

Owen spat, "You know nothing of me."

"You're a jerk who can't take no for an answer no matter how many times Rainey says it."

"I'm Ferrier that helps Washed Up get off our island. You come here, interrupting our lives, breaking hearts, and thinking you're better than us because you live out there while we're stuck here. Which is why I'm going to offer to ferry you back."

Ice settled in my veins.

"You'd try to throw me overboard," Jasper chuckled humorlessly. "No thanks."

"One moon cycle and she'll be done with you. Then you'll be left all alone," Owen taunted, his lips twisting into a dark smile. His eyes gleamed in the fire light. "Want to tell him why, Rainey?"

"Owen, what do you want?" I spat.

"You know what I want," he murmured, his gaze flicking back to me. It softened when he met my eyes but hardened when Jasper leaned into me, his cheek brushing mine. "Let's stop the games. You know what my mom says, and you know she's never wrong."

My face crimsoned, but thankfully the darkness hid my discomfort.

Jasper picked up on the tension. His fingers smoothed soft circles on my shoulder. "Dude, leave us alone. I'm not asking."

"Oh, really?" Owen challenged. "Think you can take me?"

"If we need to, we can find out."

"Goodnight, Owen," I said. My eyes fixed on the shadows dancing across the sand. "Go home. Now."

Heavy silence weighed between the three of us. Owen's chest lifted and fell with short, raspy breaths.

"You're going to regret taking him in," Owen muttered before turning to leave. "My mom's always right."

I didn't look back up until the sound of Owen's retreating footsteps disappeared.

"Is it about the land?" Jasper finally asked, his hand stilling on my shoulder. "Is she threatening to take it away?"

"No," I groaned.

Still holding my shoulders, Jasper leaned close to my ear and whispered, "What does his mom say?"

"She has visions. She's had visions about hurricanes, how to heal ailments, and even where to find a lost child who wandered into the forest."

"Storms can be predicted. She can learn about plants. The child... could have been luck." With pinched brows, his dark eyes followed the waves.

A sigh escaped me. I, too, had thought that once. "Her visions showed my grandfather on his last journey as a Ferrier. His ship went down, but he'd bowed to her concern and made extra precautions. Ones he wouldn't normally take. He credits her with saving his life." Acid slid down my throat and sloshed in my stomach, unsettling my dinner. Despite knowing all this, I still couldn't see the possibility of the future she claimed was mine.

His gaze flicked to me. "Okay, that's impressive, but what about you? What does she say about you?"

I closed my eyes and shook my head. For a moment, I allowed myself to enjoy the closeness and intimacy of his touch. A mix of excitement and dread coiled in my muscles. But Jasper was a Washed Up and wanted to go back. Other than being the last key to owning my land, he wouldn't be a part of my future.

"Is it that disparaging?"

"No," I chuckled humorously. It was just nothing I wanted now or in the future with Owen. "No, she really likes me. It's why Owen thinks I'll take her offer instead of trading for the land. I mentioned her comments before, but it's more than just hope. She keeps telling me she's already seen that I'll be his partner and the mother to his children."

He stiffened and his fingers curled against me. "Oh."

The one word felt like a mile-wide chasm between us.

Seven

THE FIRE WAS out in the hearth when we made it back home from the beach. The embers blinked as they faded and a quiet chill had settled around the house. Jasper carried the borrowed pole and the cooking supplies basket. I carried the spear and frying pan.

The windows had been left un-shuttered, but the thin sliver of pale moonlight barely penetrated the room. I lit a small torch on the wall, providing enough shadowed light to move about the room without stumbling over stuff.

From a small shipping chest, I pulled a wool blanket and handed it to Jasper.

Keeping my voice low, I said, "You can sleep in the hammock out back or on the rug in here."

He nodded and accepted the blanket.

After hanging up the supplies, I decided to catch a few hours of sleep before starting my scavenging.

When Jasper was settled, I snuffed out the torch light and crept across the room to the sleeping quarters. I slipped through the door and collided with a rigid form in the narrow hallway. A small cry tumbled from my lips, but I caught the rest by slapping a hand over my mouth.

"Mom," I gasped.

"Rainey," she accused sharply. Even without light, my imagination could see the withering look she gave me, her face pinched tight and her green eyes hard and cold.

"You should be asleep," I breathed, stepping towards my bedroom door.

"I heard about the beach," she snapped in English. She wanted him to understand what she said. And it probably had already made it around the island where he was from even though we didn't mention it.

"It's right out there," I said, and gestured towards it even though she couldn't see me. "It's really not a mystery."

"Don't get cute with me." She grabbed my arm to stay my retreat into my room. Her nails dug into my flesh, and I muffled a cry.

"What about the beach?" I said with a sigh and rubbed my forehead.

"You need to be nicer to Owen. He's a great man."

"Owen?" I asked innocently. "What happened with Owen?" *He* was the one who had been a jerk on the beach.

"Nothing except your rude mouth, which is exactly the point."

I let out a longer sigh. She was worse than him about us being together. With me getting closer and closer to finishing my trades, she brought up partnering with him daily. Any curse or groan or setback was proof I was being foolish.

Her voice turned chilly. "And what is with you bringing in a Washed Up?"

"You know why," I nearly whined, glancing down the hall. The walls were sturdy, but they didn't block sound.

"It's foolish," my mom spat. "There are other ways. Easier ways. Washed Up are more trouble than they're worth."

"Afraid I'll repeat your mistakes?" I asked, cursing the second it was out of my mouth.

She sucked in a sharp breath and then a slow, dark chuckle filled the air.

"Mom, I'm—"

"Don't," she interrupted. "You meant it. But I thought you were better than to follow in my steps."

"Mom, I'm five years older than you were when dad washed up. I'm the same age you were when I was already walking and talking and tinkering.”

“So that means you’ve successfully been better than me? You have nothing else to learn?”

I moaned and leaned against the wall, closing my eyes and letting the rough wood press into my back. This was an argument I wouldn’t win. Nothing I’d say would be right. If I agreed with her, it meant I thought she was less than me. If I didn’t agree with her, it meant I hadn’t learned my lesson.

“I don’t want him here,” she seethed, cutting into the uneasy silence.

My teeth clenched and my fists furled.

“He needs to leave in the morning.”

I didn’t even think about it. “No.”

“No?” she challenged.

Something untethered in my stomach, unleashing my tongue and thoughts.

“No, this is my house,” I said, knowing I’d crossed a line.

“*Your* house?” she sputtered.

I couldn’t take back any of my comments. I couldn’t make her agree with me. But that didn’t stop me.

“I pay the land rent. I built the house. I traded for the materials. I almost have enough to buy the land.”

“And you’ve just been gracious enough to let me live here, groveling for your leftovers? How can I ever repay you, daughter, who I fed and clothed and sheltered?”

“Enough, Mom,” I sighed again. It was pointless to remind her that, as my mother, it was her responsibility to raise me. “Enough. I know him being here brings up painful memories. We’re both tired. We both carry our weight in this house. He’ll carry his.”

“But I’m the mother, I should carry more,” she replied.

“Mom, we’re both grown,” I said. “We fill a role so the other doesn’t have to.”

“You’re twenty,” my mom started.

“I’m aware.” She was going to bring Owen up again if I didn’t do something fast. That was what she’d been leading up to. Me partnering with Owen and why my shunning his advances on the beach was wrong. That, instead of wasting time saving to buy the land or deal with a Washed Up, I could partner with the "great catch" Owen and have the land as a gift. "Since Jasper is going to be staying with us, he'll need clothes. I'm pretty sure you still have a piece or two of Dad's clothing."

Mom drew a sharp breath. A heavy silence followed.

She remained quiet, but anger and tension rolled off her in waves. I'd already jumped in deep and decided to keep going.

"Jasper is going to catch fish for us to help out while he's here. Since neither of us needs Dad's clothing and he's not coming back for them, I figured we could loan them to Jasper for the fish. He's even offered to help me with the fencing and transport in exchange for room and board. I have everything set up for the trades. *Everything*. If he can help with the prep, it'll save considerable time and I can transport them after the festival." The words came out sharper than I intended, but I was already in defense mode from her ambush about Owen. I needed to come at her just as strong.

"It's your house, do as you want," she gritted out. She released my arm and spun towards her bedroom. "Even if it is a waste of your time."

I closed my eyes. Sleeping wasn't going to work. I might as well scavenge on the beach for the smaller pieces that had washed up throughout the night.

The dark embrace of the night still hugged the sky as I picked my way across the rocks, the slosh of water the only sound. Jasmine carried on the wind, mixing with the ocean breeze.

The tides brought small treasures each night that floated in the current, depositing them on the beaches while disturbing the sands that kept older pieces hidden. The other Scavengers would wait for the morning light to find the small pieces easier, but I'd taken to scavenging at this time because I could focus on catching metallic glints without the sun bearing down on me.

My lantern's light created a warm, golden halo around me as I toed through the rocks. Although a torch or lantern made it easier for others to follow, it was only on the moonless nights that others came out this early, and often not just Scavengers. Most didn't find the smaller treasures worth as much, but nails, jewels, and trinkets could all be trade, and some for more than larger items.

Clumsy footsteps descended the path behind me, a man's panting breaths cutting over the slosh of the sea and droning out the insects.

I turned to yell at Owen for stalking me but straightened when I realized it was Jasper. Fear spiked in my stomach, freezing my breath in my throat. Had my mom driven him off? Did he not want to deal with her?

His dark hair was strewn about from tossing around on the rug, sticking out in tufts. His flannel wasn't buttoned all the way up, leaving his chest exposed. Something else twisted in my stomach over the fear and burned it away as my mouth dried. His jeans were wrinkled from sleeping in them. We needed to find him something else to wear. Something that fit. Something I could ignore.

I silently waited until he was a few feet away so my voice wouldn't carry on the wind.

"What are you doing?"

"I couldn't sleep," he mumbled, rubbing a palm over his sleepy eyes as his shoulders slumped. I willed my eyes to not track down his frame.

I knew that feeling. It was common after one of my nightly conversations with my mom.

"How much did you hear?" I demanded.

He averted his gaze to the waters, the dark waves mirroring the faint glow of the sky.

"I can't pretend I didn't hear it."

"You could try," I offered.

He lifted his shoulders. "Your mom's not happy I'm here, especially at your house."

"She'll get over it."

"Will she?"

"Eventually," I said. "You're planning to leave on the next moonless night. She'll be fine after that."

Butterflies flapped in my stomach. Thankful for the low light, I still turned so he couldn't see my face. He'd soon be gone like many before him. He wouldn't be different. My land was worth the inconvenience of harboring him and my mom's anger.

"Is she happy about you getting the land?" he asked as if reading my mind.

"No." I blew out a breath. "She thinks I should partner with Owen and make the trades for our use. She thinks I'm being stubborn and stupid and wasting time and resources by saying no to him."

Jasper rubbed his neck and averted his eyes. Toeing the dirt with his boot, he asked, "Once you buy the land, would you consider partnering with him?"

I scoffed. "No, not at all. We're not suited. I love this island. I love what I do. I'm not attracted to Owen like I am—" I stopped myself, but heat still clawed at my neck. "I'm not attracted to him. Despite what he says, his love is the sea. This island is too small for him. He had it mapped out by the time we reached our teens. He wants more."

"He thinks you're a good partnering," Jasper murmured. "He keeps trying... his mom's visions..."

"Owen says I'm a land Siren, always calling to him. The thing is, the Sirens can only snare you if you don't know what you want. I've never snared him."

"But your mom wants you to partner up with Owen? Even though you're not interested?"

I nodded. "Yeah, she thinks Owen is a great partner. She believes what his mom says. And he's from the island. I think that's the most important part to her."

He stared at me expectantly.

"You're leaving something out," he accused. "Why is that the most important thing to her?"

There was no point in lying. It wasn't a secret, and it didn't matter on the island. I finally said, "My dad washed up when my mom was fifteen."

"You said your family..."

"I said my family is from the island. The family I know. My dad was from fifteen hundred something. He was an explorer. He stayed three moon cycles and laid with many island people. They say he was very attractive and very charismatic. He took a liking to my mom and her bed."

"She was fifteen?"

"It's a little young for here, but not unheard of."

"He stayed three cycles," Jasper pointed out. "Why'd your dad go back?"

I hesitated. Some things were just better left alone. But it wasn't a secret. Everyone knew everyone's business on the island.

"He didn't know my mom was pregnant if that's what you're asking."

"It sounded like he was enjoying himself," Jasper said carefully.

"From what I heard, he didn't carry his weight here. My mom shared her portions and he let her. She shared her bed, and he enjoyed it."

Jasper was silent as he waited, his face void of judgment or emotion.

"He left on his fifth moonless night here. No one knew he was planning to leave, and no Ferrier will admit to taking him. My grandfather was a Ferrier at the time, but he claims he didn't leave land that day and the family backs him up."

"What do you believe?"

I shrugged. "My grandfather wanted to protect my mom. He didn't know she was pregnant. He didn't have to be the one to ferry him, but I'm sure he helped organize and pay for it. I think my dad got a trip back whether he wanted to or not. Or..." I let the words die in the air.

"Or?" Jasper prompted when he realized I was done.

I licked my lips and said, "Or, he's at the bottom of the ocean."

Jasper's startled gaze jumped to the ocean and then back to me.

"You mean..."

I nodded. "I have no proof. It's one theory. All we know is, he's gone and he's not coming back."

"So, your mom's afraid..." Jasper made a strangled sound and his eyes darted away from mine.

"Yeah, she's afraid I'll follow in her footsteps. She's afraid I'll be a Sea Widow."

"I..." he stuttered and stopped. He searched my face and his jaw

ticked. Finally, he nodded and said, "I'll help you finish the trade. I'll...
I'll help."

"You can help me scavenge tonight," I offered to end his discomfort.
"In the morning, you can help me clean the items of the salt or you can
fish. I may be my mother's daughter, but I won't lay with you, and I
expect you to carry your weight."

Eight

WHEN YELLOW AND orange streaked the sky, the air growing hot with the start of a new day, we headed back to the house. The half-filled cart held new items, including driftwood, a bottle, a few articles of clothing, and some metal bits to melt down.

"Does this type of stuff normally wash up?" Jasper asked, pushing his hair from his face. A sweat bead raced down his forehead. "I thought just big stuff did, after moonless nights."

"Yes. According to some Washed Up from later centuries, there are swirling pools of trash in the ocean. I don't understand it, but random things wash up. These are pretty small and take a while to float to shore. People, ships, and large items only show up on moonless nights, but there are always treasures on the beach."

I pulled up short outside of the house. A ribbon of smoke twirled from the chimney into the brightening sky, the hazy edge merging into the receding night. My mom was already up and baking bread. My stomach rumbled at the aroma of yeasty flour mixed with the salt of the sea.

"I can stay in the hammock," Jasper said, his eyes fixed on the smoke.

I glanced at him and laughed. "Afraid of her?"

"No, but this is your home. I'm transitory. I don't want to create issues."

"Sweet, but unnecessary," I said. "These issues existed before you arrived and will continue to."

"I don't need to make them worse." He ran a hand through his hair.

I shrugged. Lead pooled in my stomach and swam in my veins. I needed to harbor him, but I couldn't force him.

Even if it would be easier with someone else, someone I didn't find attractive, a part of me—one I didn't want to admit to—looked forward to the few weeks he stayed. "You're welcome here if you want to stay."

"You never bring in Washed Up," he murmured. "Everyone has said that. It goes against what your mom wants. Yet you keep fighting her on it. I don't understand... Why'd you bring me up?"

"Honestly?"

He nodded.

"Based on your clothes, I thought you had some aptitude for mechanical stuff and could be of use. I also hoped you had something on you I could use to trade if I let you stay. I thought you may actually have something worth the effort to haul you up."

He snorted a laugh. "That was brutally honest. Did I have something you could use?"

"I didn't take anything from you," I said, narrowing my eyes. "I don't steal."

"So you were going to trade me for my stuff?" he asked, raising an eyebrow.

"I figured you'd want to eat and have shelter," I replied and continued with the honesty in the fading darkness. "But you didn't have anything worth trading on you."

"You checked?" he asked incredulously. He patted his chain and pockets.

I rolled my eyes. Only an idiot wouldn't check.

"But you let me stay anyway? With nothing worth trading?"

I sighed and rubbed my forehead. Why did everything have to be so simple and complicated at the same time? His stuff didn't matter. I needed to harbor *him*.

His brow furrowed. "What? What else aren't you telling me?"

With Jasper staying with me, and my aversion to harboring Washed Up in the past, the speculations and rumors would start up. Beatrice had probably already told every person she saw and they, the same. He was going to find out, anyway. Nothing stayed secret on the island. It was best if he heard from me.

"Why did you let me stay?" He stood taller, shoulders back in defense.

"It was part of the agreement," I said, risking a glance at his face. My gut twisted knowing I had to tell him the full truth.

His features were tight as he regarded me. "What does that mean?"

A wave of nausea rolled up my throat. Blinking repeatedly, I took a few breaths to calm my nerves.

"It's an old tradition. When a plot is cleared to build a new place, the landowners harbor a Washed Up for a moon cycle. Clearing land is rare. The last plot was before my grandparents' parents. But bringing in a Washed Up, the Sirens' gift, is to show respect to them and bring good luck and fortune to the land. We're not clearing a plot, but Molly believes helping the Washed Up is imperative. We must honor tradition. She's superstitious and I'm not going to shun the Sirens' gift. I don't need to be blamed for storms or bad harvests."

Jasper stared at me, stoically. "How does that impact you and you bringing me up? The land was already cleared."

I swallowed. If he didn't stay, I'd have to wait another cycle for a Washed Up. Another cycle of delaying the trades and possibly losing them. And he'd be with someone else. "Part of the agreement with her was to harbor a Washed Up. '*To bring good luck to the reformation of the plot of land by honoring the Sirens,*'" I said, quoting Molly. "I also think it was her way to sway me to partnering with Owen."

"So you needed to bring me up as part of the agreement for the land?" he snarled.

"I had to bring someone up... You were there."

Jasper rolled his tongue against his cheek. The silence dragged on as he stared at me. The day grew warmer the longer we silently stood there. Sweat beaded on my brow from the heat and waiting.

Finally, he asked, "Would you or I have to trade for me to go with someone else?"

My heart sank, but I forced a grin. "Do you want to go somewhere else? I don't blame you. You'd have to make an agreement with them, but Willis can help. To start, they'd want a trade to take you on and then you'd work for your keep with them."

He scanned my face. His jaw ticked. Seconds felt like hours. "Regardless of your reasons for bringing me up, which I understand, I promised to help with meals and finish the trade. I just didn't realize you also needed to bring me up and it wasn't just me in a bind."

"Nothing is done here out of the kindness of a heart," I said, my mouth flattening into a thin line. "We're not mean people, but resources are limited. Harboring a Washed Up has a cost."

Jasper nodded. His expression remained unreadable.

"Did you change your mind?" The words burned my tongue as I said them. "Do you want me to find somewhere else for you? I can go to talk to Willis."

"No!" he blurted out, his cheeks reddening.

"No?" I asked, unwilling to let hope build. Too much banked on his decision. He could be the reason I got my land or had it slip through my hands like sand.

"No, I get it," Jasper sighed. "You still brought me up. You didn't have to. You've been helping me even though you really don't want to. It's a risk for you."

My muscles tightened and I swallowed down my defense. Everything he said was true.

"You're still good with our agreement?" The balance was swinging, and I needed to weigh it in my favor.

He nodded. "Fishing and helping with the fence and transport is fair for clothes, room, and board." He glanced at the hammock and then the house. "So, I should get the fishing gear so I can earn my keep?"

Dizzying relief swam in my mind, and I fought a smile spreading on my lips.

"Eh, I know you said you could fish, but I'm really doubting that after last night. We just might stick with metalwork. Well, maybe. I'll need to see what you can do first."

He shot me a glare. I laughed and punched his shoulder.

He cracked a grin. He ran a hand through his hair. "So... We're good with me staying here for the cycle, then?"

Hope bubbled in my chest, nearly choking my words, and I nodded. "You helped find and bring in today's stuff. You can help clean it and have half of it."

"To make trades?"

"You need to trade with a Ferrier to leave the island. You'll also need to build or buy a boat to cross back into your waters. The Ferrier will get you past the Sirens in their ship, but you have to finish the journey."

"There's a lot of work to be done," he muttered.

"Most of which will be easier to do inside the house." I tilted my head towards the door with a half-smile.

He swallowed.

"Come on, let's get this over with," I said and pushed open the door with Jasper trailing behind me.

Mom's back was to us as she put more loaves of bread into the hearth. The heat twisted around her, brushing my skin. My stomach rumbled in anticipation.

Jasper hovered at the door, one foot across the threshold, his head hung like a child waiting to be scolded.

I rolled my eyes at him. My nerves tingled when he smiled back at me and took the last step into the house.

I pulled the cart to the table, the oiled wheels smoothly gliding over the planks, and lit a torch by my worktable. Jasper moved to the other side, his gaze averted as he grabbed a rag from the bucket. He rolled up the sleeves of his flannel, exposing his corded muscles. The few top buttons remained askew. Shaking my head, I started sorting items on the cart.

"Find any good trades?" my mom asked without looking up from her baking, as if last night hadn't happened.

"We did," I said.

Her frame went rigid at the word *we*. She turned slowly, her eyes dark and her mouth a pinched line.

"I thought he was going to get us fish each day," she said coolly. Her eyes flicked to the dry gear above the door. "I thought he was going to pull his weight."

"Day's young," I said, and pulled out a rag. "He's also gotta get stuff to trade for a Ferrier."

"You're sharing your haul now?"

"It's not sharing if he found half of it," I said measuredly.

She snorted.

Jasper opened his mouth to speak, but I shook my head at him.

"You're looking for a Ferrier?" she asked him. She folded her arms, her green eyes burning with hate.

Jasper looked to me, while he still cleaned the metal, and I nodded.

"Yes, ma'am," he answered.

"He needs your help answering?" Mom cocked an eyebrow.

"Well you're being rude, so my guess is he doesn't want to insult you more than his presence on the island already does," I said, staying focused on the scrap metal.

Jasper's eyes grew wide while Mom sucked in a large breath.

"Rainey!" she bellowed.

"MOM!" I yelled back.

"I taught you better respect than that!"

"It's not on display right now," I shot. "You're taking out your regrets on Jasper. He's done nothing wrong yet. He's scared in a land he doesn't understand, trying to adapt to a world unlike his. He helped clean stuff yesterday, helped with dinner, and helped scavenge last night. He's trying. What more do you want?"

Her face pinched, her nostrils flaring.

"What's making you the most mad is what you think are snags in your desire for me to partner with Owen," I said, staring her in the eyes. "Jasper being a Washed Up means I met Molly's requirement without partnering with Owen."

"He's a good island man," she seethed. "You're being a stubborn fool."

"I'm not interested in him," I said and looked away so I didn't have to see Jasper's reactions to this old and tiring conversation.

"I invited him over for dinner tonight," Mom said, setting her jaw and raising an eyebrow.

"I hope you two enjoy it."

"What does that mean?" she pressed.

"I'm sure you two will have a lovely time."

"I expect you to be there," she warned.

"Can't, I have plans," I said, grabbing the first item my hands touched in the cart. A chipped platter.

"And what plans do you have?"

"I'm teaching Jasper how to properly fish."

He snorted a laugh, which made me chuckle.

"You're going to ruin your chances for a good partnering just to spite me?" my mom snapped.

"No, I'm ruining my chances at a partnering I don't want, never wanted, and will never want."

"You're saying no because I like the idea. You could stop breaking your back scavenging every day for this land and be gifted it while partnering with a good person. You're being stubborn and spiteful."

"I learned from the best," I said, leveling my gaze on my mom.

"So, Jasper knows why you pulled him up?" she challenged, her eyes dancing in triumph.

"Yes, ma'am," Jasper answered for me. He shot me a smile before continuing. "Rainey was willing to take on the extra work of a Washed Up for Molly's requirements."

"You're fine with her using you?" Mom snarled, her chances at controlling the situation were dissolving.

"Seems pretty mutual to me," Jasper said with a shrug.

"You have it all worked out, don't you?" Mom spat at me. Behind her, the air thickened with smoke.

"Seems that way," I said. I sniffed the air. "Your bread's going to burn."

Mom whirled around to tend to her bread.

Jasper shot me a small sympathetic smile and my stomach turned. I didn't want his pity or my mom's judgement.

Nine

My grandparents' house sat tucked on a hill, closer to the woods than the ocean. The towering palm trees kept the house cooler during the day and the salt of the ocean mingled with rich jasmine, orchids, and other flowers into a bouquet of scents.

The house was the same as when I'd lived there with my mom. It'd been passed down on my grandmother's side for generations, the exterior pieced together from a marooned wooden sea vessel, the thick planks smoothed from the water and bleached in the sun. They'd freshly white-washed it, brightening up the grayed wood. It was an older-style frame that included one large main room with interior room dividers to section off space.

My grandmother was tending to her garden when we walked up the stone-covered pathway. Lush flowers bloomed along the perimeter while vegetables ran in neat rows in the lot.

Grandma waved a dirt-covered hand at me, a large smile spread across her smooth face. She brushed her hands on the ground and ran a hand over her dark brown hair, held back in a bun. A few silver strands streaked it. Standing, she jogged over to us with her arms out for an embrace.

"You must be Jasper," she said. Grandma pulled him into a hug, her thick arms smothering him against her denim overalls. Her perfume of lilac oil danced in the air.

Jasper stiffened. His hands hovered in the air before he managed to gently tap her shoulders. He gave a strained smile when his gaze found mine.

"Grandma, he doesn't know you," I said, tugging Jasper free. He stepped back, but his warmth lingered in the air. My hand stayed a little too long on his arm before falling.

"Sorry, you have that kind, familiar look to you." She smiled, color staining her cheeks as she patted his face. "I'm Isla, but you can call me Grandma."

He smiled and my stomach flipped when it widened as soon as his focus turned to me.

Grandma's arms then snagged around my waist and pulled me in tight.

"It's always so good to see you," she murmured into my hair, rocking me with her embrace.

I buried my face in her shoulder. "It's good to see you too."

"I know you're so busy, but I like it when you find the time to make it over here." She pulled back to cup my cheek.

"I know, Grandma," I said, smiling. "The week after the moonless night is always my busiest for scavenging."

"You work too hard." She pulled me in for another quick hug.

"There's always work to be done," I said. I wrapped my arm around her shoulder and guided her to the door. Otherwise, she'd keep us out in the garden to chat and hug all day.

"Is this nice young man helping with your workload?" Grandma asked, swiveling around to offer Jasper a hand. She tugged him forward to walk with us.

He chuckled but joined her other side, still holding her hand.

"He is," I confirmed.

"Good." She nodded to him. "You seem like a catch."

Jasper blushed and stared at the ground.

"Grandma, you already have Grandpa, and he won't share."

She laughed and swatted me. "Don't be blind."

It was my turn to blush, but thankfully before she could continue, the front door burst open with my grandfather standing tall in the frame. His once-dark brown hair, mostly gray now, hung in long waves around his face. His warm green eyes, the same color as my mom's, shone brightly as he took us in, and his olive skin glistened in the sunlight.

In his youth he'd been a Ferrier, braving the ocean's currents and winds to help the Washed Up go back home. It was dangerous work. He'd stopped when I was seven after barely making it back. As Molly predicted, a squall had formed, taking his boat but sparing him.

"Rainey," he said, extending his arms for a hug.

"Grandpa." I met his strong embrace.

"Ah, this must be Jasper," Grandpa said, the words muffled in my hair.

"Hi, sir," Jasper said, extending his hand.

My grandpa chuckled. It wasn't our custom, but we knew what it meant. Grandpa took his hand, pumping it twice while keeping an arm around my shoulders.

"Does everyone know who I am?" Jasper asked.

"It's a small island," Grandpa said. "We know everyone's business. Including..." Grandpa's eyes narrowed on me. "...an argument you're having with your mama."

I rolled my eyes, but heat clawed at my face. "It's not like it's new or going to stop anytime soon."

"Are your parents like that, too?" Grandma asked Jasper, giving him a wink.

"Um..." He rubbed his neck and averted his gaze.

"Grandma," I warned.

"Oh, now dear, everyone has parents. Some are like your mom, some are like us, and some are not a part of your upbringing, like your father. My guess, based on his mannerisms, is he has a parent who very much loves him and encourages him."

"Yes ma'am, I did." Jasper murmured. "My dad loved me very much before he passed a few years ago. My mom passed away at my birth. My dad wanted to make her proud... I want to make them both proud." He swallowed thickly and blinked a few times.

Grandma smiled. "Sounds like a good man. I'm sorry about your parents."

Jasper shrugged and looked away, his eyes glassy. I never mourned the father I didn't know. From the stories I'd heard, he wasn't worth it. Yet Jasper mourned his mom based on his father's devotion to her memory, and his father on their history. My path seemed the easier one.

Inside my grandparents' house the hearth was cold, but the house was warm and inviting. A bowl of berries sat on the table and a sliced loaf of Mom's bread was next to it. Shelves lined the walls, displaying trinkets that had washed up, including jewels, some mechanical but had no electricity, and a few creations I'd melded together when learning. Lemon scent drifted in the air.

"Have a seat," Grandma said, gesturing towards the family table. Grandpa had taken a felled tree and made bench-style seating around a washed-up flat board. It was where I first started tinkering, and where Mom used to make her bread. I slipped into my seat, the curve fitting my back perfectly. Jasper sat next to me, his arm brushing against mine, while Grandma and Grandpa slipped into their spots across from me.

"Now, why did you venture all the way over here with Jasper, hm?" Grandpa prompted, taking a slice of bread.

I glanced between Jasper and Grandpa before taking a breath. My heart panged as I spoke. "He needs a Ferrier. I was hoping you could direct him to a good one."

"Heading home, are you, son?" Grandpa asked. A large smile curved his lips.

"Yes, sir," Jasper said. His eyes tracked to me before the table and then Grandpa.

"That's a shame. We could always use more good people here."

"Grandpa," I warned, my chest tightening. "He's a Washed Up."

"I know, dear," he said, patting my hand with his calloused one. He directed his gaze back to Jasper. "So, tell me. What do you have to trade?"

"What do you need?" Jasper asked hesitantly.

"Not for me." Grandpa shook his head. "The information comes free of charge. A visit from my granddaughter and her friend is more than enough payment. Who'll be the best Ferrier depends on what you can provide for trade. There are three active Ferriers. I was one of them, once, but my boat was destroyed, and I promised Isla I'd let Ferrying sink with it. I'm guessing you don't want Owen, or you'll have to hear him sing his love for Rainey."

Scarlet flushed my cheeks and I bit back a retort. I shot daggers at Grandpa.

Jasper nudged my shoulder. My body froze and my brain screamed at me for acting like a fool. My lips curled in a tight smile that I hoped didn't look creepy. Jasper smiled back and I relaxed a bit.

"I don't think Owen and I have gotten off to a great start," Jasper said, shaking his head. "He did offer so I would leave."

"Is that so?" Grandpa eyed me up. His smile turned into a smirk. "Owen already jealous?"

"Grandpa," I growled.

Grandpa chuckled and patted my knee. "Well, no matter who you go with, you'll have to pay them to take you out by the Sirens."

"I can fish," Jasper said and shot me a dark look when I snorted.

"Most of us can," Grandpa said. "Most Ferriers won't do it for a few fish. It's a tough trek. They'll want something that eases their burden long term."

Jasper looked helplessly at me.

"He's helping me scavenge," I offered. "Is there something he can look for or build?"

My grandparents stilled and shared an odd look.

"What?" I barked, my fingers curling into fists on the table.

"Nothing, dear," Grandma said, waving me off. "I didn't know you knew how to share treasure, is all."

"Ha, ha," I said. "He did the work, it's his stuff."

"His stuff?" Grandma gasped. "You shared your section of beach? Aren't you the one who refused to let someone use your air pump because they found stuff in *your* area?"

I groaned and slumped back in my chair, my face hot.

Grandpa stifled his laugh and continued. "The best item to trade would be a boat, but those only come in on moonless nights or you have to make it. You'll also need to make one or trade for one to get past the Sirens. Making two in the timeframe may not be possible, especially ones good enough for trade. Pots and pans, tools, weapons, or clothing are all highly sought after. It's less stuff for a person to find, create, or do without."

"Do I have any chance of that stuff washing up between now and the next moonless night?" Jasper asked.

Grandpa averted his eyes. His voice was sympathetic when he said, "Not really. Most Washed Up have to wait until the second moonless night if they want to use scavenged treasure for passage back. Otherwise, they trade something they came in with. Or help build furniture or fix a house. It'll depend on what the Ferrier needs for the other days of the cycle."

That much work would require a second cycle. He wanted to leave after one. I *needed* him to leave after one. The thought of him leaving already settled hard on me, and the cycle had just begun. If he stayed two... My mouth dried.

"He has a watch," I said. I didn't mention the chain he wore. That type of jewelry was usually sentimental.

Jasper raised an accusatory eyebrow at me.

"I told you I checked," I huffed.

"A watch doesn't matter here," Grandpa said. "We don't care what the sticks say on the face of it. If you found a ring or bracelet or necklace, a Ferrier might be willing to provide passage if they wanted to gift it to a loved one or thought they could trade up for it."

Jasper's hands fell to his chain, rubbing over the lump of his t-shirt. "So, I'll need to be here for two months?" he asked, a catch in his voice. His eyes bounced to me before he cleared his throat. "That'll be okay? Can we work that out?"

"There's no need," I said quickly, my heart hammering in protest. "Pull your daily weight and I can give you something to trade for passage. If you help me finish the fencing so I can do the transport on time, I can trade you my boat that you'll need to cross the Sirens."

"But you need your boat," Jasper said, his brow furrowing. "Two months will be okay. Will I need to ask someone else after a cycle?"

My heart thudded louder and more violently in my chest. He was okay with two months? He was already making plans? What happened to wanting to go back immediately? Fear and excitement curled in my veins.

"We'll make sure you get to leave when you want to." I swallowed the lump in my throat. Two months seemed like eternity to have him underfoot and making me act weird.

"Should I work on trade with another islander for room and board for a second month?" Jasper asked again, his voice scratchy. His dark eyes stared at his hands.

"I didn't say that. I said we'll get you back when you want to. You want to go home. We'll make the one cycle work. I can trade my boat to help." I forced the words out around the dryness in my mouth, staring at the tabletop.

Grandpa sucked in a whistly breath between his teeth. "That's a generous offer," he said, nodding at Jasper. "You best make sure you earn it. A boat is a lifeline here."

"If I have to stay an extra month, I'll earn my keep," he said. He folded his arms. "I can't take something of yours."

I waved him off. Why couldn't he see I was trying to help him? "I'll make you earn it. There's food to catch, stuff to clean, a fence to build and transport to set up. You'll be a second set of hands for a few weeks."

"Uh-huh," Grandpa drawled, a mischievous grin tugging at his lips. "Sounds like you have a plan."

Grandma *tsked* and shook her head at me like I was a fool. She leaned into Grandpa, snaking her arm through his. He instinctively leaned his head against the top of hers. "Sometimes we can't see past our own noses."

"Or get too caught up on the words said instead of the meaning," Grandpa replied.

I rolled my eyes. Placing my elbows on the table, I cupped my chin in my hands and asked, "Who do you recommend as the Ferrier?"

Grandpa looked Jasper up and down. "He's a fit fellow who should be able to help with the trek across, unlike some of our Washed Up. That opens up the possibilities. Fredricka is looking for a new boat for shore fishing. Marcus is looking for something to help him and his partners with transporting their food to sell. I'm going to guess Owen wants something sparkly to catch someone's eye, but Jasper already said Owen isn't a match."

My attention jerked to my grandfather. A twinkle played in his eyes, and he chuckled. He patted my hand. "I know, dear. It won't work on you. You find your own sparkly stuff."

"She keeps rejecting him and Owen wants to propose to her?" Jasper asked, his eyes darkening.

"Propose?" I parroted.

"Ask you to marry him?" Color tinted his cheeks.

"Oh, partnering," Grandma said, nodding. "He's talked about that since they were kids. He's been seriously trying for three years. He keeps trying, she keeps refusing."

"Three years?" Jasper said, his eyes widening as they tracked to me.

I looked away.

"The boy should learn to accept no," Grandpa said. "Rainey's made her point. I don't care what Molly says."

"Rainey is his land Siren," Grandma said with an eye roll.

Jasper looked to me, his brow furrowing.

"Sirens aren't real wants," Grandpa added, reiterating what I told Jasper earlier. "They're what will lure you from what you want."

"One theory," Grandma said, bobbing her head.

"Anyway," I interrupted, "Thankfully, I don't have anything sparkly to trade him, so he's off the table for more than one reason. I only have my boat. The last two I was able to scavenge went to the house and building the hearth. I probably have things we could put together to make something for Marcus."

"When you have it ready, let me know," Grandpa said. "Then I'll set up a meeting with Marcus. He'll be less likely to try to barter for more if I'm involved."

Ten

To beat the sun, I took Jasper through the woods to get fresh water. We had a dozen canteens and a barrel to fill. The fresh crisp air of the forest was refreshing, as was the shaded canopy. Birds chirped above us and the river babbled towards the bay.

"Is there always fresh water?" Jasper asked.

"We have rivers and lakes through the hills. We all use the streams."

"Does anyone live by the stream to make getting water easier? They could trade for it."

"Water doesn't belong to anyone here. Besides, the riverbeds flood and could wash away a home."

"So no one can build on a river?"

I shook my head.

"Well, well, well," a familiar voice called out.

I groaned.

"He always finds you..." Jasper whispered.

"You two are always together," Owen taunted from behind us. "You normally don't work with anyone. Or socialize. What does he have over you?"

"Just ignore him," I grumbled, filling my last canteen.

Jasper nodded as he finished with the barrel. He lifted it to put the lid on and Owen banged into his side as he moved to a small outcrop of rocks dotted in the river.

Jasper lost his hold on the barrel. It fell back into the river, emptying its contents and splashing water on him, soaking his clothes.

Jasper cursed and righted the barrel.

"Oops, you should be more careful," Owen mocked. "You need to make sure you earn your keep, and spilling more water than you bring won't do it."

"What's your problem?" Jasper barked, his face dark.

Owen turned and squared his shoulders. He was a few inches taller than Jasper and used it to look down at him. His blue eyes burned with hatred. "My problem is that Washed Up keep coming here and playing games with people, knowing they're leaving. You leave scars on our island."

"What game am I playing? Survival?"

"You'll be like the rest. You'll come here. Turn some faces. Break some hearts. And then pay tokens to escape back to your world, leaving people behind who will mourn for you while you forget about this place."

"Like your father did?" Jasper asked.

"And hers," Owen said as he turned towards me. "You planning on repeating the pattern? Laying with her, impregnating her, and then begging to leave?"

I sucked on my teeth.

Jasper's face reddened about as much as mine did, his lips curling into a snarl. "You son of—"

"You'd be the first to take his offer," I spat, interrupting Jasper. My fists furled at my chest, ready to swing at Owen. "You've already offered to ferry him. You sit here accusing him of others' choices knowing full well you accept their payment to take them away. You profit off those escaping back to their world. Off the pain. You help make Sea Widows."

Owen's face pinched up, his nose flaring, and he shot me a murderous look. His wrath twisted back to Jasper and he stepped closer, his fingers curled into fists.

"So, your concern is that I'm going to break someone's heart?" Jasper asked Owen. He stepped out of the water, leaving the barrel in the current. His dark eyes assessed Owen. His damp white t-shirt clung to his torso.

"We have enough Sea Widows, we don't need more," Owen said, staring at me.

"Owen, we are not partners, nor will we be, despite what your mom says. She's wrong. What Jasper and I do is none of your business. Besides, we have more Sirens' Daughters than Sea Widows."

"So you're not denying it?" Owen yelled. His face elongated, teeth bared.

Something inside of me snapped. I saw red. I wanted to break his face. Claw him with my nails instead of my words. Show him I was a daughter of the Sirens and my foremothers' blood ran in me. Whatever I was, Sirens' Daughter, Sea Widow, or just a Scavenger earning her land, it was by *my* choice.

I lunged at Owen.

Jasper spun around and grabbed me around my waist. I gasped at the sudden stop. Regardless, I lashed out towards Owen, but Jasper held tightly to me, grunting as I gained inches towards Owen.

Owen swallowed and anchored his feet. His eyes darted around my squirming form, trying to find where I was going to attack.

"He's not worth it," Jasper hissed, his breath hot against my ear. My stomach curled in something more than anger.

"Put me down," I yelled and kicked at him, lashing out to go after Owen and to stop whatever effect Jasper had on me.

He grunted and twirled me around to face him instead of Owen, keeping his hands on my sides. The touch was electric and too distracting. He stared me in the eyes. "Are you okay?"

"Yes," I spat to loosen his hold and effect. His face was an unfocused blur as I twisted to see Owen. "Perfect."

Jasper sidestepped to block my view of Owen.

"Rainey, it'll only cause issues for you," he soothed.

The warmth of his touch was intoxicating, taking my breath. I swallowed and stepped back. "I'm fine. I won't kill him today."

"Good enough," Jasper said with a smile. His fingers lingered for a bit longer before he went to retrieve the water barrel.

Owen stood on the rock, his face a wall of hate as he glowered at me.

I ignored him as I gathered up the canteens and helped Jasper refill and seal the barrel. When it was properly sealed, I showed him how I rolled it to reduce the effort of carrying it.

"Rainey, you're not acting like you," Owen said, his words clipped. "I bet my mom would have some thoughts."

Mom was in the garden when it came into view. Her dark hair was pulled back in a braid and her overalls were clean despite being in the dirt. She cast me a bored look over her shoulder but otherwise didn't acknowledge us.

"She's not like her parents," Jasper whispered, leaning over my shoulder.

"I think she was, before my dad," I answered. "She was loving and caring. She still is. It's just... since I reached the age she was when she had me, she's gotten more protective, more paranoid. She wants to protect me. Her parents were kind, and she blames them for letting her be naive. She doesn't want her life for me."

"But look at what you've done." Jasper nodded towards the house.

"It made it worse. Now, everything I do is seen as a way I'm putting her down."

"Why did she move in with you, then?" Jasper asked.

"I think she was afraid I'd hermit away. She doesn't want her life for me. She wants me to have a family. She wants me to be happy. We just disagree on what will make me happy."

"Why didn't she partner with someone else? Lead by example?"

I shrugged. "We have Tillie, a counselor by your term, who talks with people, but my mom won't talk to her. She wants her anger. Some people, Sirens' Daughters, prefer to wait for the Washed Up, have a few months' relationship and then move on. She didn't move on, but I don't think she still wants my dad. I think she wants her possibilities back. It's not uncommon for children to be born to Washed Up who have left, and the children's mother and her partner or partners to have more children together. Sometimes they share their house with a

Washed Up and have more kids. We're used to Washed Up. Sea Widows aren't as common as you may think."

He stared at me, mouth agape.

"My mom would prefer if I lived her dream so she can see it play out. She just doesn't want to get hurt again."

"But you don't want to partner?" he said, sending me a quizzical look.

My cheeks flushed. "I don't know. It's never been a main goal of mine."

"There have to be others besides Owen."

I nodded. "There are few others around my age in the village."

"What about the other villages?"

"Yes."

"Still tagging along, I see," Mom groused from the garden, her back still to us.

"Good afternoon to you, too," I offered saccharinely.

She glanced at me over her shoulder.

"Afternoon, ma'am." Jasper nodded at my mom. He offered me a forced smile.

"Any plans this afternoon?" The benign question sent the hairs on my neck up.

"Just finished getting water." Jasper maneuvered it by the house.

"And then?"

Hesitation stilled my response to say *fixing things*. That is what I did every afternoon. My patterns didn't vary much. Catching sight of the boards I'd prepped for Molly's pastures, I smiled. Might as well get started now. "I'm going to show Jasper how to put up a fence."

"Lucky you," my mom told Jasper.

After loading the boards onto a cart I'd built, we pulled them to the sand-covered pathway to Molly's house. Her plot was one of the largest, inherited over the centuries.

"How far does her plot go?" Jasper asked.

"She has ten acres."

"Is that a lot?"

"More than most."

"The plots aren't all even sizes?" His brows furrowed as he glanced back at me.

I stared too long before moving my gaze back to the path.

"Maybe at one time?" I guessed. "Lots have changed sizes as people married, had children, and divided up the land for their children. Molly's great grandparents—her mother's mothers—each had adjacent lots. The land went to her grandmother, an only child, and then her mom, another only child. Same with Molly."

"Her parents passed away?" He asked.

"A couple years ago."

"That's sad."

It was, but I had nothing to add other than a nod.

"Are only children common?"

"Most have one or two, some three, like Willis. A few families have more."

"Land is inherited on the maternal side?"

"Usually, but it's up to the families."

We reached the grassy area Molly had designated for the pastures.

"You already have the poles placed?" Jasper stared around in awe. Evenly placed poles dotted the land creating a grid.

"Yeah, I put them in based on where Molly wanted them." I'd spent many evenings putting them up while Owen had been on his ship. It was one thing to avoid him on my property or in town, but this was his home.

"Damn," he mumbled. "What can't you do?"

Words escaped me. He shot me a smile that warmed my core before he moved to grab a board from the cart.

We worked through the heat, the trees offering some protection. A slick lather of sweat covered my skin and stuck my shirt to my body. My focus kept drifting up to Jasper, his shirt plastered against his hard body. My mind flashed with images that sent me guiltily staring at the sand or sea when he'd look up at me.

When fatigue, my nerves, and the fading sun caught up with us, I called for a rest. With his help, I got more than double what I normally would. Not needing to balance the board on one side and secure on the other since he secured one side, we were able to move quickly.

"One or two more days and we should be done." I wiped at the sweat on my forehead, my dry lips parted. I rolled my shirt over my hands to better clean my face. The cool breeze on my bare midriff felt amazing.

Looking up, I found Jasper's dark eyes watching me until he caught my gaze and glanced away. Something delightful twisted in my stomach.

"I'd say fish for dinner, but I'm too tired," I said. "How does dried-meat sandwiches sound?"

"Yesterday's lunch?" His warm gaze returned to me.

"Yep."

"Sounds delicious."

Eleven

On our third and final day of the fence-mending, Molly ventured out to us. The sweet aroma of oranges danced in the gentle breeze. Instead of fierce heat, clouds blotted out the intensity of the sun and cooled the lands.

Soft pattering sounded on the sand, drawing my attention from Jasper's rolled-up flannel sleeves and bare chest. Expecting to see Owen, I stood straight with a glare fixed on my face. Instead, it was his mom.

"Molly? Isn't it too hot for you to be in the sun?"

"Rainey," Molly sang, extending her arms. Her orange, geometric print shirt swam on her and smelled of oranges and cinnamon. Her brown hair coiffed up in a bun but tendrils escaped it, framing her face. Her piercing blue eyes matched Owen's, but her genuine smile stood in contrast to his smirk.

I stepped into her embrace, accepting her warmth. She clung tightly to me, rocking me as she patted my shoulders. Despite being around my height, she seemed to stand a foot taller with her squared shoulders and confident stride.

"It is so good to see you," Molly said. "I meant to come down yesterday but ended up napping instead."

"What do you think?" I fanned my arms out to the squared pastures.

"It looks amazing, Rainey, as I knew it would."

"Now why are you really here?" I smiled knowingly at her. "You like the mornings and nights. This is when you're normally sleeping."

"Always direct, as I appreciate. Owen said you may be considering changing your mind about the land?" Her sharp gaze snagged on Jasper.

"I said no such thing," I stated, failing to rein in my temper.

Jasper came to stand beside me. My anger dissipating as I turned to him. Sweat glistened in the sun but he still smelled of ash and cinnamon.

"You have a helper?" Molly's brows furrowed. She tilted her head to the side and hummed. Her normal vision stance.

"Molly, this is Jasper. He's a Washed Up." An uncontrollable smile curved my lips.

His arm brushed against me as he wiped sweat from his brow.

She shook her head in disbelief. "You brought a Washed Up to your home?"

Her surprised gaze shot to me, assessing, before a large smile spread across her face.

"I found him. He's helping me finish the fencing and the transport. He also knows about the requirement to harbor a Washed Up." There was no point in lying. Molly was considered a Visionist, someone who could see the future. Her more distressing characteristic was her innate ability to detect lies. It created a lot of distress for me as a child, but I found being blunt and honest earned her respect.

"He's helping you," she parroted, staring at me like I had sprouted wings.

Jasper chuckled, earning Molly's gaze. He nudged me with his shoulder.

I hushed at him, causing him to double over laughing, clutching his stomach. The rich sound filled the air. I couldn't resist grinning in return.

"Jasper, you say," Molly said, taking a tentative step forward. Her smile dimmed and her eyes clouded.

"Yes, ma'am," Jasper answered. He stood, brushing his hands on his jeans and leaving streaks of dirt. He extended his hand to her and smiled.

Molly blinked repeatedly. Her mouth opened as if to respond but no sound came out.

"Molly?" I asked, touching her arm.

She startled and quickly forced a smile.

"Oh, I don't shake hands, but... I do hug," she said, her voice catching. She swallowed even as she extended her arms out to Jasper.

Jasper shot me a confused look but hugged Molly back.

Her arms clutched him, her face pinched tight as she trembled in his embrace. A sob rocked her body.

"Ma'am?" Jasper asked stiffly.

Molly sucked in a breath and chuckled hollowly.

"I'm so sorry," she sniffed. "You just... you just remind me of someone."

I stared at them. It couldn't be Owen's father. He'd left a picture when he went back, other than the color of blue eyes, he looked exactly like Owen. I shook off the comment.

"Please, have a seat," I said, touching her elbow to direct her to my cart.

"I'm just being..." Molly murmured. She rubbed her large stomach, rounded with a child ready to join us in a month. "Emotional."

"Can I get you something?" Jasper asked, running a hand through his hair. "Some water? Or bread? We still have some cookies Isla—er, Grandma—dropped off this morning."

A veiled snooping mission, Grandma had dropped off cookies yesterday and this morning. Although different recipes, both had cherries in them.

Molly chuckled, her normal melodic sound returning. "You are a sweet boy. Please just sit with me."

Jasper shot me a look but moved around to sit on the cart next to her.

"I see why Owen is upset," Molly said, sinking back and letting out a groan.

My stomach twisted at her mention of Owen.

"Molly—"

She waved a hand at me. "Owen is a determined child. It doesn't mean he's right."

I licked my lips, drawing the top one in between my teeth. Finally, I asked, "What did he say?"

"That you'd changed your mind." She cast a knowing look at Jasper. "I must have misunderstood his meaning. I thought I was coming to gift it to you."

"Oh," I mumbled, looking at my hands, my heart sinking to my stomach.

"Rainey, it's okay," Molly said. She took my hand. Holding it in hers, she ran her thumb over mine. Her skin was calloused from sewing but tender and comforting.

"I know you think..."

"I still know it," Molly said firmly.

"Think what?" Jasper asked. He cringed at my frown.

"Rainey will be the mother of my grandchildren," Molly said matter-of-factly. "Owen's children."

"Oh." Jasper leaned back, sucking in a breath. "The vision." He directed his wild expression at me.

"They've been mostly true."

"They're always true," Molly shot back, her eyes hard as she regarded me.

I grimaced but didn't argue.

"I see." Jasper rubbed his neck.

"Jasper, you weren't supposed to land here," Molly said, staring into the distance, her eyes unfocused, lost in her own visions.

"Ah?" Jasper tried. "I didn't mean to..."

"No, no," Molly said, shaking her head. "I... I don't make any sense."

Jasper jumped when Molly reached across, grasping his hand with her left one, her right hand resting on her belly. "Jasper, this changes everything. This wasn't supposed to beI—"

Molly dropped his hand and grasped her head, a whimper escaping her lips.

"Molly!" I yelled, kneeling and grasping her knees.

Jasper slipped away to the water jugs resting in the shade.

"I'm okay," Molly muttered, rubbing her temples.

Jasper reappeared with a glass of water in his hand and knelt beside her.

She took a heaving breath and looked up, her blue eyes watery with unshed tears.

"Here." He lifted the water for her.

With a trembling hand, she took the glass and sipped, her eyes never leaving Jasper.

"What is that?" Molly murmured, reaching a hand towards Jasper's neck. It hovered without touching him.

"What?" Jasper asked, looking down.

"That necklace..." She tilted her head to get a better look.

Jasper's hand flew to the chain tucked under his shirt. The only visible part was the glint on his collarbone where the neckline dipped.

"Oh, my dad gave it to me," he said, lifting it. The links were made of twisted gold.

Molly gave a small sad smile and nodded. "It's beautiful."

"He said it belonged to my mom. I've worn it for as long as I can remember. It's all I have of her."

"Jasper." Molly clasped his hands and sucked in a breath. "Do me a favor."

"Um..." Jasper said, his eyes darting to me.

I shrugged.

"Never take it off. Those chains are old good-luck charms. The twisted links are meant to keep the luck tucked inside."

He ran a hand over it.

"It will keep you safe on your journeys," Molly insisted.

We startled when Owen's voice sounded in the distance. It was then I noticed the sun had started to dip into the horizon, splashing the sky in a dazzle of colors.

"Oh my, I've lost track of time," Molly said, moving to hoist herself up.

Jasper jumped to his feet, offering her his hand.

She smiled and took it.

"Your father... raised you very well," she managed, her voice catching.

"Molly, I can walk you home," I offered.

"Thank you, but no, dear. I will be okay. Besides, I'm sure you two are hungry and want to get to dinner." Her face pinched, doubt darkening her expression. "Maybe you'd like to join us?"

Owen's voice sounded again, closer and more annoyed.

She cast a glance back at her home. The structure was built a century ago but freshened up over the decades. A whitewash had recently been applied, and fresh flowers draped over hanging baskets. The colorful blooms sent a fresh, heady aroma into the air.

"Maybe another time." I forced a smile.

"Are you going to be alright?" Jasper asked, continuing to support her arm. "Do you need someone to stay with you?"

She chuckled and patted his cheek. Her normal large smile spread across her face, and her eyes sparkled in amusement. "I will be fine, Jasper. My partner is at home. He'll brew me some tea and rub my feet."

Jasper looked to me for confirmation.

"Yes, he's very attentive," I agreed.

Jasper began, "If you need—"

"Mom!" Owen's voice ripped through the air. A door slammed.

Molly sighed and closed her eyes.

"Mom!" Owen's voice crooned closer.

Before any of us could respond, Owen's blond locks appeared over a mound.

"Rainey!" Owen bellowed. "Rainey, you still down there? Have you seen my mom? She's not in the house."

"Yep and yep," I called. "She's with me."

Cresting the dune, his gaze landed on her. His frame deflated in relief.

"Mom," Owen breathed. The relief vanished when he noticed Jasper holding her. "Why are you touching my mom?"

"Owen," Molly snapped.

Jasper cocked an eyebrow at Owen but didn't move away.

"Mom, I was worried about you, and here you are with... with..." Owen flicked his fingers in the air towards Jasper.

"Jasper, honey, his name is Jasper," Molly corrected sharply. "Where are your manners?"

Owen pulled back like he'd been slapped.

"I was going to start dinner." he defended. "I came to make sure you were okay."

"I'm headed home," Molly said, and started over the sandy terrain. Both Owen and Jasper flanked her like sentinels. She paused, her hand resting on Owen's wrist. "We need to talk."

Owen's gaze flicked to me and Jasper. "I was thinking, Mom..."

"Oh, this will be good," Molly said, resting her hand on her stomach.

"Rainey hasn't met the agreement," Owen said.

"Hey, I have it almost finished," I interjected, shoving a finger in Owen's face.

"Almost is what you've said for the past three cycles." Owen folded his arms, staring down at me triumphantly.

"This time—" My gaze cut to Jasper. His dark eyes met mine. I swallowed down the rest of my response. I finally had my Washed Up.

"What's your point?" Molly asked Owen as she waddled towards the house.

"We could accept other offers. I'm sure there are others interested in it, so they don't have to petition the village to clear land or move to a different village. It was once used for crops. We could change it back into a field to grow sisal for rope. The business is taking off, and John wouldn't have to travel so far for supplies. There's a lot happening and maybe it's time to reconsider."

Molly's brow furrowed as she contemplated.

Finding another plot could take years, and many more trades. My grandparents' land wouldn't support the workspace I needed nor had the easy access to the water. Besides, it was willed to my mom, not me. It would be hers to do with as she wanted. Or, as Owen said, I'd have to go to another village.

My stomach flipped and I clutched the cart's handle. My knuckles whitened from the strain to not attack Owen for setting the new seeds into Molly's thoughts. He was right. It was a good idea. But this was my plot. I'd shaped and leveled it after years of overgrowth. I'd built a home. Owen was trying to force my hand.

Molly hummed. Deep lines wrinkled her forehead. Her eyes rolled back as another vision no doubt danced in her mind.

I didn't dare breathe or say a word to draw her attention to me. For her to say she didn't want to sell the land anymore.

Regardless of my stillness, Molly's gaze found me, deep and contemplative.

"Rainey, I have no desire to go back on our agreement." Her gaze moved to Jasper before tracking back to me, and she added, "Everything is changing. I believe the land will be yours by the next moonless night."

Twelve

WITH THE FENCE DONE, I started back on my finds. Not wanting to jinx the trade agreements, I didn't want to prep my boat and supplies until it was confirmed.

"Is this good enough to salvage?" Jasper glared at the metal he was working on.

I put aside the wooden chair that had washed up. I'd spent an hour sanding the wood, dried and brittle from the salty sea. Next, I'd apply several layers of oil over the next few days.

Jasper's eyes followed me as I walked around to inspect it. Grease darkened his t-shirt, arms, and face. The car door panel sat sprawled out in front of him as we worked to separate each layer and section without damaging other pieces. The metal door, a seventies monstrosity as Jasper called it, could be sectioned out for multiple projects. It was a huge score, if usable.

I ran my hands over the piece, feeling for soft spots and cracks. My arm brushed against Jasper's hand, tingles racing up. Instead of pulling back as I expected, he seemed to hold his breath, waiting.

For the past two days, we'd worked around the shop. Careful of our space. The room seemed too big and small all at once. Everywhere I looked, my sights always locked on Jasper. Yet, we seemed separated by a giant chasm, one filled with time and uncertainty, and Molly's words.

Thankful for the distractions of the trade and finds to clean, I tried to busy myself to not think about him or watch him. For the most part, my attempts failed.

"I think this section might be too soft," Jasper pointed to a section by the handle.

"Feels okay," I said testing the spot, careful to not move my fingers too close to where his hand lay.

"Seriously? I think we have to cut the part out."

I made a throaty response and tested the spot again.

"No, around here," his gentle fingers grazed my hand, and guided it to a section that was obviously unusable. Instead of moving away, his fingers started to curl around my hand. My heart thudded loudly in my chest.

"Rainey." Mom's voice was like a crack of lightning.

We whirled around, our hands separating. Guilt clawed at my face even though I wasn't certain what I was guilty of.

She leaned against the door frame with her arms folded, her plaited dark brown hair swinging at her side with a few tendrils askew. Her green eyes narrowed in on me, a smirk on her lips.

Salty ocean air gusted in through the open window, stirring the dust and fanning the lamp on the wall. Streaks of pink and yellow clouds curled across the sky, bringing the first sliver of the moon. The day had sped past faster than I'd thought.

"Do you know what tonight is?"

I stared at her, my mind racing but coming up blank. "Um..., a night..."

She released an overly dramatic sigh that made me roll my eyes.

"What happens the first quarter moon night ...every month?" my mom asked.

I grimaced when it hit me.

"What is it?" Jasper asked, leaning over the table.

"We have a gathering," Mom said, sending Jasper a brittle smile.

"A gathering?"

"We have a feast in honor of the Sirens and what was provided." Mom tilted her head to stare down at him.

"Oh, the festival?" Jasper asked. I nodded. "Why is it the first quarter moon?"

"Because other villages join in," Mom said. "They can't make the trek after scouring the beaches. They need travel time."

"Oh, aren't you going to settle the agreements and schedule transport tonight? Especially since you're harboring a Washed Up?" Jasper asked with a large smile, earning a dark look from my mom.

"I will." My gaze fell to the metal crab trap I'd found. If I could remove the lid, it'd make a sturdy base for Marcus's food cart assuming my grandpa was correct. I'd just have to find a frame that could support wheels. I'd used my bracketing for the wheelbarrows. I'd have to fashion some more. Hopefully they'd be time before we had to leave.

"Planning on staying tonight after the trade talk?" Mom asked a mischievous look in her eyes that unsettled my stomach.

"No."

"Why not?" Jasper asked.

"Yes, why not, Rainey?" Mom smiled at me.

"I have too much work to do to worry about dancing and eating around a fire."

"You see this?" Mom waved a hand in my direction and sent Jasper an imploring look. "She'd rather work than enjoy a feast meant to thank our Sirens for all the things she brings up. She makes trades and leaves."

"I don't have time to waste," I protested. "Stuff washes up every night. Good stuff. I need to make sure I can make trades. I used all my metal to frame out the wheelbarrows. Hopefully we can find some more for Jasper to use."

The words were bitter on my tongue. Jasper shot me an odd look, his lips curved down, but I ignored both him and my tongue.

Mom watched me for a few beats. Something flickered behind her eyes before she turned to Jasper.

"What about you, Jasper? Are you going to enjoy the festival?"

A snarl rippled on my lips.

"However long Rainey stays, I stay."

Warmth blossomed in my chest and veins.

"She's harboring you," Mom spat. "She doesn't control you."

He smiled at her, his silence his answer.

"Unbelievable," she hissed. Sucking in a breath, she focused back on me. "It isn't fair you aren't letting him see the island life. The festival is a favorite event. You should let him enjoy it."

Suspicion weaseled out the warmth I'd felt, settling heavy on my bones. She was up to something, but I couldn't figure out what.

"Well, hopefully, you'll stick around," Mom said, folding her arms triumphantly.

My stomach twisted at her elation.

A thick silence hung between us. When I didn't ask why, she volunteered the information.

"If you do, you can join me for drinks with Bretti's father."

"What?" I roared. Bretti's father, Bartholomew, owned the cows I was set to trade for. What was she doing? Was she interfering? And why now? My gaze snagged on Jasper's, and my stomach dropped.

She smiled at me, her eyes twinkling in delight. "He rowed in early with drinks. I chatted with him. Offered him a loaf of bread for his travels. We decided to meet up later."

I stared at her. Mom never gave her tradable breads away.

"What did you do?" I seethed. Suspicion winning out.

Jasper stepped around the work table next to me.

"Nothing!" Mom barked. "I asked for some time to speak with him."

"About what?" I gritted out.

"This and that." A wicked smile cut across her face.

My jaw worked but no words came out.

"Guess you'll need to stick around the festival to find out."

My muscles tightened, every fiber of my body wanted to explode. Curses rolled on my tongue. She wanted to ruin my trade agreement. There was no other reason she'd want to talk to Bartholomew.

Jasper placed a hand on my shoulder, startling me out of my thoughts.

"That means you can stick around, too."

Distrust twisted in my heart. Whatever she was up to had to do with my trade and Jasper. She wanted us both there.

Jasper's hand moved to my shoulder, squeezing in support. I sucked in a ragged breath and then another. With each breath, my mind cleared more and her eyes narrowed watching his hand. She'd never bothered with any of my trades before. Why would she now? Why else would she want to talk to him? She knew me enough to know it would drive me crazy. Get me to stay.

Then there was Jasper. A Washed Up. He was an obstacle to her plans with Owen. He'd agreed to my terms, so the only thing to do would be to distract him. Get him to hang around less. Reality hit me. She wanted to find him a lover. The thought sat heavy in my veins. Even if I wasn't interested in Jasper as a partner, it wasn't her business to intervene. To scheme.

"I can't go to the festival other than to discuss my trade," I tried, grasping onto my last chance to back out of going and avoid her plotting. "I don't have anything to bring as my share."

Mom's smile grew and I knew I was doomed.

"I have you covered," she said. A glint flickered in her eyes. She gestured to a dozen large herb bread loaves on the hearth. "I even made extra for Jasper so he can go. You have no worries."

She must have spent all night and morning on the loaves. I cursed and curled my toes.

"Thank you, ma'am," Jasper said with a shy smile. "That's very generous."

Mom smiled back. It looked sincere and my spine stiffened. She turned to me with a Cheshire grin before she headed to the sleeping quarters.

"Don't thank her yet," I whispered. "She likely made you loaves so she can sic other women on you."

"What?" Jasper said, eyes widening.

"She's trying to get someone to lay with you, so you'll go to their house at night instead of here. My mom is never generous unless she wants something in return." The words felt no better once said than in my head.

"Being generous means you don't expect something."

"Exactly. She's helping you to help herself."

"But I thought you had to harbor a Washed Up for a cycle," he said.

"It's harboring you," I said. "You'd work here, eat here, have the option to sleep here, but you'd likely want to go there nightly. She's trying to make sure we don't lie together."

He froze, eyes large with concern.

I laughed to break the tension, but my stomach knotted. The night was going to suck.

Thirteen

Music filled the air, and the pulses carried on the wind to the ocean, a mixture of our songs for the Sirens and tunes brought by Washed Up. Roasting meats crackled on spits, the aroma mingling with breads, fruits, and wines. All the shops had boarded up for the night except the few selling last-minute treats to the islanders from different villages. Candles swayed in glass and metal enclosures, the lights flickering and dancing off the trims and panes of the shops. Warm light bathed the buildings and cast long shadows down the alleys. The main lane had glass oil lamps suspended over the street while the side street lamps glowed brightly. A cacophony of voices greeted us as we neared the growing crowds.

A small group of people sat together with drums, flutes, and other instruments. A small gathering of elders had taken up dancing despite it still being early.

"So, what happens?" Jasper whispered into my ear. His warm breath sent a shiver down my spine and I stiffened to regain my senses even if instead I wanted to melt into his touch. My dad's trousers hadn't fit Jasper but we'd traded three of the garments we'd scavenged with Willis for a pair of pants and a shirt.

"We move around to different tables to eat," I explained. "We sit and talk. You can dance. So far, I only see our villagers. As others arrive, it'll get noisier and more packed. They use tonight as a socializing event more than honoring the Sirens. It gives everyone a reason to mingle and what most hope will be new partnerings between the villages."

"So a big matchmaking situation?" he chuckled.

"Pretty much," I said. "But the food is really good."

As we picked our way through the streets, I led him to a small shop with a table out front. He stuck close, his arm brushing mine. I scanned the streets, thankful I hadn't seen my mom or Owen yet. Perhaps I could finish my trades and head back before seeing either.

"They make cookies and cakes," I explained. Various pastries lined the table. "They're not like what you have, from what I'm told, but they're really good."

I picked up a pear cookie, the crumbly texture sweet and tart.

"We can just take something?" he asked. His stomach rumbled.

"Yes, we brought food to share," I said and grabbed a second cookie. "My mom made twelve loaves of bread so she could have us here. She's plotting something, but since we're here, we might as well enjoy the food."

"So, it's a potluck gathering?" He grabbed a cherry cookie. He seemed to almost gravitate towards anything cherry flavored as my grandma picked up on.

"No clue, but we get to participate and enjoy the food," I said, licking the pear filling from my finger.

"So, people use this as a means to find partners? Dates?"

I shrugged and nodded. "I avoid them for that reason. My mom tries to get me to stay, but I'd rather be in my shop. But this is a good means to make trades when I need to."

"Do you have anyone else at these things who asks for dates like Owen does?"

I choked on the cookie I'd just popped into my mouth. The beginnings of a blush clawed hot on my neck.

"You okay?" he chuckled and rubbed a hand on my back.

I jolted from his warm caress, inhaling a piece of cookie.

Coughing, I nodded and pounded my chest. Finding my breath, I croaked out, "When my mom gets me to stay longer, she'll try to get me to dance with others or sit and eat with them."

"Do you?" he asked, glancing at me.

"Sometimes, so she'll leave me alone. But after she leaves, I'll stay for a few minutes and bolt. I used to stay and have fun when I was younger, but I've been more focused on the land the last couple of years." I smiled. "However, tonight she'll try to set you up with others. Speaking of which…"

I nodded towards Larissa. The young woman smiled shyly at Jasper as she approached us, her russet hands twisting in her curly, light brown hair. She wore a soft blue dress that brushed her knees. The top curled around the back of her neck, revealing her collarbone and shoulders.

"Hi, Larissa," I said.

Her copper eyes shot to me, widening in surprise.

"Hi, Rainey," she said, smiling too brightly. "I didn't know you were coming tonight."

I sighed. My hope of finding Bartholomew and being done was quickly dwindling. "I'm surprised I'm still here, too."

After a nod, her eyes shifted back to Jasper.

"Hi," she said, color creeping up her cheeks. "I'm Larissa. You must be Jasper."

Jasper nodded and his lip tugged up in a half smile. "I am. Nice to meet you."

An unexpected twist of jealousy turned my stomach, followed by a wave of annoyance. He was leaving. I needed him for the land. Nothing more.

Maybe it was for the best. My attraction to Jasper was growing and becoming more awkward. My heart twisted painfully in protest.

He stepped closer to me, his side brushing against mine. A new heat washed over me, singeing my annoyance and dissolving my previous thoughts.

Larissa's smile faltered. "Are you two…?"

"Are we what?" I challenged. Another jolt twisted my stomach. I didn't need to witness her flirting with him.

Jasper draped his arm over my shoulders. The touch made me jump but I quickly settled back, letting my back nestle into his arm. His warmth tingled my skin.

"I guess so," she muttered. Her lip curled into a snarl.

"It was really nice to meet you, Larissa," Jasper said, shooting her a bright smile as his fingers rubbed small circles. "Rainey was just going to show me where the beverage tables are. I hope you have a pleasant evening."

His smile remained as he guided me around Larissa and towards a cluster of stands, none of which had beverages. He stopped us in front of a table with different seaweed on it, finally removing his arm.

I rolled my shoulder, missing the feeling of his hand. Realization dawned on me for what I was doing, and I squared my shoulders.

"What just happened?" I asked. I glanced back at Larissa, who was watching us with pursed lips and narrowed eyes. Why hadn't she continued to pursue Jasper?

"She was trying to see if we're a couple." Jasper picked up a piece of blue seaweed and sniffed it. He grimaced.

"W-What?" I stammered. I was only harboring Jasper...

"You said your mom was going to try it," he said, offering me a piece, too. I shook my head and pointed to the purple seaweed. He grabbed two.

"I know what my mom is going to try. But why would Larissa ask if we were a couple?" I said, gesturing to both of us and feeling like an idiot. Deep, burning splotches pulsed on my face, which I assumed was bright red.

He chuckled. Amusement flickered behind his eyes.

"What?" I barked. Were my reactions that noticeable? Sirens. Maybe he did need to partner with another so I could act normal again. The thought settled heavily in my heart.

He shrugged, still smiling. "Can't say."

I rolled my eyes and took a bite of seaweed to stop whatever stupid thing was going to pop out of my mouth.

"Where to next?" Jasper asked, sidling closer. I closed my eyes, enjoying the contact until I shook my head to clear the nonsense. I was making this into something it wasn't. He was a Washed Up and was leaving.

Before I could answer, the chords of a guitar danced in the air. The musicians started a new song about the sea and a man named Johnny told him to leave his ship.

"A sea shanty?" Jasper asked, lifting an eyebrow.

I shrugged. "It's a song a sailor who washed up sang," I said, my foot already tapping to the tune.

Younger couples took to the open center, arms intertwining, knees lifting, and hands clapping. They twirled around, switching partners as they wove through the street in a square. Their laughter rang out, mixing with the melody.

"Do you have that dance, too?" I asked, nodding toward them.

"Can't say we do," he said. He popped the seaweed in his mouth. "But it looks like a folk dance. Or square dance. Or..."

"So, you have no idea," I chuckled.

We fell into step around the dancers, skirting the open square. The sun dipped below the horizon, painting the sky in rich purples, blues, and reds. A breeze stirred, picking up the cocktail of aromas from the food. Although the village around trumpeted with life, I only noticed Jasper's hand brushing against mine. If he wasn't a Washed Up...

....No, it didn't matter. He was. And he was leaving.

"Is there water?" he asked, finishing the seaweed and rubbing his hands on his jeans.

"Yes, and I'm pretty sure you informed Larissa I was showing you to it."

"Well, we don't want to be liars," he chuckled. A smile tugged his lips. He reached for my hand but then froze midair, staring at it like it was misbehaving.

"What's wrong?" I asked, looking to his hands. They looked clean enough.

"Nothing," he said, shoving them in his pockets. "Where's the water?"

"This way."

I licked my lips as a chill settled on my skin. Chiding myself for my foolish heart's wants, I turned to head toward the other side. He matched my pace and kept close as the streets started to teem with more villagers, happy with spirits and food. I sucked in the salty air and blew it out slowly to settle my nerves.

"There's more people here than I thought," he said, taking in the throngs milling around us. "They're mostly from the island? Or Washed Up?"

"All villages can get Washed Up. We can get a dozen or more a year in our village. I don't know how many stay in other villages, but many do."

He nodded as he watched the myriad of faces drift by.

"I can see why," he murmured. His eyes took in the scenery.

My stomach twisted at the thought, and I pursed my lips. I let the idea hang in the air like a fine mist, warming my skin and stupidly sending skitters of possibility to my heart and nerves. My mind and heart warred. One wanted to create distance while the other wanted to see all that was between us.

We reached one of the beverage tables where large barrels were set up with taps.

I plucked two cups from my belt pouch and handed one to Jasper.

He stared at it.

"It's clean," I said.

"I know." He turned it over to study the carved wooden cup. "We used them on the beach. Do you always carry them on your waist?"

"If I'm traveling or hunting, I do. It's easier that way."

"I should make one, too." He nodded towards my belt.

I didn't mention he didn't need to bother since he was leaving, but the words lingered on my tongue.

Fourteen

"Rainey," a familiar voice called.

"Bretti," I said, forcing myself not to grimace. "How was your travel here?"

He smiled, his green eyes lighting up. "Very good. Even better now that I see you here."

I swallowed down a reply and tried for a polite smile. Based on the smothered cough-laugh from Jasper, I wasn't very convincing.

"Do you know what's in the barrels?" I asked.

"Two are water, the middle one is ale." He smiled. "We brought it with us."

"Bretti is from one of the farms," I told Jasper. "They usually bring an ale to the festivals."

"His father has cows, too," Jasper murmured.

"Yes." A curse for my mom about mentioning the trade burned my throat.

"I didn't know you knew that much about me." Bretti stepped closer, the sweet tang of wine on his breath. His eyes shined in merriment, his bare arm brushing against mine. "I can't wait to discuss more tonight."

I stepped back, closer to Jasper, only stopping when my back was against his solid frame. His heat seeped into my back. My core tightened in a delightful way. "Bretti, I've known you since we were kids. I'd be an idiot not to know where you're from or what your family does."

He shrugged and his smile turned dark. "You are always welcome to come for a visit. I could show you our farm and animals. Perhaps teach you a few things. Instead of trading for cows for land...we could make a different kind of arrangement for a piece of our land."

My heart pounded in my ears. Jasper moved closer. His warm breath tickled my neck, pulling me out of my thoughts.

Bretti reached for my cup and filled it with ale. He handed it back to me. I stared at the cup and swallowed.

"Something to think about, hm?" he crooned, winking at me.

I startled when Jasper's arm reached around me to offer his cup to Bretti.

Bretti scowled at him but filled it up.

"Bretti, this is Jasper." I stepped around Jasper, turning cold without contact.

"Washed up?" Bretti sneered, returning his cup.

"Yep," Jasper deadpanned.

I sipped the ale awkwardly.

"This is great," I offered, lifting my cup in Bretti's direction. I then looped my arm around Jasper's, and warmth pooled in my center when his hard gaze softened.

Bretti's scowl deepened. I steered Jasper away as I spoke.

"We'll have to stop by later and see if any is left. It's very good."

"Did your mom send him?" Jasper asked as we ventured down the street, leaning in so I could hear him over the music and laughter.

"No." I shook my head. "He always asks me to dance."

"And do you?"

"I used to, before I focused on the land," I said and shrugged. "He's a good dancer. I've usually had an ale or two by the time he asks. I dance a few dances and then go home."

"With him?" Jasper choked.

"No," I snorted.

"With anyone?" he asked carefully.

"With anyone? No, I go to my home."

"Does anyone come with you?"

"No. Well, I guess sometimes my mom does. When I get too loud after ale, she'll lead me home. Otherwise, she'll meet me there a couple hours later."

He chuckled, his shoulders relaxing. "I have a hard time seeing you drinking or being really loud."

I shrugged. Years before, I had been more likely to leave with someone I was interested in, but my focus turned to the land and romance became a distraction. As it was seeming to be again.

Before us were three tables: one with flowers, another with breads, and the last one with different mushrooms.

I picked up two matching hibiscuses and handed him one. I tucked mine behind my ear. He turned his over.

"They are great for when we get sweaty," I said. "They help mask some of the smell. People wear them behind their ear, or in a pocket, or on a bracelet or watch."

He nodded and tucked it into his watch band.

"Are these your mom's breads?" He nodded at the loaves.

"No, her breads are gone. They get snatched up first by locals. I doubt the first song had stopped by the time they were gone. Try a mushroom on the bread."

"Why?"

"The mushroom enhances this type of bread's flavor."

He did as I suggested but winced, forcing a snort from my lips.

After swallowing down the last of it, he said, "I can do without that."

"You can at least say you tried it. It's from the village on the southern side of the island. The mushrooms only grow there."

He sipped his ale, grimacing and sliding his tongue against his teeth to get rid of the taste.

"He's like a baby chick, following you wherever you go." Owen's voice sliced through the night.

I threw back the rest of my ale, washing the bread taste out of my mouth and providing me a moment to regain my composure and brace for the confrontation.

Jasper's dark eyes slid to him.

"Owen," he drawled, holding his almost-full cup in mock toast.

"What are you two up to?" Owen asked, folding his arms over his chest as he stepped closer into our space. Like the other villagers, he wore dark trousers and a colorful shirt. He'd washed and combed his normally wind-snarled curly hair.

"I'm going to get more ale." I shook my empty glass.

"I can help you with that," Owen said, reaching for my hand.

"No thank you," I retorted, the ale already warming my body. I yanked my hand back and bumped into Jasper. My body rubbed against him. The touch sends a different heat to my core. My toes curled and a flush spread across my cheeks.

Owen just stared at me, his jaw ticking. He did a double-take and rolled his eyes. I followed his gaze to see Bretti picking his way through the crowd.

No amount of ale could help with both of them.

"Jasper," I said, hooking my arm around his waist and sinking into his hard but warm side. "You need to drink your ale so we can get more."

"You can have mine while we walk," he said, offering me his cup. He wrapped his free arm around my shoulders, anchoring him to me. "I'll grab some water."

"There's another beverage table over this way," I said, sipping his ale.

"Rainey." My mom's sharp voice made me freeze.

I sighed and slumped against Jasper, enjoying the contact and the way my veins warmed. "Why now?" I croaked. I turned to face my mom.

Mom glared at Jasper's arm around me. Behind her was Marn, a girl a year younger than me. Long blonde tresses from her Washed-Up mother, who'd stayed, hung around her shoulders. Her blue eyes shone brightly on her fair skin.

"Hi, Marn," I said, cutting off my mom's introduction. "Are you here to talk to Jasper, too?"

"Rainey," Mom scowled.

"Hi, Marn." Jasper choked back a laugh and rubbed my shoulder. "It's nice to meet you."

"It's nice to meet you too," she said, stepping closer with a pretty smile.

I may have bared my teeth trying to force a smile.

Marn's eyes widened as she shifted on her toes.

"I'd love to chat longer, but Rainey is taking me to a water table," Jasper said, tightening his grip. "I ate some bread that wasn't baked by her mom and need to wash the taste out of my mouth."

My mom's eyes lit up at the compliment, competing with the anger warring on her face. She opened her mouth to say something but only air came out.

"See you around, Marn," I said and twirled around with Jasper in tow towards the beverage table.

"Is this how this evening is going to go?" Jasper asked. He leaned his head towards mine so I could hear him over the thrums of the music as we neared the musicians again.

"Sure looks like it," I muttered, the ale sitting funny in my stomach.

As we neared the table, two familiar faces smiled back at us. Grandma and Grandpa stood with their arms linked, leaning into each other.

"You two look flushed," Grandma said, reaching her free arm out to hug me.

I hugged her with one arm, the other still around Jasper. Grandma reached out for Jasper and brought him in, too.

"Mom is up to her normal stuff," I said, rolling my eyes.

"What is she doing, sweetheart?" Grandpa ran a hand over my hair.

"She's sending many young ladies and guys to us tonight," I said.

They shared a look and suppressed a laugh.

"What's so funny?" I asked, raising an eyebrow.

"Your mom has not been known to play matchmaker," Grandma said. "This sounds out of her intentions."

"She keeps pushing me about Owen," I whined.

"Any others talking to you tonight?" Grandpa asked me.

"Just Bretti," I said.

"Your mom sent Bretti?" Grandma's eyes widened.

"No, she doesn't like him," I said, shaking my head. "He just finds me at every festival."

"Ah," Grandma said, her smile returning. "She doesn't want you to leave. It must be why she wants to talk to Bartholomew. To make sure too many visits out there aren't required."

I didn't question how my grandma knew about my mom setting up a time to talk. Nothing stayed a secret.

But the pieces clicked together. It made too much sense why Mom was helping. She'd prefer that I take Owen's offer over a possible one from Bretti, which would require me to move across the island. "I don't know why she doesn't want me to leave. We only fight."

She patted my arm with a sympathetic smile and turned to Jasper.

"And how about you?"

He shrugged. "I've been introduced to two so far." His eyes traveled back up the hill we'd descended. "Looks like number three."

I followed his eyeline and saw Mom walking towards us with Annabelle. My fingers tightened on his waist.

"Looks like you're right about your mom," Grandma chuckled. "She looks quite determined."

"Oh geez," I groaned. Annabelle was drawn to Washed Up. She lived the life of a Sirens' Daughter. She and her partner had shared their bed with a Washed Up three years ago. Once they were both pregnant, they'd sent him back to the Sirens. They were looking to add to their family again. The thought of them sharing Jasper sent a spike through my heart and curdled my stomach.

"Is there someplace we can get away from them?" Jasper ran a hand through his hair, leaving it askew.

"For tonight, sure," Grandma said, bobbing her head.

He spun towards her. "What does that mean?"

"You can hide tonight. Tomorrow, based on what I see now, Marianna will invite ladies and Owen over for lunch, or dinner, or both."

"Seriously?" he sighed.

"Yes," Grandma laughed. "Oh, yes. I didn't believe it was possible. But she has the idea in her head now. Once that happens, nothing is going to detour her. She'll have a date set up for every day."

Jasper sighed in defeat. His gaze tracked to me. Fear and annoyance shone in his eyes.

I looked to Grandma and Grandpa. "So, who would be willing to let him sleep at their place for a month? Get him away from Mom. I have some stuff I can trade."

Jasper frowned. "But you have to harbor..."

I blew out a breath. What in the seas was I going to do? She was messing everything up.

"There's an easier way," Grandpa said.

"I'm not drowning him," I said.

Grandpa chuckled. "Nothing that severe."

"What, then?" I asked with a sigh.

"Pick one," Grandma said to Jasper.

"Pick one?" he echoed.

"Select one to see while you're here and the others will go away," Grandma said.

Jasper flinched. "I don't think—"

"Or," Grandpa said. Mischief glinted in his eyes. Jasper turned hopefully to him.

"Or pretend to see Rainey while you're here. It'll stop Marianna's meddling and Owen will stay away until you leave."

I snorted even as heat flushed at my face. "That won't stop Mom or Owen."

"Owen's not going to chase you if you're openly with someone, especially a Washed Up," Grandma assured. "He'll wait and rub it in after Jasper leaves."

"Oh, I can't wait for that," I deadpanned. Realizing I'd roundabout agreed to it, I stared straight forward, not seeing anything. My mouth dried. "That won't stop Mom."

"Your mom will just add it to the list of imaginary slights," Grandpa said. "It won't stop her complaining, but the ladies won't come around if they think you're partnering, no matter what your mama says. They are afraid of you."

"Me?" I asked, splaying my fingers across my chest.

"I'd make your decision soon, Marianna is almost here," Grandma said, nodding behind me.

I looked at Jasper, eyes wide. He met my gaze, his dark, hooded eyes reflecting the flickering lanterns. Heat pooled in my stomach and lower. My gaze fell to his soft lips. He smiled, the right side higher than the other. Without thought, my lips curved into a matching smile.

"Rainey," he murmured. His voice was deeper than normal.

I swallowed, unable to look away from him as need and desire tightened my core.

Jasper's hand cupped my face as he tilted his head. Heat wove through me and I leaned into his touch. His lips met mine and tingles rushed my spine.

Two things happened simultaneously as my body melted against his and my arms wrapped around his neck, pulling him closer and deepening the kiss. First, my grandma squealed in delight, clapping her hands triumphantly. Second was my mother's bitter cry of, "No!"

She stomped toward us, her footsteps lost in the ruckus of the festival, but her intensity and hatred charging the air.

"Rainey, what is wrong with you?" Mom screeched, yanking me away from Jasper.

I blinked slowly, taking in Jasper's hazy expression. His hands still lingered in the air. Instead of the red heat of embarrassment spreading across my cheeks and neck, my face and body flushed with delight.

My mom shook me, pulling my thoughts to her as she berated me and my choices. Her voice turned into a drone as I stared at Jasper. The same look of awe and fear reflected in his eyes.

Annabelle hovered behind my mom. She clasped her hands, her heated gaze sliding between me and Jasper.

"Rainey," Grandma sang.

I turned in her direction, unseeing.

"Your grandpa was going to introduce Jasper to Marcus," Grandma said, a dark gleam in her eyes and a smirk twisting her lips.

My heart hit my stomach, the world and reality whirling around me.

Jasper was leaving.

I'd kissed Jasper, in front of everyone, and he was leaving.

My fingers flew to my mouth and I nodded, staring at the cobblestone path. The rocks blurred as my vision swam trying to focus on everything.

Jasper wrapped his arm around my shoulder. Without thought, I leaned into him.

"Rainey," he whispered, his voice hoarse. He rested his forehead against my head. His ragged breaths matched mine.

"Rainey," my mom yelled.

"Rainey," my grandma sang.

My name is like daggers to my brain. I rubbed my temples.

"Let's talk," Jasper murmured against my hair.

My mom ranted something disparaging towards Jasper.

"Marianna," my grandma scolded. The one word shot through the group like a gunshot, silencing everything else and leaving a ringing in my ears.

Mom sucked in a breath, her fingers twisted in the air, her face distorted in anger. She opened her mouth like a fish, but no sound came out.

"Rainey, hon," Grandpa said, his deep voice pulling my attention up. "Why don't we go talk to Marcus now?"

"Marcus?" I asked, searching my brain.

Jasper stiffened next to me, and then I remembered. Marcus was the Ferrier we were going to ask about helping Jasper. My breath left my lungs.

"Rainey, can we talk?" Jasper asked again, his voice urgent.

I nodded. "Yeah. After we talk to Marcus."

Fifteen

MARCUS SAT with his feet propped up on a table, a mug filled most likely with mead in his hand. His loud laugh filled the air, overpowering the music around him.

For a moment, I considered turning around, but Jasper stood next to me, his hand perched on my shoulder.

"Marcus," Grandpa called.

Marcus lifted his mug in salutations before his eyes slid to me and then Jasper. He studied us with narrowed eyes before standing. His stocky frame was just below seven feet. Dark brown hair stuck out in tufts around his head and on his dark brown chest.

"Washed Up," Marcus said with a nod to Jasper.

"Yes, sir." Jasper started to extend his hand but let it hang in the air before returning it to his side.

"Rainey." Marcus smiled at me, his black eyes gleaming in the lantern light.

"Marcus," I said. Acid slid down my throat, pooling in my stomach as I considered what we needed to discuss. It was a ridiculous reaction.

Silence fell.

"So you need a Ferrier?" he finally asked Jasper, brow pinched as he took in our stance.

"Um," Jasper murmured. His gaze darted to me.

Grandpa smiled and winked at me. "It'd seem Jasper is working with Rainey to get the needed trade set up to pay for his stay and ferry ride."

The air hung thickly on the group. My breath caught in my throat.

After a beat, Marcus's gaze turned to me, dark and assessing. "Rainey, you brought in a Washed Up?"

Jasper's frame shook with his suppressed chuckle. I stole a glance at him.

"Yeah, I brought him."

"Why?" Marcus asked.

Jasper watched me.

I rubbed my temple but told a half-truth. "It was late, he'd likely go unfound. He looked like he was from a later century and maybe able to help with some of my stuff to trade."

"Uh-huh," Marcus said. "And you're letting him help you with your finds?"

The price of help was sometimes too much.

"Marcus," Jasper started, licking his lips. "I appreciate your time tonight. I'm thinking through everything. If I wanted to stay through the first moonless night..."

A cheeky smile flashed across Marcus's face. His mirthful gaze fell to me. "I see. Considering your options?"

"You want to stay for two cycles?" I sputtered. I stared at Jasper's torso, unable to meet his gaze or anyone's as hope and fear filled my stomach.

"Maybe longer," he whispered. "It's what I want to talk about." He tried to catch my eyes. Through his cotton shirt, I could feel his heart rate quicken. The thudding matched my own.

"Looks like the kids have some things to discuss," Grandpa said, arching his eyebrows at me. The same smirk was still in place. "Might need some time."

"Looks that way," Marcus agreed with a chuckle. "Jasper."

"Yes, sir." Jasper's fingers tightened on my shoulder.

"I don't have a trip planned for this cycle. You're the only Washed Up this cycle and none are going back from other ones in our village.

"I can't speak for other villages, but we usually don't ferry other villages' Washed Up without a steep markup. My fees are simple."

Jasper nodded, his mouth a thin line.

"You'll need to make your own boat to cross the barrier. I have an emergency one on my ship, but it's mine. You can't make it swimming. Once you cross over, I have no control over where or when you are or what happens. My agreement is to get you to the Sirens' barrier. The rest is up to you."

I opened my mouth to ask what that meant. A shake of my grandpa's head stopped me.

Marcus waited a beat for me to close my mouth and continued, "I expect a trade equivalent of my time and risk. Ortun says you might be able to make a cart for my partners and me?"

I nodded. "We have the materials for the basket. We need to build a frame that can hold it and put wheels on it."

"We?" Marcus asked, his eyebrows shooting up.

I bit my lip.

"It's your choice, Rainey," Marcus said. His hard expression softened, and a sad smile tugged at his lips. "Just make sure you're okay with the costs. All of 'em."

He meant more than the parts. It was the possible trades. It was my feelings. It was the possibility of falling into my mom's footsteps.

"What do you mean, you want to stay longer than one cycle?" I asked. We nestled against a wooden building at the edge of the street. Long shadows covered us, made darker by the lanterns swinging in the gentle ocean breeze on the intersecting street. "I promised that I'd make sure you could go back in one."

Our nook was the first private place I could find amongst the bustling activities and everyone trying to talk to us about our kiss and Jasper's announcement. I needed a quiet place to think. My mind raced as fast as my heartbeat at the prospect of him staying longer. But that just meant I had more of a chance to be hurt. More of a chance to follow my mom's footsteps. The reality of my choice to defy my mom and Owen for a cycle weighed on my heart.

He ran a hand through his hair, only his silhouette visible as my eyes adjusted to the darkness.

"So much is going on," Jasper began. He sighed and slumped back, resting his head on the building. "There's a lot to do."

"You don't have to help with my cow contract. I already told you that. You have enough with making a boat, fishing, and the cart. I'll help with the cart, too. We'll get it done." My stomach turned at my words.

"Rainey," he whined.

"What?" I spat.

He growled. "First, the cart is to pay for me. You shouldn't have to help with it."

"I said I would help."

"I know, and I said I'd help with the fencing *and* transport. Why don't we focus on the animals for this cycle since it's the highest priority, and then I can focus on if I stay or go."

"If?" I choked, regretting the hope blooming in my chest.

"Rainey," he murmured. He shifted off the wall. His aroma of ash and cinnamon stirred as he slipped his hands against my cheeks, filling my senses.

"Jasper," I croaked.

"I've been here a week, and everything is chaos. I don't know what I'm doing or seeing or overall feeling. It's a lot. But I do know I'm attracted...er, interested...ah, I don't know how to phrase it, but there's something between us."

"You're a Washed Up," I said. "It's just the newness." I was hoping my heart would believe it. Instead, it thudded in my chest and sent curls of want through me.

"No," he barked. Softening his tone, he continued, "No, the newness is everything else. I feel like...like I belong here. I haven't felt that way in a long time. I don't know why I feel it. I need to spend more time on that before fleeing back to Florida. I...I can't return here if I leave, and I don't know what here is, really. I know what life is like back in Florida. Yeah, I have a place, school, car, friends, but none of it makes me feel like I do here. Like I do with you."

"Jasper," I breathed. I blinked at the tears welling in my eyes. He didn't know what he wanted, and he was lassoing me into his troubles. All those things he listed would be chips in his resolve if he stayed, especially his friends.

"Rainey, I'll work with you on the trades and the cart so you feel better about this, but can we agree to me staying through at least the second cycle? So I can think, and help, and not regret rushed choices?" His voice was tender as he rubbed his thumbs against my cheeks.

"I know you didn't want a Washed Up, especially one that stayed an extra cycle, but you pulled me up because you thought I could help. Let me. I'll carry my weight."

I rubbed my cheek into his left palm, his warmth caressing me.

"Jasper," I murmured, unsure what I wanted to say.

The air changed as he leaned in, his lips brushing against mine. My body responded, pushing into his touch. His hands slid to my hair.

"Rainey." My mom's voice sliced through the air.

My eyes fluttered open and I placed my hands on Jasper's chest. I stepped back, panting.

"Jasper," I choked. An imaginary dagger stabbed my heart as sense took over, chilling the moment. "Jasper, we can't...we can't do this."

I took another step back, shaking my head. "Jasper, you're going home. You'll want to. We can't. We can't."

"Rainey," he said, reaching towards me, but he stopped himself, letting his hand drop to his side. His head rolled back, eyes sliding shut. "I understand."

I swallowed the lump in my throat. My body was numb as lead formed in my stomach. This was the wisest choice. Even if it tore me apart.

"Rainey," my mom's voice called again. "I'm talking with Bartholomew now if you want to come."

Sirens. Why now? My mind raced thoughts as fragments. Jasper. The trade. Jasper. My mom. Jasper.

"Coming." I closed my eyes for a beat, letting the breeze cool my skin and clear my senses.

"Rainey," Jasper said, taking my hand.

I curled my fingers around his, glancing at his shadowed frame. The contact felt so right.

"I'll talk to your mom. I'll tell her I overstepped. I'll apologize to your grandparents. I'll make it right."

As he said the words, my heart shattered and rebuilt. I could spend the next few weeks avoiding his touch, avoiding saying too much, going numb. Or I could enjoy the time I had with him. Enjoy the experience. Live as a Sirens' Daughter.

It was my choice to be alone, as a Sirens' Daughter, or a Sea Widow. My mother made her choice, one she regretted and reflected on me. I could show her a choice could be made and let go without losing a piece of myself. I could be an example to help my mom rebuild, grow, change.

It was a long shot, but until we had common experience, she'd only see me as besting her. Avoiding her and her choices.

I was being foolish and letting my heart make decisions for me. The same as I had with being a Scavenger. Or bartering for land and building a home. If I didn't chase my wants, let my heart lead me, I'd be my mom. A Sea Widow.

I stepped closer to him, resting my other hand above his heart. The beating anchored me to him. Sliding my hand up his chest and neck, I curled my fingers through his locks. I drew his head towards mine until our lips touched.

He groaned and released my hand to cradle my face.

"Rainey?" he murmured, pulling back. "I don't know the message you're sending me."

That made two of us.

"Jasper, honestly, I don't know either, but don't talk to them. They know I'd punch you if you crossed a line with me. It's sweet that you offered, but no one will believe it."

"Then what do you want to do?" he asked, stroking my hair.

Another "I don't know" hung on my lips. But I knew what my heart wanted.

"Rainey!" Mom hollered a few storefronts down. "Come on, or I'm going alone."

I let out a shaky breath.

"How about I go talk to Bretti's father?" I offered. "We'll work on the order and your cart. We can talk about the logistics of you staying another cycle afterwards."

"Are you okay with me staying another cycle?"

"Yes," my heart answered before my brain could stop it.

Sixteen

Bretti's father, Bartholomew, stood a few inches shorter than Bretti. Gray hair hung past his shoulders, tied back to hide his balding spot. Yellow, hawk-like eyes perched above a Roman nose, long and angular. His constant frown belied his generally jovial attitude.

The thunderous laugh that rang out of him meant he'd had at least two meads already. Hopefully, that meant he'd be amenable to whatever my mom was doing and still agree to our trade.

"Rainey," he cheered as I neared, his frown tipping up slightly in his version of a smile.

"Bartholomew," I said, smiling at him.

Bretti sat at his side, an empty mug next to him. He glowered when his gaze met mine and snarled when he saw Jasper.

"Bretti," I said.

Jasper slid up next to me.

With a glance at him, I slipped my arm around his elbow, skimming my hand down his arm to clasp his hand.

He smiled, tightening his fingers around mine.

Bretti glowered as he sat back in his chair and folded his arms over his chest.

"Rainey," Bartholomew repeated, pounding his fist on the table.

Jasper flinched but held his ground as Bartholomew stood. Although a few inches shorter than Jasper, when he stood, the older man peered down his nose at him.

"So, you've found a new beau?" Bartholomew asked. With long strides he stalked around Jasper, taking in his appearance and grunting.

He finally stopped in front of us and ran a hand through his long beard. "I like him, but he reminds me of someone."

"A good someone?" Jasper asked with a cocked eyebrow.

Bartholomew cracked a grin and pointed a finger at him.

"I like him," he said. Without looking back, he called, "Bretti, come here."

Bretti growled, slowly running his hands down his legs before standing. His eyes cut to me, dark and stormy as he sidled up next to his dad.

"Sir?" Bretti gritted out.

At his tone, Bartholomew rolled his eyes and slapped Bretti's shoulder, making him flinch.

"You had a chance," he snorted. He turned back to me. "Looks like you found a good one."

I didn't bother to tell him Jasper was leaving. I didn't want to think about it. Especially with Jasper wanting to stay an extra cycle.

"He's a Washed Up," Bretti seethed.

"Your great grandma was a Washed Up, too," Bartholomew spat.

"But she stayed," Bretti said. A dark smile spread on his face. "Jasper's leaving."

"You're not staying?" Bartholomew asked, shooting Jasper a perplexed look.

Jasper licked his lips and squeezed my hand. "I'm staying through at least two cycles... Rainey and I are discussing stuff."

"Hm," Bartholomew said, rubbing his chin. "You'd be stupid to go back, but what do I know? I'm an old man who's lived a life he's loved."

His rich laughter filled the pavilion again.

"Rainey," Mom called behind me. "Let's sit."

Unease gnawed at my stomach.

Bartholomew's gaze shot behind me as he stood straighter and squared his shoulders. He ran a hand over his hair and straightened his beard before calling out, "Marianna, I'm so glad you could join us tonight."

"Bart," Mom said. She hid her shy smile with a cough as she stood on the other side of me.

Shyness was not usual for my mom. What was she planning?

"Come, come, sit," Bartholomew said, sweeping his arm towards their table. "Bretti, grab us refills, please."

Bretti snarled but walked off with their pitcher towards the ale kegs.

Taking his seat, Bartholomew said to me, "You want four cows?"

"Yes," I answered.

"I want four wheelbarrows and four scythes," he confirmed. "As we agreed."

"Now, Bart," Mom interjected before I could agree.

A pregnant silence fell on the table. All of us shifted to stare at her.

Sirens, she was here to discuss *my* trade. My vision tunneled and the sound of my breath echoed in my ears.

"Marianna?" He leaned in towards Mom, his eyes twinkling.

"Bart, I know your cows are the best, there is no denying it."

"Thank you," he beamed.

"Rainey is one of the best Scavengers on the island," Mom stated, her expression going neutral.

My mouth dried. Compliments about me from Mom were rare, and never shared in front of others.

"That she is," Bartholomew agreed. "It's why I'm willing to trade some of my cows."

"With that said," Mom continued as if he hadn't spoken, "Not only does she find amazing things, but it's also her craftsmanship in fixing them up and customizing that is unmatched anywhere."

My eyes unfocused. I recognized her face and voice, but the words sounded nothing like her.

Bartholomew hummed, leaning back and folding his arms over his chest. His eyes tracked to me. "Did you bring in a ringer?"

I met his gaze, my eyes wide with surprise, and shook my head.

He chuckled, turning back to Mom. "Are you trying to renegotiate the terms of our trade?" he asked.

"No—"

"Bartholomew," Mom scolded cutting me off and causing him to flinch when she used his full name. "If you thought your child was being taken advantage of, wouldn't you step in?"

She leaned against the table with her head cocked to the side. Her green eyes were hard and unyielding.

I swallowed. Guilt twisted in my stomach even though I'd done nothing wrong. This was her pose when she'd caught me in a lie, or I'd disobeyed one of her few rules.

"You think I'm taking advantage of her?" Bartholomew echoed, rolling the words around like they were foreign.

"Four wheelbarrows and four scythes for four cows?" She cocked an eyebrow.

"I've fed and housed them. I'm losing out on the milk I could sell."

"Please," Mom said, swatting his words away. "You use the sloped common fields to feed them. Your village has it open for livestock. You're also not feeding them anymore or housing them."

He sucked on his teeth, staring at Mom before his gaze flicked to me. He snorted. "Based on your expression, you weren't expecting her involvement."

"No, sir," I admitted. Despite my heart hammering and fists furling, I tried not to glare at my mom. I wasn't sure what I'd say to her or if I could stop myself from saying it.

"Do you agree with her? That I'm taking advantage of you?"

I stared at him.

"Bartholomew," Mom admonished, drawing our attention again. His cheeks redden at his full name again. "I think you are taking advantage of her. She's said nothing of the sort to me. She speaks her mind freely. She learned it from me. I didn't want to have this conversation with you without her present. She's already mad enough that I'm doing it. She looks ready to explode at me. She'd be madder if she found out afterwards."

I sat back, bumping into Jasper. He squeezed my shoulder and we shared a look.

She'd never spoken up before. Granted, I'd made the agreement and was okay with it, but it was my final piece for the land, and would have agreed to almost anything to secure it.

"What's your offer?" Bartholomew finally asked.

Mom looked at me. A soft smile skittered across her face before she returned her focus to Bartholomew. "Rainey will make you two wheelbarrows and two scythes."

I stared at her, my heart racing. That would save so much metal. One wheelbarrow could be traded and I could keep one for my use. Or repurpose the pieces.

"Marianna—" Bartholomew started, but Mom held a hand up to stop him.

She went too low. She was going to sabotage it. "I'm good with our agreement," I blurted out.

"And I will bake you three loaves of bread of your choice each cycle for the next year," Mom answered ignoring me again.

"Mom?"

"I live there, too," Mom said without looking at me.

Bartholomew shot me a look before his gaze turned back to Mom. His expression softened when he said, "I'll agree to your terms, Marianna, only if you deliver them personally."

What? He was considering it. Everything swam in my vision.

"Deal," Mom replied.

Excitement skittered through me, fluttering in my stomach. I couldn't force the smile from my face. Lightness swayed my body.

"I have them done and can deliver the items anytime," I beamed. I squeezed Jasper's hand.

Jasper slid his arm around me.

"Deliver in a week, and the cows will be ready!" Bartholomew cheered, raising his glass in the air.

I clanked my glass against his. My dreams were finally coming true. The land would be mine.

Seventeen

Morning sun filtered through the cracks in the curtains, the bright beams piercing my eyes. I groaned, blocking them with my hand, and rolled over, bumping into Jasper. Stars popped in front of my eyes as I scrambled to right myself.

He moaned and rolled over, snuggling deeper into the blanket, draping his arm over me. We lay sprawled on the living room carpet, blankets from the sofa spread over us. Both of us were fully dressed in the same rumpled attire from yesterday.

My hand caught on a knot in my hair as I ran my fingers through it in an attempt to gather my wits. The house was quiet. The embers burned in the firepit, but no bread lined the cupboards and only the faint smell of the sea and ash lingered in the air.

The front door creaked open, my mom's small form slipping in before silently closing it. Her tousled hair matched her disheveled dress.

"Mom," I croaked. The word came out hoarse. My throat was dry and burned as I tried to talk. I slipped out from Jasper's arm and clambered to my feet.

"Rainey," she breathed, her hand flying to her chest. "You should be asleep."

I swung my hand at the curtains. "I should be scavenging."

Jasper stirred, grunting as he flipped over, and patted the spot where I'd been.

"Sh, or you'll wake him," Mom said, a smile teasing her lips.

I stilled, staring at her. "Who are you and what have you done with my mother?"

"What?" She stifled a yawn.

"You just got home. You care if Jasper sleeps. You're not chastising me for last night."

"Time for that later," she said. "I have bread to make now."

"Where were you?" I asked, unsure if I wanted to know. She stayed out later than I did, but never till the morning.

"Out," she replied, putting sticks in to stroke the fire.

"With?"

She giggled.

My stomach turned and I looked away. This was the first time, to my knowledge, my mom had stayed out with someone. My mind raced backwards through the foggy night's events. It caught on a memory, and I blurted out, "Bartholomew?"

Her face reddened and a devilish smile spread across it.

"Mom?!"

"What?" she said, shuffling her ingredients onto the counters. "We're adults. We both have kids. I know you've been with boys and girls. It's one of the reasons you stopped going to the festivals. So you wouldn't be distracted from your trades."

"Are you seeing him again?" I asked, ignoring her comments on my youth. A boyfriend or girlfriend never lasted a full cycle with my attention.

It was like my youth reversed. There'd been a time when I told her about my flings and everything in my life. She'd encouraged my excursions until Owen became serious about wanting to partner. Then the two had a like mind when it came to my love life or lack of one.

She smiled at me and shrugged. "At least once a month for a year."

"You...planned it?" I asked, the color draining from my face.

"No, but it'll be a nice benefit. His partner passed several years ago. We're both interested."

I opened my mouth to protest but stopped.

Her eyes narrowed in on me, her smile dimming as she waited.

"What?" she asked, fear darkening her words.

"Mom, I'm happy for you," I said. I threw my arms around her before thinking better of it. Even if she ambushed my agreement, she worked it out in my favor... and hers.

She stiffened, but then patted my back.

"You planning any more babies like Molly?" I asked, ducking before she could smack me with her spoon.

"I have plenty of years to have more children," she said, doubt creeping into her voice. "I don't know if we want that. I'm just having fun. I've been talking with Tillie since Jasper washed up."

My eyes flew open at that comment. She was finally seeking help. I smiled at her.

"Then have fun, Mom," I said, nodding at her. "I'm really happy for you."

Her eyes shot to Jasper, who twitched as the day pulled him from sleep.

"Be careful," she said, pointing her spoon at me. "Don't let him break your heart, and don't break his."

I stared at her. What happened to my mom?

"And," she murmured. "You now have the metal necessary to finish the trade he needs to leave."

There she was. Bitterness tanged in my mouth, dulling my joy. To help me or not, she'd bettered the trade to get rid of Jasper.

A curse flew from Jasper's mouth as he kicked the outside worktable.

"Too used to electrical tools?" I asked.

He glowered and I shot him a grin.

"Honestly, yeah," he said, wiping his hand across his brow and smearing grease over his temple.

I bumped him aside with my hip and took over the forge welding. Leaning back, I checked the connection and grinned.

The crab trap sat securely on the metal frame made from the metal of one of the wheelbarrows.

"Now, we just need four matching tires," I said, moving to my stash behind the house. After unlocking the shed, I ducked inside.

"How many tires do you have?" He slid past me in the tight corridors.

"Dozens. I only grab bicycle-sized or smaller. Some other Scavengers grab larger ones, but I don't have a use for them."

"How do you inflate the tube inside?" he asked, squishing the rubber between his palms.

"I have a pump that washed up." I nodded towards the house. "It's highly coveted. People will trade food to use it."

He nodded with furrowed brows. After a moment, his gaze shifted to mine, dark and troubled.

"What's wrong?" I asked, looping tires around my arms to check sizes compared to the cart.

He shrugged and toed the ground.

"The cart's almost done," I said. I forced a smile, but it fell when he grimaced. The cart would buy him passage with Marcus. He'd still be able to leave after one cycle, even if he said he wanted to stay.

As my mother had planned.

We hadn't spoken much since the previous morning, the high of the festival fading in the sun's rays and leaving us back where we had been—disagreement on Owen and Jasper.

A gust of ocean breeze flew in, picking up sandy dust and stirring the rubber smell in the small space.

I walked out, waiting for him to follow so I could close the door.

He leaned against the front of the shed, taking the tires from me as I relocked the door.

"What's wrong?" I asked again. My mind raced. Had he changed his mind and didn't know how to tell me?

He chewed his lip, his gaze tracking the crashing waves of the ocean.

"Jasper?" I rested my hand on his bare arm. His sleeves were rolled up from working. Strong muscles flexed beneath my touch.

His eyes darted to me, and a smile tugged his lips.

"Want to eat on the beach tonight?" he breathed.

"Okay, but are you going to tell me what's wrong?" I asked, taking some of the tires from him and turning towards the house. Regardless of what he said, there was work to be done. Heaviness settled on my heart. I couldn't focus on Jasper staying or going in one or two cycles. He was going, it was just a matter of when. My land was permanent, though, and something I could work toward.

"I'm just amazed at how quickly you finished the cart," he said.

Not what I was expecting.

"You're sad because I work fast? This is my livelihood."

"No, it's not that. You're a force. I thought it'd take longer. It's just... it's making my possible departure more likely."

I gulped when he said, "possible." My heart thudded at the possibility. Could "if" be playing on his mind?

"Jasper? Are you...are you...?" Hope bloomed in my chest and clogged my throat.

Jasper stopped midway up the path. His face showed the war inside him. "Rainey, I like it here."

A stupid smile wobbled on my lips. "But?"

His eyes shot to me, glossy with emotion. My heart thudded in my ears.

"I've been here a little over a week. Can I make any decisions based on that?"

Reality settled as a ball in my stomach, his doubts weighing heavily, but I forced a toothy smile. It wasn't "if," but the finality of a decision he was warring with.

"No one is forcing you to make any decisions right now. Regardless of what you choose, it's your choice."

"Is it? You don't want to weigh in?"

I swallowed and averted my eyes. Of course I did. "Jasper, I can't make choices for you." No matter that I wanted to.

"What do you want to happen?" he asked, his voice soft and fearful. He stepped closer. After placing his tires down, his hands cupped my face. His gentle thumb brushed my jawline.

I shook my head. "It doesn't matter." I bit my lip and blinked my eyes, turning from him. He was right, it was less than two weeks and I'd been caught up in the whirlwind between him and finally finishing the trades for the land.

Space. We needed space. He needed to work on his boat and have room to think everything out, and I needed to deliver my items.

His lips softly touched mine, shattering my thoughts.

"It does matter," he whispered. "Your opinion is the most important."

Dark waves capped in white moonlight lapped at the beach as the tide rolled in. Flames from the fire flickered in the air, sending glowing embers on the breeze and blinking out in the distance.

Jasper sat next to me, reclined back on his elbows, staring at the water.

"It's nights like this I miss my dad the most," he murmured. He stared across the black ocean.

I glanced at him. The moon reflected in his eyes and bathed him in an ethereal glow. His dark hair caught shards of the moonlight as it fluttered in the light breeze.

Moments passed as I watched him, waiting for him to continue. When he didn't, I slid my hand over his, nestling our fingers together. He shot me a smile.

"Did you go to the beach often?" I asked.

"Yeah, he was fascinated with the ocean. He was from Kansas but moved to Florida so we could be by the sea. We always lived within walking distance of it. We'd go daily to watch either the sun rise or set or both. He said the ocean reminded him of my mom." The last few words caught in his throat. He blinked and swallowed.

"How long has it been?" I whispered, scooting closer and resting my head on his shoulder.

He leaned his head against mine before answering. "He passed two years ago. Car accident. He died instantly, no pain for him."

"But more for you?" I whispered.

He sniffed but didn't answer. Instead, he turned his hand so our palms touched and his thumb caressed the top of my hand.

"You have friends and extended family?"

He nodded noncommittally. "I never met my mom's family. My dad was an only child and his parents passed when I was a kid. I have some good friends."

I nodded, but my chest tightened. His going back or staying had to be his choice. I didn't want to carry the burden of his regrets if he stayed and didn't like it. Even if I knew what my heart wanted.

"What about you?" he asked, rubbing his forehead against mine. "Where are your friends?"

I laughed. "I have friends. I've spent a lot of time organizing the trade for the land, and don't see them as much as I did. When I get the land, I'll have a party."

He chuckled. "You party?"

"I can let loose." I bumped his shoulder with mine.

"I saw you with only two ales," he said smiling, leaning in so his mouth hovered close to mine.

"Hm." I brushed my lips against his.

He repositioned himself to deepen the kiss, running his free hand along my cheek and into my hair.

With my free hand, I laced my fingers through his hair, pulling him closer.

"This is a public beach," Owen's voice spat behind us.

I sighed against Jasper's lips.

While still cradling my face, and his lips barely above mine, he said, "Yes, and we're part of the public."

"You're a Washed Up," Owen drawled. Sand kicked up as he walked closer. "You're not even staying. Even if you stay for two whole cycles."

I stiffened, tugging my lips between my teeth. My gaze shifted to the side.

Jasper let a breath out through his nose and rested his forehead against mine.

"Forgetting that, huh, Rainey?" Owen taunted.

Forgetting wasn't the correct term. Ignoring felt more fitting.

"Owen," Jasper said.

With a dismissive wave, Owen continued down the shoreline, his form becoming a dancing silhouette in the moon's light.

"He reminds me of someone back in Florida."

My gaze jumped from Owen to Jasper. I hadn't missed his use of Florida versus home. Either it meant something, or hope was stealing my sense.

"Who does he remind you of?"

His dark eyes met mine before he settled back and pulled me against his side. I rested my head on his shoulder and he rested his head on mine.

"A friend since childhood, Erick. He also made a big show about wanting to be a lawyer like his dad and mom, but I never believed it. Like Owen does with his interest in you and the vision. Over-the-top shit, too, like quoting laws and codes about everything. He'd call out court TV shows for incorrect stuff. It could be a real drag to hang out with him, but he was always trying to protect us, in his way."

"If he didn't want to be a lawyer, what did he want to do?"

"Dude was an artist. Wanted to go to art school and work on manga. He even did some tagging—um... graffiti art on buildings he didn't own, which is illegal. His parents had to bail him out of jail and make the legal issue go away. Afterward, all he could talk about was being a lawyer. I only know about it because I overheard his parents talking to my dad about it. My dad had been a lawyer before I was born. He did mostly pro bono—helped people in need with a legal rep for free—after I was born. He had experience with the situation and offered advice. Anyway, after that, all Erick did was talk about being a lawyer."

"Did he continue his art?"

"Nope. Well, not where others could see it, at least. But he still sketches on his tablet when no one is around and doodles when he's thinking. It's a waste of talent. He was a year ahead of me in school and took loaded semesters. He graduated college in three years. He's finishing up his law degree and studying for the bar. He has several top firms interested in him. He's living his parents' dream for him."

Other than his friend wanting to please his parents, most of the details he said meant little to me. His world's legal system was vastly more complicated than ours and had too many loopholes for everyone to understand, which was stupid. But Erick meant something to him. "Are you close with him?"

Jasper laughed and shrugged. "He's my roommate."

He'd mentioned his roommate on the first day, too. So, he was someone Jasper would miss during the time he was away. "The one with a new car?"

A smile curved his lips. "You listened to me. Yeah, he got a new car. A gift from his parents for ranking top in his class. We were going to take it up the coast after finals."

Jasper had a whole world beyond our Sirens. Longtime friends, plans, and dreams that wouldn't, couldn't happen on the island.

Swallowing down the thoughts, I asked, "How does this relate to Owen, besides appeasing his mom?"

"I think he uses you as a cover. He knows you don't want to date him, but as long as he chases you so openly, others leave him alone. Whatever desire he's hiding, he uses his show of affection towards you to mask it."

Something clicked into place. What Jasper said made too much sense. Owen had always called me his land Siren. Calling him back to the land. "Our Ferriers have a saying."

"What's the saying?" Jasper asked.

"Unless you know your heart's true love, the Sirens' song will pull you to the bottoms below."

"Is that true for Washed Up, too?"

Heaviness settled in my stomach. When he went back, he'd have to face the Sirens. Still not wanting to spend the night harboring on what-if thoughts, I shoved the idea of him leaving to the side.

I shrugged, watching the water lap at the sand, leaving a foam trail as it slinked back into the ocean. "I'd guess so. The Sirens snare sailors with their song. The Sirens reach their heart and lure them in with promises. The Ferriers must know their hearts' wants to keep grounded. My grandpa always said for him, it was my grandma. His heart belonged to her, so the Sirens could never have it. Most Ferriers have a person as their anchor to the island. Owen has always claimed it was me. Claimed I was his land Siren. But that would mean I lure him back from what he wants. I'm keeping him from his wants."

Jasper narrowed his eyes, searching the ocean for answers. "What does that mean for Owen? What does he want?"

His truths were his and I could only speculate. The only thing more important to him than the ocean was his mom's visions. "He knows what his heart desires, and if what you say is correct, I'm not what brings him back each voyage."

Eighteen

THE SKY WAS DRAPED in black, the moon dancing on the horizon when I slipped out of the house. Jasper lay sleeping on the floor, wrapped in blankets.

He had a choice to make, but my presence would only dilute his thinking. Whatever he decided needed to be done with a clear head. The space would also let me untether myself from whatever had happened between us. My emotions had been dictating my choices more than logic.

I checked my boat tucked in the shed with the wheelbarrows and scythes readied for the voyage to Bartholomew's village. Jasper had helped tie down everything in preparation for the journey, including my metal-frame cart for my boat when I needed to travel in the woods.

Rowing around the island would take a week or two, depending on the current, but walking through the island with the heavy items would take longer. The paths would be clear enough to move the goats to the next village for shipping, but not ideal for hefting two wheelbarrows across by myself.

As an afterthought, I walked the distance to Molly's house. A twirl of smoke billowed from the chimney. Molly sat outside, a blanket draped over her shoulders and a steaming mug in her hand.

She turned toward the sound of my approach, a smile on her face.

John, her partner, sat next to her, sleep tugging on his dark eyes. He smiled at me, too, but his loving gaze returned to Molly. He held her free hand between his, rubbing circles.

"Rainey," Molly whispered, and nodded to a chair next to her.

I licked my lips and scanned the faint glow of gold cresting the horizon.

"He's sleeping," Molly said, patting the seat again.

With Owen asleep, I took the seat.

"I'm headed off today to bring the animals back," I said. A curl of excitement skidded through my veins.

"Congratulations," John said.

"Thanks," I beamed.

"I'm proud of you, Rainey," Molly said.

I stilled, waiting for the "but."

"You could have taken the easy way, partnered with Owen, and had the land, but you took the harder way. Earned the land."

It wasn't the "but" I was expecting.

"I know what you believe—what you know—" I started.

Molly smiled a tired, thin-lined smile, and shook her head. "My vision isn't wrong."

I stared at the table, shifting my feet beneath me.

"Rainey," she said, placing her mug down to take my hand. "I am proud of you. However it happens, when you choose to be a member of my family, you will be happy, too."

I nodded and pushed my chair back.

"Rainey," Molly said, letting my hand go.

I turned my face towards her but didn't meet her eyes.

"I can't wait to celebrate when you return to your own property."

I slid the boat from under the tarp and shoved it free of the shed. After relocking the shed, I slipped the rope tethers around my shoulders and tugged it toward the ocean. The crown of the sun peaked on the horizon, casting rich oranges and yellows on the rippling waves. The breeze kicked up, wafting in the salty brine of the ocean. I'd miss scavenging for a few days, but with the land secured, I could cut back on the intensity of it.

"What are you doing?!" Jasper's voice rang out like a gunshot.

For some reason, I started running towards the ocean like I could outrun the guilt of leaving him behind, outrun not telling him I was going, outrun my feelings, outrun the thoughts of him leaving.

His breathy pants drew nearer as he ran through the sand. Without the drag of the boat slowing him down, he circled in front of me, cutting off my path.

The boat was too awkward to cut around him. I could either run into him or stop. He braced his hands to steady my shoulders.

"What are you doing?" he asked again, his face dark with anger.

"I'm going to start my trades."

"Why are you sneaking out?"

"Sneaking? I'm normally up at this time. I'm doing nothing wrong," I seethed, pushing against his hands.

He let his hands drop from my shoulder but grabbed one of the ropes and pulled it from my grasp.

"What are you doing?" I shot back at him.

He slipped the rope over his torso. "It was built to be pulled by two people."

I rolled my eyes but didn't protest.

"We had an agreement. I help with transport. Now why are you trying to leave without me?" he asked when we reached the water.

I untethered the ropes and tossed them in the boat.

"Rainey," he murmured, catching my arm. He pulled me into an embrace, his arms warm and comforting around me.

I took a moment to inhale his scent, to memorize his strong hold and the feel of him pressed against me.

"Do you not want me to come?" He pulled back to look me in the eye.

"We need space to think."

"Think about what?" he asked, furrowing his brow.

"You don't know what you want," I said, stepping backward.

He ran a hand through his hair. His chest heaved and he let out a long breath. "Rainey, I don't know if staying or leaving is best, but I know I want to be with you."

My heart swelled but my brain popped it. "As you said, we just met. It's too soon. You need time to think about what you want without me around."

Jasper chuckled humorlessly and shook his head. He took a step toward me, regaining the one I'd stepped back. He cradled my face and smiled down at me with a hazy expression. His lips met mine in a gentle kiss.

Stupidly, I kissed him back.

"This trip will be easier with two people," he said after pulling back.

He wasn't wrong. Two people would cut the time down to row around the island considerably.

"Show me the island you love," he said, getting behind the boat to shove it into the water.

The thought sent heat skittering through me. It would just be the two of us most of the time for the couple of weeks it'd take. But he needed time to think, and I needed to create separation. But my heart protested. I could have all the time I needed after he left. I could enjoy the few borrowed moments with him. My heart drowned out the logic of my brain.

Together, we pushed into the waves, jumping inside as we crested the first peak. The rip tide pulled us back into the depths of the ocean.

Leaning over the boat, I tossed a bracelet I'd made from -washed-up pearls. "Siren mothers, may our passage be safe."

The waves rippled by, snagging the offering. The pearls caught the sun's glint before slipping away in the current. An accepted gift.

Waves lapped at our boat as we rowed through the waters around the island. The sun had risen and dipped below the trees. After taking a swig from my canteen, I wiped my brow. My arms burned from the hours of rowing, and my body cramped. Together, we'd traveled much farther than I could have alone.

"I think we should pull over for the night." I nodded to a sandy shore a few yards from us. "We can camp in the trees."

"How close are we to the next village?" Jasper asked, shading his eyes with his hands to scan the horizon.

"A few hours or so, but I don't want to get caught in the tide or try to dock in the dark. I don't know the harbor well enough. I also don't want to have the items on the shore overnight. Stealing isn't common, but Scavengers are scavengers."

"Makes sense," Jasper said, helping steer the boat to the spot.

After pulling the boat ashore, we used the straps to tug it up to the tree line with us. I dug out a tent I'd borrowed from Willis.

"Do you know how to set one up?" Jasper laughed, watching me tug at the pieces.

"I'll figure it out," I said, kicking it for good measure.

"I camped with my dad. I'll set it up. You start a fire?"

I nodded in agreement and quickly set up a firepit. Securing some fish, I dressed them and tossed them in my pan.

I knelt to the ground, my muscles easing as I finally gave them rest. A chilly wind blasted from the ocean, bringing salt and stormy smells. The fire danced in the breeze, flickering before righting itself.

Jasper eased down next to me, his legs and arm brushed against me.

"That wind's different," he said, casting a look to the ocean.

"Storm," I said.

He wove his arm around my shoulder, drawing me to his side. I let him, resting my head on his shoulder. He leaned his head against mine, his gaze watching the fire.

Stealing a glance at him, the fire danced in his dark eyes, the oranges and golds reflecting back. He caught me watching him, and a slow smile spread across his lips.

I cupped his jaw with my free hand. He leaned into it, closing his eyes for a moment. I arched, meeting his lips. They tasted of the sea, salty and full of life.

He shifted, his torso pressing to mine. Jasper cradled my head before his right fingers traced down my cheek and rested on my neck.

With my free hand I braced myself against the ground, pushing myself to my knees. He leaned back to reposition himself, his hand moving to my waist. His warm fingers teased against my exposed skin between my pants and tunic. I lifted my leg over his, settling down on his thighs with my legs on either side of him.

His other hand shifted to my waist, his fingers splayed across my sides. I wrapped my arms around him, pulling us tighter together. I could feel his heartbeat in his chest against mine. His hardness pressed against my core, coiling heat in my center.

The fish sizzled, the crackling skin spraying oil into the fire.

"Shit," Jasper yelled, his eyes flying open.

I hopped off him, reaching for the pan. In a moment of stupidity, I grabbed the hot handle to pull it from the fire. Searing pain shot through my hand and I swore, yanking back.

Jasper pulled his shirt over his head and using it as a mitt pulled the blacked fish from the fire. He then gently took my hand and poured water on the burn. His touch was feather soft against my damaged skin.

"I have a first aid kit," I choked out, my hand throbbing. He moved to the boat, still holding my trembling hand.

I grabbed my knapsack and dug in it with one hand until my fingers caught on the silver vial.

He squeezed the yellow mixture onto my hand, the scent of aloe and lemons tingling my nose. The mixture numbed the throbbing.

"Your hand is pretty burnt," he said. His dark eyes flicked to mine.

I licked my lips, his taste still on them. His scent dusted my skin. My gaze moved from my hand to watch the fire shadows dance on his face, casting him in waves of dark and light. His eyes shone with concern intensified by the fire. Then I noticed his shirtless torso. The outline of muscles created from hard work. My pulse kicked up and I swallowed. My center warmed and my thoughts became only of him.

"Rainey," he choked.

Startled, my eyes darted to his. Heat from the fire and embarrass-ment reddened my face.

"What?" I breathed, my eyes moving to his mouth.

"You can't..." he groaned and shifted his hips.

My attention moved to his jeans and warred between his chest and pants.

"Can't what?" I muttered.

"You can't look at me like that," he gritted out.

I met his stare. "Like what?"

"Like... like..." He swallowed, shifting again. "Like you want to... lay with me."

I stilled, staring unfocused at him. My muscles tingled, alive and craving. I did want to lay with him. I did want to touch him. For him to touch me.

I tilted my head, unable to stop the smirk that lifted my mouth. I stepped closer. He shifted, stiffening as if expecting to be attacked, but didn't back down.

I rested my uninjured hand on his chest. His muscles twitched below me, and my smirk grew to a grin.

Jasper stood taller, his eyes focused on my face, waiting, watching.

I ran my hand up his neck to his face and fisted my fingers in his hair, pulling him closer. He remained immobile, shallow breaths from his nose his only movement. My face was mere inches from his. His eyes dilated, darkening with each inch of distance I closed.

"What if I want to lay with you?" I whispered before placing a gentle kiss on his lips. His lips parted and his hands flew to me, one on my neck anchoring my mouth to his as the other found the small of my back to push me closer to him.

He pulled back, panting. After running a hand over his mouth, he stepped back, eyes darting around the ground. "Rainey," he choked.

I hummed, closing the distance again. I arched to meet his lips.

He groaned against me. For a few moments, he deepened the kiss before pulling back again. "Rainey, we can't," he panted, shaking his head.

"Why?" I asked, embarrassment hardening my words.

He pulled me back to him, his kiss greedy. He tilted his chin away, resting his forehead on mine. "Because...I don't know. I want to...but..."

"But?" I asked, a cold chill stealing down my spine.

He leaned his head back, rubbing his thumbs against my jawline. "We just met. I don't want you to regret laying with me."

"Why would I regret it?" I asked, furrowing my brow. He wasn't my first. Some Washed Up had preconceived notions about sexuality and virtue. Their morality was more about depriving wants than being kind.

"I don't have condoms," he admitted.

"Condoms?" I asked, searching my mind for the meaning. "Oh! Oh, we have other means here."

But I didn't have any with me. I didn't normally need them. I also didn't know how to make the concoction. A villager grew the necessary plants and created the tonic.

He leaned forward, brushing his lips against mine.

A crack of lightning ripped across the sky. The silver veins clawed through the clouds, bathing the ocean in holy light before the heavens opened, drenching us. The moment broke.

We scrambled to grab the fish and duck into the dry tent.

Shivers stole through me as I huddled beneath the covering.

"The rain will help with the taste," Jasper said, picking the fish up by the corner. Ashy water dripped from it back into the pan.

Smirking, I took my own piece, eating it in three bites. It did little to satiate my hunger, but the storm's dampness and the bit of food allowed my tiredness to catch up with me.

"It'll be an early morning," I said with a yawn. "We should get some sleep."

I tossed off my drenched tunic and tugged off my pants, leaving on my damp tank top and underclothes. I grabbed the blanket from where it'd been tossed in a wad and pulled it up as I snuggled to sleep on the soft tent mat.

Jasper cleared his throat.

I tracked my gaze to him.

"What?" I asked.

His face was flushed as he stared at me, unmoving.

My eyes tracked down to my discarded clothes. Modesty, I'd forgotten his world's modesty.

"Blankets, warmth, body heat." I patted a spot by myself.

Following suit, he tugged off his jeans—that needed more than a rain bath to be clean—and settled down by me. His heat greeted me and I snuggled against him.

He draped a warm arm over me and tugged me close, burrowing his face into my hair for a pillow.

"Night, Rainey," he murmured.

"Night," I whispered, lacing my fingers with his. We had limited time, but I didn't need to regret anything.

Nineteen

Morning broke. The smell of rain still lingered on the chilly air. The sun barely crested the horizon, staining the sky in shimmers of yellow and pink. When I exited the tent, the ground was damp, but my boat was still intact as was the tarp covering my items to trade. The Sirens had watched over us.

I started a new fire to boil water for washing, the glowing embers sending curls of heat against my cool skin. Jasper stirred, his groggy grunts carrying on the wind.

"Rainey?" he called, fear tugging at his words.

"Out here," I replied, tossing my rain clothes into the boiled water to ward off whatever festered in them overnight.

He stretched as he came out, his ab muscles rippling.

My lips parted and I chuckled.

He came up behind me, wrapping an arm around my waist as he nuzzled into my neck. His warm breath tickled me. I could get used to his cuddly emotions in the morning. I stiffened. He wasn't staying. I shouldn't get used to anything.

"You okay?" he murmured in my hair and then kissed me behind the ear.

I twisted around so our torsos were touching. His warm skin was welcoming against my chilled skin. I wrapped my arms around his neck, taking advantage of the time I did have. After locking my fingers in his hair, I arched to kiss him.

He groaned against me, returning the kiss.

"You said the village is about two hours?" he asked after breaking the kiss, keeping his body wrapped around me.

"Yeah, if we get to Bartholomew's early enough, we can make the distance to where the goats and pigs are."

"Same village?"

"No, we'll go to several villages on the southern side of the island. Different parts of the island are better suited for varying stuff. Sunny, the pig farmer, will ship the pigs and goats back while we'll sail back with my boat."

We came into the port as the sun arched in the sky, basking the ground and bleaching the sand. The port had three docks jutting into the ocean. One was narrower than the others, and at the end a trellis arched over benches. An offering site for the villages to the Sirens. Our village often used Sirens' Cove, but each village had its own area to honor our Siren foremothers.

Jasper's eyes scanned the scenery, taking in the port and small village.

"This is like a quarter the size of your village."

"Yeah, we're the largest. This is the second largest."

"Second?" His eyebrows arched as his gaze tracked to me.

"Yeah, some of the other ones are offshoots of our village. They built villages to help with the resources we needed from the area."

The village sat on sloped land. Naturally bare of trees, the area had plush grass for livestock. Although the fresh bite of the ocean tickled the wind, the livestock and clover added another layer to the aroma.

After looping the straps over our shoulders, we tugged the boat onto the shores.

"Do you want me to stay with the boat while you get Bartholomew?"

"No need," I said, pointing at two specks cresting the hill. "They saw us coming a while ago. Visitors to other harbors aren't common outside of the festival. Most trade is done then, too."

Bretti flanked Bartholomew's side. His black windswept hair fluttered in the breeze. His sharp yellow eyes matched his father's and a deep snarl marred his face.

"He's still here?" Bretti gritted out, his hands shoved into his pockets.

Bartholomew cut an amused look to his son and nodded in my direction. "Let me see them," he said.

I pulled back the tarp, revealing the two wheelbarrows and two scythes.

Bartholomew let out a long whistle, sauntering up to peruse the agreement.

"Rainey, your work is exquisite as expected," he said, running a hand over the metal belly of the wheelbarrow.

"Do they meet your expectations?" I asked, already knowing they did.

"Aye," Bartholomew said. "Follow me, I'll show you the cows you're trading for."

Before I could lift the wheelbarrow out of the boat to follow him, he flicked his hand at Bretti. "Get the stuff, they're ours now."

I stepped aside from the boat. A triumphant smile spread across my face.

A dark glower passed over Bretti's face and his jaw ticked, but he moved to grab a wheelbarrow.

Jasper reached for the other one, but Bretti barked, "They're ours, don't touch them."

Jasper pulled back, his hands empty in the air. He bowed his head slightly in an apology and bit back a smirk.

Bartholomew rolled his eyes and waved Jasper forward. "He's being a bitter fool. Let him. Sulking and pouting certainly will win Rainey's heart."

Bretti's face turned crimson, and he ducked his head to avoid eye contact.

Jasper chuckled at my red face. Slipping an arm around my shoulders and pulling me close, he directed me forward.

"You," Bartholomew said, pointing at Jasper, "don't look like a pouter."

"Pouting catches bird poop, according to my father," Jasper said. A smile flickered across his lips at the memory.

Bartholomew barked out a laugh. "That's a common saying here, too."

Their farm was modest. A house sat squat on the property, tucked beneath towering palm trees. It was about the size of ours with a grand room and bedrooms. Three barns flanked it with troughs and water wells.

The four cows looked like cows: large, squarish, and black and white. The coats looked healthy, and their bellies appeared well-fed.

"Do they meet your approval?" Bartholomew asked in formality, a glint of pride reflected in his eyes.

I nodded. "Molly should like them. If she doesn't, you'll know."

He chuckled and nodded in agreement.

"I hope you two can stay for lunch," Bartholomew said with a wink at me. "I have stew on the pot and some nice currant wine."

I nodded in agreement.

"I'll get things ready," he said. "Take a look around. We'll eat when Bretti finally makes it here, the fool."

I chuckled and nodded.

Walking towards the tree line, I found a large oak. I leaned against the trunk, basking in the smell of wildflowers and the sea. The breeze was still chilled from the storm and rippled through the leaves, shaking droplets of water on me. Jasper wordlessly nestled beside me, digging his feet into the grass.

He leaned back, closing his eyes, his chest rising and falling with his easy, rhythmic breathing.

"Does this spot remind you of home?" I asked. My words felt intrusive in his private thoughts.

He flinched, opening his eyes to meet my gaze. A lazy smile spread across his face as his hand lifted to caress my cheek. Pivoting, I faced him, our shoulders on the tree touching.

"Reminds me of some of the farms, but most of the farms look different. They're inland."

"Places where you can't see or smell the ocean?" I furrowed my brow. Some Washed Up talked of such lands, so dense and distant from the shores that you could live not knowing they existed.

"Yes, much of the land is like that," Jasper said. "Is the other farm close?"

"After lunch, we'll row to the next village where the farm is."

"Will we need to camp again?" he asked, a mischievous and hopeful look in his eyes.

I swallowed, recalling last night and the *almost*. I leaned in closer until I could feel the warmness of his breath on my cheek.

"We can still camp if you want to." I looped my arms around his neck. "Jeri would likely let us crash on her property, but we could camp under the stars."

"Is she expecting us today?" he asked, a wicked smile dancing on his lips.

My core tightened with heat.

I shook my head before I thought better of it. "We reached Bartholomew's faster since there were two of us paddling."

He smiled triumphantly at me. Despite not bringing up my attempt to ditch him, he gave a knowing look and hummed.

Jasper closed our distance, his lips brushing against mine. He licked my lips, and I parted them. His tongue slipped inside as he cupped the back of my head. A moan escaped my mouth and my hands slipped under his shirt, tracing over his muscles.

"Don't do that on my property," Bretti's voice barked at us.

Jasper groaned, leaning his forehead against mine.

"It's not your property," Bartholomew countered, walking around from the back. Sweat beaded on his brow and dampened his shirt. "I put some bread out, too. It's not as good as your mom's, though."

"She'd be flattered to hear that." I smiled.

We followed him to a small table set outside. Eight tree stumps dotted around it.

"Make sure you tell her, then," he said with a pointed look.

I chuckled. "If you have a favorite kind of bread, I can let her know for your trade."

A smile danced on his lips. "I'm hoping I can pick a few loaves up with this delivery."

I blinked hard to not blanche knowing what he really meant. Sure, he wanted the bread, but he was looking forward to more private time with my mom.

"Dad, the boat is ready for the cows, but Lily's partner has gone into labor," Bretti muttered.

Bartholomew cursed, pursing his lips as he rested his elbows on the tables.

"What's wrong?" I asked, uncertainty twisting my stomach.

"Lily's my best first mate next to Bretti. She was going to help me take the cows. With Ginny in labor, she'll want to stay close to the farm."

"Can anyone else help you with the cows?" I asked, swallowing the lump in my throat.

Bartholomew cut his eyes to Bretti.

"I'm not helping," Bretti chortled, casting me a dark sneer. "Looks like you're outta luck on getting the cows by the next festival."

"You won't help your dad?" Jasper murmured. He buttered his roll, casting Bretti a dark look.

Bretti growled and slammed his spoon on the table, rattling our bowls. "I'm not helping her." He jabbed a finger at me while glaring at Jasper.

"Why?" Jasper asked, ignoring Bretti's posturing.

"Yeah, why, Bretti?" Bartholomew prompted, raising an eyebrow at him.

"Trade's not with me," he sniffed. "We apparently aren't friendly, so I don't do favors."

"We're not friends?" I asked. My brows scrunched. "Since when?"

His eyes jumped and he pulled back to stare at me, mouth agape.

Bartholomew stifled a laugh.

"Seriously, I'd like to know. We've hung together at festivals since we were kids. We even danced."

His cheeks tinted red, but he sent Jasper a triumphant smile. "Yes, we did dance."

Jasper sipped his water and looked at me. "Can I have the salt?"

Bretti glowered.

"Have you danced with Rainey?" he asked, folding his arms over his wide chest like he was a victor.

Jasper's eyes darted around before he shook his head. "Nope, we've only kissed."

I laughed while trying to swallow and choked on my water.

"Hm." Bretti sat taller, squaring his shoulders. He lowered his head to stare at Jasper from under his brows with a sneer. He tilted his head to me and smiled brightly. "I figured out the trade for my *friend* to have me help transport the cows."

"What's that?" I asked, taking the bait.

Jasper and Bartholomew both shifted to stare at him.

"I want a kiss from my good friend, Rainey."

The wind whistled, the trees swayed, and birds cawed, but no one at the table made a sound.

"What?" Jasper finally choked, pushing himself back. He turned, his breathing heavy as his eyes narrowed in on Bretti.

"Bretti," Bartholomew moaned, rubbing a hand over his forehead. "What a fool."

I stuck my tongue in my cheek as I considered his words. Nodding, I said, "Fine, I'll give my friend a kiss so he'll help his father."

"Rainey?" Jasper whined.

Head still bowed, Bartholomew tracked me with his eyes as I stood and moved towards Bretti.

Chest puffed out, he sat straighter in his seat.

The intensity of Jasper's gaze weighed me down as I stepped towards Bretti, but I didn't look back at him.

Bretti puckered his lips out, his eyes hooding closed.

My hand trailed on the tabletop until I reached him. Bracing on the rough corner, I leaned over, pressing my lips to his cheek.

His face slackened and his eyes widened in surprise and embarrassment.

Bartholomew hooted, pounding his fist on the table. "Ha, ha, oh Bretti, she got you! That is a friend's kiss!"

I straightened, meeting Bretti's dark glare. I winked at him, a smirk tugging my lips up.

I returned to my seat, Jasper's dark eyes watched me, amusement flickering in them along with something else. Perhaps jealousy or annoyance.

I placed my hand on his shoulder as I settled back on my log, leaning into him. His body rippled with silent laughter, causing me to giggle.

Bretti made a strangled noise, but I couldn't look at him or I'd burst out in a belly laugh.

"Jasper?" Bartholomew asked, his laugh fading.

"Yes, sir," Jasper said. He wrapped an arm around me and tucked me against his side.

"Hm," Bartholomew hummed, staring at us. His eyes finally tracked to meet Jasper's. "Are you enjoying island life?"

"Yes, sir." Jasper nodded and squeezed my shoulders.

Bartholomew's hawkish eyes narrowed in on me before returning to Jasper.

"Have you put any thought into the next few months?"

Jasper didn't stiffen or go hoarse. Instead, he leaned his head against mine and answered, "Rainey and I are talking about things."

"Oh?" Bartholomew asked, his eyes bright and wide as they turned to me. "Is that so?"

I swallowed and forced a smile. Jasper and I had talked about two months. Everything else was iffy and undefined. And instead of taking this time to think, he was traveling with me.

"Well, if you decide to be a fool, she always has a friend here," he said, flicking his fingers in Bretti's direction.

Jasper tensed, his muscles tight where we touched. "I don't plan on being a fool."

Twenty

AFTER LUNCH, Jasper and I returned to my boat bobbing beside the dock. The sun arched above us, bathing us in heat and light.

I waded into the shallow beach, letting the water lap away the sand and dirt clinging to my feet and pants. Jasper joined me, his hand finding the curve of my waist.

A light twinkled in the distance.

"Fisherperson?" Jasper asked. His fingers started to rub slow circles into my hip.

"Possible," I said. Based on distance, it was very unlikely.

"Or?"

"Siren," I said.

Silence embraced us, heavy with unspoken questions and answers. Fear and hope.

Many had a story of the Sirens helping them get safely ashore when out at sea to fish. How they protected our island from the beyond. Or the bountiful treasures they provided us from the sea. Our Siren mothers protected us, but we knew not to cross them. We offered gifts and ceremonies in their honor. Before Jasper, I hadn't thought much about the Washed Up and their journey back through the Sirens. Jasper would see them when he returned, something I had never done. Yet, I knew they were out there, and he likely still thought them myth.

Our Ferriers had their own sayings and warnings but for their own return. For our islanders. I had no clue what warnings the Washed Up were given, if any. Before Jasper started back, we'd have to talk to my grandpa. Make sure Jasper had a safe journey.

The final thought settled on my heart like lead, stealing my breath. Jasper's warm fingers tightened on my hip, pulling my thoughts back to him. Now wasn't the time to worry about his departure, be it one, two, or more months. Now was the time to enjoy his fleeting moments still here.

"Do they look like the fairytale books?" he finally asked, his voice soft.

I shrugged. "I haven't read your books like that."

"They have an upper body of a human with a lower half like a fish," Jasper said. He tugged me in closer, resting his head on mine. Despite the short days, his touch had grown familiar and addictive.

"They are more beautiful than humans and take the colors of the rainbow in their skin and hair," I said. "They have womanly upper halves and serpent-like lower halves with fins. When they choose to terraform, they can, for a short time, take on human legs."

"Razor-sharp teeth?"

"Yes," I said. My tongue flicked against my own, feeling the flattened ridges.

"You mentioned several possible origin stories," he started before pausing. He pressed his lips into a line and scrunched his face.

Silence hung between us before he said, "Which one do you believe?"

He didn't appear to be mocking me or setting me up. Genuine curiosity flittered behind his eyes as they shifted to look at me.

"They are our foremothers. For whatever reason, our ancestors couldn't join them in the sea. Our legs became permanent. Regardless of the generations removed, they still watch over us, protect us. We are theirs."

"When you walk into the water, does it feel different?" He selected his words carefully as he thought through the question.

"Do you mean, do I feel powers dwell within? The need to lure men to their watery graves, or feel like I am growing a fin to join them?" I asked with a laugh.

He flinched. "I didn't mean it like that."

I wrapped my arm around his torso and squeezed, his taut muscles hard against my fingers. His heat soaked through, igniting my own.

"I know," I said. "The water is a part of our blood. We are born to it. But I don't morph when I enter, nor do I want to swim away. I am where I belong. On the Solstices, we have ceremonies in the waters in Sirens' Cove. No one has been overcome by it."

"The Sirens... Do the Ferriers anger the Sirens?" Jasper asked. "Doesn't it disrespect their gifts to return Washed Up?"

The question stilled my nerves and froze my blood. Leaving was still on the forefront of his mind.

"What's wrong?" Jasper asked, shifting back. His eyes, bright with concern, searched my face.

"Nothing," I lied quickly.

His face lit up with realization. "Rainey," he started and sighed, running his other hand in his hair.

Before he could continue, I blurted out, "The Ferriers have their own rituals to not anger the Sirens when they take Washed Up back. They bring offerings. Each Washed Up is sent to us for a reason. It could be to teach us something, to live here or to bring us new blood for our lines. Just like no one is required to harbor a Washed Up unless settling a new plot, it's not a gift if we are required to tend to it. We've returned Washed Up as far back as our history goes."

"Oh..." Jasper said, his eyes widening.

"Their gifts are to help us. Even if we don't see how."

Unable to find a suitable place to camp overnight along the way, we landed in the next village as the moon crested the sky, warring with the sun, their battle painted in bold colors across the sky.

The boat, much lighter now, was easier to carry across the sandy beach. The harbor was really more like a few piers that pierced the ocean with two larger ships. If needed, they could possibly be Ferrier boats, but they were better suited for island travel with their medium build and low sides.

A few dozen houses spotted the landscape, trees sparsely dotting the land, but the forest in the distance choked out the view of the setting sun. The terrain was rockier and more uneven than Bretti's village.

"Goats?" Jasper asked, staring at the landscape.

"Yep." I nodded. "Jeri lives closer to the forest line."

Jeri's house stood tucked into a hillside. Mismatched metal siding was tacked on a wooden frame. Portal windows allowed light in but kept rain out. Her barn sat off-center, tilting slightly away from the ocean. Goat bleats pierced the still air.

"We're staying with her tonight?" Jasper asked, his eyes reflecting the ocean.

"Or we can camp in the forest," I smirked, dropping my lead on the boat. "We have a tent..." I stepped closer to him. His eyes, dark, intense pools, tracked me.

He sucked in a breath, standing taller when I wrapped my arms around him. His hands slid down my sides, dipping below my waistband. I stood on my toes to reach his mouth with mine. "We can continue last night sans a rainstorm."

"Rainey?" Jeri's harsh voice rang out.

Jasper chuckled, the deep sound echoing in my heart.

"Everyone's timing... is so..."

"Interruptive," he said. He stroked my hair before pulling back to stare behind me.

"You brought someone?" Jeri asked.

She stood a few feet behind us wearing black muck boots to her knees, pants that once had been black but were caked with earth and grime and everything else, and a shirt stained with even more. Red tresses escaped her braided binds, frizzing around her face. Her normally green eyes were dark in the fading light.

"Jeri, this is Jasper," I said, waving between them. "Jasper, this is Jeri."

Jasper nodded, curling his fingers around my shoulder in an attempt to not offer his hand for a shake.

"Jasper, huh?" Jeri asked, her eyes narrowing. Snapping her fingers, she grinned and shook her finger at Jasper. "I remember you from the festival."

We both stilled. In the blur of faces, I didn't remember seeing many after we met with Marcus. The night had turned into a blur of kissing, dancing, and retreating home full of mead and want.

"You do?" he choked.

"Oh yeah, you had a bunch of people in a tizzy. That Owen boy." Jeri gave me a knowing look. "Now I understand why. Good catch, both of ya."

My lip quirked up in a smirk. "I have the pans as promised for the goats. They are enameled cast iron."

"Not that junky coated stuff? Non-stick, or whatever they call it?"

"Nope, true cast iron," I said, nodding towards the cart. "I cleaned them up. Two pots and a pan."

Jeri clapped her hands excitedly, darting to the cart. "I'll have to fry up tonight's dinner in them!"

"Can I stash my boat in your barn for the night?"

"Yep." Jeri nodded. "No one will steal it, but no point in letting the kids joy ride in it and ruining it. You two are joining me for dinner?"

I nodded and then looked to Jasper.

"Yes, thank you," Jasper said.

"Such manners," Jeri chuckled. Her lips curled into a grin.

"We'll settle up and be ready," I said.

"Thanks again." Jasper leaned down to gather his share of the ropes.

"Jasper," Jeri called.

"Yes?" he asked, his eyes meeting hers.

"You better not hurt our Rainey, or you'll deal with me." Jeri jabbed a thumb against her chest. "The whole island... well except for one or two... will come for you."

I closed my eyes and swallowed down the anger and love rivaling to come out towards Jeri. She meant well, but I'd handle my business.

Jasper's eyes widened and he stammered, "I-I have no intentions of hurting her."

"Good, and keep it that way," Jeri said and then waved him off, focusing on her pans.

"Mind if we clean up?" I asked.

"Fresh water finished boiling a few minutes ago. Wash up. I have blankets on the floor ready for you. I thought it would just be you, Rainey, but I'm guessing you two can share the spot?" She cocked an eyebrow at us.

Thankful for the darkness as the blush stole across me, I nodded. "We'll be fine, thank you very much."

After washing my body clean, I donned a new tunic and trousers, leaving my boots to dry out by the fire. My toes squished in the sandy grass.

Jeri had built a fire, and in our honor, had invited a few friends over for a feast, each bringing something to enjoy. Three others had joined us: Phillip, Ursula, and Manny.

I snagged a few fish while Jasper cleaned up, allowing myself time to not gawk at his physique. He joined me after a few minutes, clean and smelling of Jeri's lemon soap.

I ran my fingers through his wet hair, smoothing it down before spiking it back up.

His hands traced my sides, resting on my hips. Leaning down, he kissed me gently.

"Oh, time for that later," Jeri sang. "Feast time now. We have fish from Rainey, goat cheese, goat burgers, milk, and fruit."

"Sounds delicious," I said over my rumbling stomach.

We sat together on a large log, sides pressed together.

"Rainey, I don't remember the last time you had a boyfriend or girl-friend," Phillip, a local farmer, said. His ruddy hair shot with gray matched his thick beard. He sat next to Jeri, casting her longing glances, but she never returned them.

Jasper cut his eyes to me, a grin tugging at his lips.

"Last time I remember," Jeri said, rubbing her chin, smearing grease from the burger on her cheek, "was a couple summers ago. You snuck out into the forest to meet up with others you met at the festival. That was before all the trades to own that plot of land."

"Really?" Jasper asked, cocking an eyebrow.

"You and Lorilynn lasted almost a whole moon cycle. You and Henry two weeks. Those are the longest I know about before you got bored and quit showing up."

I sucked my lips between my teeth, staring intently at my plate as Jasper tried to snag my glance. The island knew everyone's business and enjoyed sharing it.

"Didn't she see Bretti for a bit?" Phillip asked.

Jasper's eyes shot up to Phillip.

Jeri scoffed and swatted his arm. "No, you idiot, she danced with him but would never meet him in the woods. He tried for years."

Phillip held his arm where Jeri had hit him, a smile dancing on his lips as he stared at it, then Jeri.

"But you never saw a Washed Up," Jeri said. She gave me a pointed look.

Jasper shot me a triumphant smile.

"Yes, everyone seems to like to point it out."

"Again." Jeri swung her gaze to Jasper, dark behind the fire. "You hurt our girl, we'll all come for you."

Jasper swallowed and curled his arm around my shoulders. His warm fingers rubbed circles. I sank into his side, a jolt warming my center.

"Understood," he said with a smile.

Jeri fought a smile. With a wave of her hand, she nudged Philip and gestured to the open field.

Phillip removed a harmonica from his pocket, weathered and chipped, but it still played.

To his right, Ursula lifted a ukulele from her side. Long, braided blonde hair wrapped around her head and hung over her shoulder.

Together, Phillip and Ursula started up a tune. One about our Sirens. Jeri and I joined in, clapping and stomping our feet.

Manny, the other one to join us, jumped to their feet, twirling in time to the music. "Come on, this here is a party," they sang and pulled me up by my arms. They swung me around and then pulled me close. We bowed towards each other, stomping our feet, before kicking out and twirling away from each other. I circled back and grasped Jasper's hand. His hand went limp in mine, and his eyes bulged in horror.

"I can't dance," he hissed.

I laughed and pulled him with me. "Just follow me."

He smiled, and my stomach flipped, sending butterflies to my throat. "Always," he said, trying to mimic my footwork.

Manny yanked Jeri up. She protested, but her smile won out and she joined in the twirling. Manny and I bumped backs before spinning our partners back around. I released Jasper and Manny released Jeri, the four of us stomping in time and twirling.

Manny swooped down next to Phillip. Unintelligible words passed between them, but a reddened Phillip took up Manny's spot in the dance as Manny pulled out their own harmonica.

We all panted as the song came to an end.

"Time for a slow one," Manny called out. Their tenor voice started on a sea song about waiting for love to return. Ursula joined them, her haunting voice leaving the heart yearning.

I went to sit, but Jasper wrapped an arm around my waist and pulled me tight against him.

"I know how to sway," he whispered in my ear. His breath sent tingles down my spine and tightened my stomach.

I moved my hands from his shoulders and wrapped my arms around his neck. He leaned forward, resting his cheek against mine. I closed my eyes, savoring the movement, letting his warmth heat me. Before Jasper, I hadn't known this was something I wanted. Now I craved it. His touch. His warmth. Him.

Letting my heart have its moment, my brain reared up, reminding me we only talked about two cycles. The first one was already almost halfway done. Reality splashed like cold water over me, numbing me, and I stiffened.

"What's wrong?" he whispered against my ear, his voice alarmed.

"I..." I started, but closed my eyes and turned my head.

"Rainey," he murmured. When I didn't respond, he repositioned to try to look at my face.

I shifted from him, blinking back the emotion. I knew he was leaving. I knew he was a Washed Up. I'd tried to have fun, had fun, but it wasn't fun anymore. My heart panged, tremors rippling through it, fracturing me at the seam. I'd been a fool. I'd fallen for him. I'd fallen for a Washed Up who was going to leave. I'd be my mother, after all. Mourning a man who left. In my attempt to be a Sirens' Daughter while earning my land, I was running the path to be a Sea Widow.

A bitter laugh ripped through me thinking about the land I'd have. I'd earned it. It was mine, and it'd only cost years of hard labor and breaking my heart.

"Rainey," he growled again, snapping me from my thoughts.

"What?" I murmured, my voice thick with emotion.

Misreading the conversation, Jeri whispered behind us, "Take the loft in the barn. Blankets are stored up there. It'll give you more privacy than my house."

I blinked, my vision blurry with unshed emotion. Jeri was already leading a beaming Phillip up to the house. Ursula and Manny smiled at me, and with hands clasped, walked down the dark trail together.

In a matter of moments, Jasper and I were alone in the yard. The sky was light above us, bathed in stars and the waxing moon. The full moon would grace us in the next night, the Siren song at its strongest and the deeper waters the most dangerous to travel.

"Rainey, what's wrong?" Jasper asked, his voice urgent. He caressed my cheeks, his eyes searching my face, growing more alarmed by what he saw.

"Jasper," I choked, emotion stealing my words. I bowed my head to avoid him seeing me, seeing the pain I couldn't hide.

"Rainey, please," he begged. "Please, look at me. Talk to me." He leaned over, trying to see me, trying to make eye contact.

"Jasper, it's just... too much," I said, copping out of telling the full truth.

"What's too much? The trades? The long day? Me? What?"

"Jasper," I said again. Closing my eyes, I steeled my nerves and feelings and looked up to meet his stare. His brown eyes shone with concern, his face pinched as he tried to figure out what was going on.

As I came into my words, the surroundings came into focus. His closeness. The smell of cinnamon and ash I'd come to associate with him flooded my senses. His care. His gentle touch on my face. His entire focus on me.

Without thought, I grabbed his face, pulled him to me, and kissed him. I couldn't get enough. Didn't want enough. I just wanted.

"Jasper," I breathed as I trailed kisses along his chin and down his neck.

Twenty-One

MORNING RAIN PATTERED on the roof. Drips trickled down from small gaps, dampening the floor.

Jasper's arm tightened around me as he nestled closer in sleep.

"Jasper," I whispered, trailing kisses down his jaw.

He shifted against me, pulling me closer. Before he was completely awake, he was returning my kisses.

"Good morning," he murmured against my lips.

"Morning," I said. "We have a long walk today."

He groaned, flopping his head back on the blanket pillow.

"We need to talk about last night," he murmured, eyes still closed.

Unsure if he meant our conversation or our trip to the loft, I kissed his lips instead. My fingers traced his exposed chest and farther down, resting on his naked hip.

"It's your turn tonight," he said. He rubbed circles on my back through my shirt. His hands roamed lower, dipping below my pants' waist.

"I can't wait," I said, rubbing my hand across his groin. "We should start soon."

"We were supposed to talk last night. You may have distracted me." He chuckled. "Where are my clothes?"

"Um, your shirt is somewhere down there, and your pants are by the ladder," I said, waving my hand behind me.

"I'll be kinder with your clothes than you were with mine," he said and then kissed me hard.

"You weren't complaining last night," I teased. I'd fallen asleep in my shirt and pants, leaving them rumpled for the day.

"I'm not complaining now," he said, standing and providing me with a show.

I licked my lips and whistled.

He shifted himself, casting me an amused look. "You're going to distract me again?"

My glance darted to the window on the ground floor. The gray morning filtered through. It would be a rough, damp passage if we left now, anyway.

I sent him a cheeky smile, causing his smile to fall and his eyes to dilate.

"We have time," I said, bending my finger at him.

Without hesitation, he knelt to the floor beside me. His mouth was on mine. A groan escaped my lips, and he deepened our kiss. My brain tried to protest, remind me of his departure, but with each kiss, my heart and soul smothered it silent. Need gripped me, my fingers tightening on him, pressing him closer to me. I needed to feel him everywhere. He acquiesced, his hands sliding against my jaw and fisting in my hair. Then one was cradling my neck as the other slid down my back. There were too many clothes separating us.

Greedy fingers tugged at my shirt. His fingers traced over my breast and I arched into his hand. His thumb brushed over my nipple, circling around it.

"Jasper," I panted, my want and yearning filling the room. My center ached for his touch. For him.

"Rainey," he growled. The vibration spiked through me, unleashing any restraint I had.

Pushing up, I rolled him over, straddling his waist as I continued to kiss him. His naked body, taut beneath me, promised so much pleasure. Trailing kisses down his hard chest and over his abs, my stomach tightened, my nerves on fire with each touch. I cupped him before running my tongue the length of him.

As his fingers caught in my hair, he arched into me.

"I'm selfish," Jasper said, holding me to him. I felt his heartbeat through my shirt, still racing. A yearning song to my own. I was still completely clothed. "And two tonight for you."

I chuckled, and said, "We'll see."

He ran his fingers through my hair, gazing unfocused at my face.

"Rainey," he murmured.

"Hm." I kissed his cheek.

"I really like it here." He swallowed.

"I didn't know you liked smelly, dank lofts," I said, gasping when he tickled my side. "Had I known, I could have had you housed in Willis' barn."

"I like being here, with you," he said, his gaze honest and focused on me. "Anywhere, with you."

My insides melted and I nestled closer to him.

"I like you here, too," I whispered. I ran a finger on his jawline.

"So every time I want to talk about what upset you last night, are you going to give me fellatio?"

I choked a laugh. "So proper and scientific."

"Cunnilingus for you tonight," he said with a straight face as his eyes flashed in amusement. "A couple times."

"Can't wait," I said, rubbing against him. My body already thrummed at the thought.

"Then we're going to talk about last night," he said.

I groaned.

He chuckled, pressing me tightly against him.

"How long of a walk do we have today?" he asked.

"Not sure with the goats," I said. "Without, a long day. With the rain, we'll get a late start. We'll need to camp early tonight for the full moon."

"Full moon?"

I nodded, my lips finding his again for a light kiss. "The Sirens' song is the strongest tonight. We celebrate in their honor. I brought a flask of wine for it."

His dark eyes deepened, and he swallowed. "Wine and campfire in the woods?"

"Mhm," I said, my hand trailing down his side.

"Will today put us behind?" he asked. His body shifted, giving me more access to explore. A gentle hand cupped my breast as his other one ran the length of my back. With a feather soft touch, he trailed kisses over my jawline.

"I planned on delays with the goats," I said, tilting my head to the side to give him access to my neck. "It'll be a couple days' travel with them now. We should be fine."

"Then what?"

"Sunny will transport the goats with the pigs. Jeri doesn't have a vessel that can make the trip. Sunny's boat can handle it and they like to stock up on goods outside of the festival time."

"We row home, then?" he asked.

My heart stalled at his expression of home. A stupid grin grew on my face, and I kissed him.

"They'll eat as they walk," Jeri said, slipping leads over the goats. "They'll also want to explore. Let 'em, but keep 'em leashed or you won't catch 'em again."

"Thanks." I nodded and took one lead. Jasper took the other.

The rain had rolled away, leaving a fresh scent over the land. The sun dried the ground, providing us a smooth track until we entered the forest, still damp with lingering rain.

"You know where we're going?" Jasper pushed a branch from his face. The thick air clung to our skin, dampening our shirts.

"Ocean to the right of us and the sun in front of us," I said. "So, yes."

He smirked at me. "What predators lurk in the forest?"

"Nothing like what you're used to," I said. "We have deer and some hogs and goats that escaped farms. There are some wolves, but we leave them alone and they leave us alone. There's plenty here for us all."

The sun was still in the sky when we set camp. Jasper tended to the tent as I secured the goats to a fallen log, giving them ample lead line. The sticky post-storm air hung thickly in the air. A sheen glistened on my skin and dampened my shirt. I tugged it away to provide airflow. I left my boat on the track with wheels I'd built for it years ago. The thick rubber tires traversed the land with ease. I pulled out my pot to boil water and the dried meat I'd packed for the forest stay of our journey. I didn't want to hunt and bring the smell of fresh blood towards the goats or us.

As the water cooled, the spindly smoke cloud twirled in the air. I set a fire up to ward off animals throughout the night.

Jasper finished with the tent and walked up to me. He slipped his arms around my torso, resting his hands on my abdomen.

"You smell," he whispered into my ear, sending tingles down my spine.

I giggled and swatted at him. "You're not a fresh flower, either."

He kissed the spot where my jaw met my neck and slid his hands to my waist and under my shirt. His warm thumbs rubbed circles into my flesh.

With a fluid motion he removed my shirt and tossed it aside. His hands splayed on my torso, one moving towards my chest while the other dipped into my pants. He turned me around so I was facing him. He leaned down, kissing me urgently, and his hands pushed my trousers down.

"Step," he said between kisses.

I obliged and stepped out of my pooled pants.

Keeping his hands on my waist, he walked me backwards while kissing me. My mind only thought was of him and his touch. Despite his promise of focusing on me, my hands took over, pushing his shirt over his shoulders and head. I flung it away from us, not caring where it landed.

He chuckled. "Told you I'd show your clothes more respect."

I reached my hand down his pants, holding him. He groaned against my mouth and pushed into my hand.

He moved one hand away but returned it quickly with the wet wash rag from the pot we stood beside. Methodically, he moved the rag over my bare skin, wiping away the grime and dirt. As he traveled it over my flesh, he kissed each freshly-cleaned spot. I gripped his shoulders as he moved lower and then finally his hair as he anchored himself on his knees.

Insects sounded around us and the fire burned low. The orange glow flickered off the tent's material and danced against the trees. Through the tree canopy, the speckled sky blazed in rich purples. The moon hung large and bright. Tomorrow it'd start waning for the next moonless night less than two weeks away.

A lump formed in my throat thinking about the few weeks that had passed. We hadn't talked much about the next cycle or what would come after it. Mostly because I had stopped the conversation. All I knew was that I didn't want it to end. I didn't want to say goodbye.

The flask of wine lay in my knapsack. After digging it out, I wordlessly offered my hand to Jasper. He slid his hand over, lacing his fingers with mine.

A dark river raced through the forest a quarter of a mile from our camp. At a narrow part, I stepped into the water, letting the cool current splash against my skin. Jasper followed me, still holding my hand. His watchful gaze took in the surroundings: the river, the bloated moon hanging low in the sky, outshining the stars, and the swaying of palms in the wind.

He slid his other hand along my hip, bringing us closer. His nearness charged the air and my body heated. I wrapped my free hand around his neck, bringing him down to my lips. He was a Washed Up, a gift of the Sirens. Be one month, two, or more, he was mine now. My heart twisted, sharp shards stealing my breath.

He broke the kiss, his dark eyes hooded as his unfocused gaze took me in.

"We should thank the Sirens for their gifts," I said, my voice huskier than expected.

His fingers skimmed over my hips below my pants, leaving heated tracks.

He nodded, waiting silently for my lead.

I sipped from the flask and offered it to him. He too took a sip.

"We have a feast in their honor on a full-moon night, often in the cove or on the beach," I said to Jasper. "Since we can't join in, we will send the Sirens our honors in the water for all they do for us and helping us have safe travels now."

He nodded.

"Siren mothers," I whispered.

The breeze kicked up, rustling the trees and skittering through my tangled hairs loose in the braid.

Jasper squeezed my hand before releasing it so I could dig in my pocket.

"Thank you for the gifts." I rested a glittery trinket on the nearest rock. Silently, I said, "*And Jasper.*"

The current lapped over the rocks, taking the gift in its watery grasp. The treasure slipped beneath the surface into the dark depths.

"Rainey," Jasper murmured in my ear.

I wiggled, moving to capture his lips with mine.

He returned the kiss before tilting his head to the side. "Rainey, I..."

"It's okay," I whispered, my voice hoarse with the emotion I kept trapped in my throat.

"Rainey," he said. He placed a hand on my cheek, gently holding it in place. The cool waters raced by my ankles in contrast to the warmth from Jasper.

I blinked, pressing my lips into a thin line. Too many emotions swam in my veins and ached in my soul.

He swallowed, averting his eyes before finding my gaze again. "Rainey, I want to stay."

"What?" I asked. Hope burst in my chest, replacing everything else.

He took an uneven breath; his eyes mirroring my fear. "If you're okay with it, I'd like to stay on the island. Permanently."

"Are you sure?" I choked out. He had a life there. One very different from the island. "Your family, friends? Erick? You're almost done with your degree."

He leaned over, brushing his lips against mine. "Yes, I want to stay on the island. My family is gone. My friends...they'd understand. Erick would fist bump me for finding happiness. My degree was to pay bills. This is where I want to be. But are you okay with me staying?"

I smiled against his lips. "I'd be okay with that."

He leaned back. A smile beamed on his face. He reached his hands behind his neck, unclasping his chain. He held it in his hands with the ends dangling in the air, reflecting in the full moon's light. He took a deep breath. "Rainey, I know it was fast, but I know how I feel."

My body stiffened. Tingles raced down my spine. My face twisted in fear and hope for what he was going to say next.

"Rainey, I don't know how much works here. What your traditions are. But I know mine. I'm in love with you. I want to stay on the island, with you. I want... I want to give you my chain," he blurted, cheeks flushing.

I stared, mouth agape at him. The words. So many words. All words I wanted but didn't know I wanted until he said them. Words that warmed and frightened me. Words I couldn't repeat yet.

He held his arms out awkwardly between us, the chain pinched between his fingers, ready to reclasp it but unsure what to do.

"Jasper, it's your mom's...are you sure?" I asked, placing my hands on his.

He met my gaze, his eyes bright with emotion. "Yes, absolutely."

I shifted around so he could loop it around my neck and clasp it. The metal, warm from his touch, sat lightly on my skin and heavy on my heart. My fingers traced the intricate weave.

His fingers gently brushed against my neck after he finished hooking it.

I turned back to him, cupping his cheek and pressing my lips to his. "Jasper, I want you to stay," I said against his lips. "With me."

"Okay," he whispered.

The Sirens had answered.

Twenty-Two

THE GOATS HAD us up and moving before the sun cracked the sky.

Jasper and I held hands as we trekked through the forest, welcoming the break of day. The fresh breeze off the ocean tickled the leaves and brought a briny smell.

"Do you plan on being a Scavenger with me?" I asked, the words hard to form. Fear tugged at my stomach that he had already changed his mind. Twirling my thumb around my fingers, I waited for his reply.

"I enjoy working with you," he said with a nod. "If you're up for it, we could work together, maybe enlarge the work area outside with an overhang shelter."

I snorted. "Don't like working inside with my mom?"

He chuckled, a blush stealing across his face. "It's crowded with us and her annoyance of me."

I waved away his words. "She'll get over it. She's just certain you're going to leave and break my heart." A part of me thought it, too.

Jasper hesitated, his toe digging into the dirt. He tugged my hand back. I pivoted to face him.

"What's wrong?" I asked. The notion of my mom being right, and that he did want to leave, gnawed at my resolve.

"Rainey, I'm staying," he said. His eyes searched my face. "I want to be with you."

"I believe you," I assured him even as I flinched.

"But?"

"Forever is a long time," I said and swallowed. "I've seen people who were certain they wanted to stay leave after a few cycles."

"Why would I want to leave?" he asked.

I shrugged. "You miss family or friends. You miss electricity. You miss the perishable conveniences of your world."

"I don't miss them," he said, closing the distance between us. He wrapped the lead around his hand so he could fit his hand on my hip. "I want to be here. I love you."

After several days of walking and camping in the woods, we reached Sunny's as the moon appeared in the hazy blue of the fading day.

Their home was one of a few dozen sprawled on sandy cliffs overlooking the ocean. Corrals ran in grids across the farms.

Sunny waved at us, their blonde hair pulled back in a bun. They wore overalls and thick waders.

The goats ran into the offered corral, darting for the hay and fresh grain.

"You made good time," they called.

After wiping their hands on their faded blue jeans, they joined us at the gate.

"The goats were easy to travel with," I said. "The storm delayed us a bit, but we made up time."

Sunny's gaze cut to Jasper. Their blue eyes narrowed as they traveled from his head to his rubber-sole shoes and back up.

"Who are you?" they snapped.

"I'm Jasper," Jasper said.

I smiled and looped an arm around his waist. He snaked his arm around my shoulder, tucking me into his side.

"Oh," Sunny said, a smile brightening their face. "I see! Well, that is a surprise. I'd never thought Rainey would be involved with a Washed Up."

Jasper shot me a dark look, his mouth a thin line.

I chuckled and bumped my hip against his. "You could take it as a compliment."

"Oh, I do," he assured.

"What does Owen think of him?" Sunny asked, a smile tugging at their lips.

I rolled my eyes, causing them to laugh.

"Owen has a way about him," Sunny said.

"So everyone is aware of Owen's attempts and he still tries?" Jasper asked.

Sunny's gaze met mine, searching for how to answer.

I shrugged. "Owen hasn't been shy about it."

Sunny eased back, their blue eyes jumping to Jasper. "Owen has been claiming he's going to partner with Rainey since they were kids. It was when they stopped being friends."

Jasper's fingers tightened on me. "He's been doing this for that long?"

"Ever since Molly told him her vision," I said. An odd acidic sensation twisted in my stomach. "We were best friends until then. We explored the island. Played on the beach. Then he was focused on her vision and trying to make plans for the future."

"I see," Jasper said, but his face was scrunched in confusion or annoyance.

"Rainey and Owen were inseparable, like siblings, but Owen went... well, you've likely seen how he is."

Jasper's rigid form shifted beside me. His jaw ticked as his fingers rubbed circles into my shoulder.

"I don't have feelings for Owen like that," I whispered.

Jasper's gaze bounced to me, a smile curving his lips and brightening his face. "I know. I just don't like that he's bothered you for years. No is no."

"Enough about Owen." Sunny waved for us to follow them back to the house. "You're here to trade so you can finally have that land! I've got some water simmering on a fire. I'll put the goats in a corral. Put your boat in the barn and then go around back to the watershed. Clean rags are ready for you. Sorry, Washed Up, no fancy bathroom here."

"Thank you," I said and led Jasper back towards the barn.

"Is everyone going to remind me I'm a Washed Up and you don't get involved with them?" he whispered, leaning in close.

"No, after a while, they'll forget." I shrugged. "It's new. Since working for the land, I haven't seen many people outside of business transactions. They mean all the best by it. You'll always be a Washed Up, but staying like Willis means the name has respect. Everyone knows everyone's business. We are separated on the island, but we're an island. We purposely find reasons to get together at least once every cycle. We have other holiday and seasonal celebrations."

"Beyond the moonless night and the full moon?"

Next to the wash bin, I pulled my shirt off and tugged my pants down.

Jasper's eyes watched me, dilated and dark.

"Yes, we have other celebrations," I said.

"Like what?" he asked, distracted.

When he didn't move from watching me, I closed our distance. His breath came out of his nose. I slipped my hands under his shirt. The warmth of his skin was inviting. After pushing it over his head and tossing it aside, I looped my arms around his neck. My mouth hovered next to his.

"We celebrate the changes in the seasons," I said and pressed a soft kiss to his lips. "Each one is marked by a celebration. We also have harvest celebrations when different items are ripe. We make it a habit to stay interconnected. We need each other. We rely on each other. And, as annoying and frustrating as it can be, knowing each other's business helps us stay safe and keep others safe."

"I'm fine being Rainey's Washed Up," Jasper said. He pressed a hot kiss to my lips before stripping down to clean up.

We set camp behind Sunny's barn, tucked under the tree's canopy. A warm fire flickered in the firepit, the flame tendrils twirling towards the sky. My belly was full of the feast Sunny provided: bacon-wrapped cod filets with baked potatoes.

Jasper nestled beside me, draping his arm around me. His heat soaked through my tunic, going to my center.

I shifted to my knees, arching one over Jasper's legs.

His dark eyes tracked me and his hands came to my hips. He leaned forward, his lips brushing mine. I deepened the kiss, wrapping my arms around his neck.

His hands slipped under my tunic, rubbing against my stomach. One skimmed up to my breast. He cupped it and ran his thumb over my nipple. I pushed into his hand and pressed my core against his length. He groaned and pressed back.

My greedy mouth met his in a scorching kiss. His hands moved to my hips, pressing me to him as he deepened the kiss. With smooth circles, he rubbed his thumbs under my trousers, rubbing lower until I squirmed against his touch.

I pulled my shirt off, tossing it to the side. His kisses tracked down my chin, neck and to my collarbone and then breast. His hands moved to my waist, lowering them.

His fingers slid lower until they slid between my folds. I gasped and pressed into his hand. His thumb circled my center, igniting my core. My head lolled back and I moaned.

Pressing hot kisses back up my neck, his lips found mine again. Hot and urgent, his kisses matched his caresses.

"Rainey," he murmured like a prayer. "I love you."

I deepened our kiss, unable to get enough of him. My fingers fumbled with his zipper, but still freed him and wrapped my fingers around him. His hardness pressed into my hand. My stomach tightened, need pooling in my core.

"Jasper," I panted.

He sat up, forcing me to lean backwards to keep our embrace. His mouth trailed down, leaving sizzling kisses on my heated skin. He lowered my back to the ground, his kisses following his hands down. With quick work, my trousers joined my shirt.

"Jasper," I said, resting my hands on the side of his face. I leaned to the side, forcing him to meet my gaze. His eyes were dark and hazy with lust and need.

He stilled and licked his swollen lips. "Yes, Rainey?"

"I love you."

Twenty-Three

DAYS LATER, my feet crunched on the sand as we trekked back up the beach. We hauled the emptied boat behind us.

The thinning sliver of the moon pierced the sky, hanging low as night crept across the horizon.

"How close are we to a new cycle?" Jasper asked, staring backward at the waning moon.

"Tomorrow will be the last of the moon. The next night starts the new cycle."

He shot me a grin. "I've made it longer than your other interests."

"Ha, ha," I deadpanned, though a smile tugged on my lips.

As we cleared the tree line, we were greeted with glowing lanterns swinging in the trees.

"What's going on?" Jasper murmured, stopping short to stare at the people milling around the property.

"Rainey and Jasper are back," Molly cheered. She separated from the group, her hands rubbing her belly as she sauntered to us. "Some night fishers saw you coming."

Cheers rippled through the group.

She finished the distance to us, her eyes gleaming as she took us in. "I had no doubt you'd reach the goal," she beamed. "I have a small party set up to celebrate the newest plot change in generations. Once the animals all arrive, we'll finish changing the council record."

A large smile broke across my face. I'd made it, I'd earned the land. My land.

"Congratulations, Rainey," Owen muttered, coming to stand by his mother. His jaw was set tight, and he averted his eyes.

Jasper sidled up next to me, his arm around my shoulder. I wrapped mine around his torso.

"Once you set your boat up, we'll bring out the pies. I hear Jasper has a sweet tooth." Molly shot us a smile before rejoining the group.

Owen stared at us. His gaze dropped to my neck. His jaw ticked and his eyes narrowed.

"What's that?" he hissed.

My hand flew to my neck, ready to swat away a bug when it landed on the exposed gold chain. My fingers rubbed on it.

Owen's gaze jumped to Jasper, anger burning bright.

"Rainey," Owen gritted out. "Is that his necklace?"

"It's hers now," Jasper said, squaring his shoulders.

"Is that so?" Owen said, his eyes boring into me.

"Yes, Jasper gave it to me." I refused to look away.

"You know the vision," he spat. His hands fisted at his sides.

I sighed, a long one that had been building for years after hearing about his mom's vision and our supposed destiny.

"Owen," I started. I stopped, shaking my head. My words would mean nothing. The argument was so old, we could have it without the other one around.

"He's a Washed Up. He's going to hurt you," Owen seethed.

"I'd never try to hurt Rainey," Jasper growled.

Owen snorted. "You'll bore with our island and life like many of them do and leave."

"That's your father," Jasper spat. "Willis stayed. Others stayed."

Owen grunted and rolled his eyes. "You know nothing of this island. You're a washed-up outsider. You don't belong."

"Owen," I scolded, drawing his attention back to me.

"Whatever," Owen muttered, and turned on his heels. "We'll talk later. Once he leaves."

Without another word, Owen merged with the crowd and headed towards the ale table.

"He's..." Jasper snarled, running a hand through his hair.

"Stubborn," I filled in. "Don't let him bother you."

"He bothers me because he upsets you. I'd just ignore him, but he targets you."

"I've fought the fight with him for over a decade since his mom first shared the vision. We'll—" I stopped myself. The next part was so habitual.

"We'll what?" Jasper prodded.

"Nothing," I said, shaking my head.

"No, tell me. You can distract me later," he said with a wink.

My center warmed and I cracked a smile.

"I was going to say, 'We'll continue having it forever,' but if you stay, it'll be a moot point," I said.

Jasper drew me to him, wrapping his arm around me. He brushed his lips against mine and murmured, "No 'if.' I want to stay."

Others joined us, each congratulating us on the trade. Their words were a blur in a sea of my own thoughts. I'd gotten the land. I'd done it without partnering with Owen. I'd done it without shortcuts.

"Rainey," Willis' voice rang out, distinct from the drone of those around us.

"Willis." I greeted him with a smile and nod.

"I knew you'd complete it," Willis said, lifting his mug in a toast to me.

I lifted mine in return, both of us taking a drink of the ale. My body warmed and eased with the liquid.

"Jasper," Willis said, turning his attention to him.

"Willis." He nodded.

"I've been hearing rumblings that you are considering staying," Willis said.

Jasper's eyes widened, and he shot me an incredulous look. "How does he already know?"

Willis and I both snorted a chuckle.

"Nothing stays private here," I said.

"It wasn't hard to tell, son." Willis cocked an eyebrow at him. "You've had the lovestruck look since I met you."

Heat crept up my neck, but Jasper laughed and shrugged. He pulled me closer, his fingers rubbing circles into my shoulder.

"Well, Rainey, I'm proud of you," Mom's voice sounded behind me.

We whirled around to find Mom standing there, ale in one hand and her other arm wrapped around Bartholomew.

"I see," I said. A grin cracked on my face.

"Jasper, the night after next is the moonless night," Mom said, giving him a pointed look. She pursed her lips before continuing, "Marcus said there isn't an arrangement made."

I stilled, staring at her face, trying to find her meaning.

"No, ma'am." Jasper shook his head. "I have no intentions of making an arrangement with a Ferrier."

A smile spread across my mom's face. My stomach flipped at the unexpected display, my fingers curling in preparation of the surprise attack.

"I'm so happy for both of you," she said. A genuine smile lit her face. For a moment, her eyes narrowed on Jasper. "If you hurt her, I'll... Sirens." Mom swore to herself. "Sorry, I'll need to talk with Tillie about that." Forcing a smile to Jasper. "I'm trying to be happy for you. You've done nothing but help my daughter. I'm trying."

"Mom?" I questioned before I could stop it.

"Rainey, you were right," Mom said with a bob of her head. "I was seeing you through the lens of my youth, but you are not me. I know you asked me for years. Your grandma and grandpa asked me, too, but I finally started talking with Tillie. When Jasper went to help you, especially when his trade was already built, it shattered a lot of what I knew —thought about Washed Up. I have a long way to go, but I'm working through..." She blew a breath out. "I'm working through everything. It's just a long road."

My face twisted in different emotions: surprise, fear, hopefulness. I didn't know if this was a setup or her genuine response.

She chuckled, watching me react before sobering. "I'm sorry, Rainey. We obviously need to talk about everything. We can do that another night. I'm proud of you. Enjoy your success."

She and Bartholomew slipped back into the crowd, leaving me with bees in my stomach.

"What just happened?" I croaked out.

"I think your mom was happy for you," Jasper said, leaning his head against mine.

"But..."

"Looks like she's finding happiness, which is helping her find it in other things, too."

"I guess," I mumbled, still watching my mom snake through the crowd smiling and laughing.

Guests started to depart. The moon had arched over the zenith and was headed for its rest when Molly found us again. She folded her hands together, her eyes darting around.

"Molly, are you okay?" I asked, cocking my head to the side.

Molly met my gaze, her eyes bright with emotion.

"I've been contemplating what to do," she said.

My stomach tightened and dread clawed at my throat. Was she going to change the arrangement?

Seeing my expression, she hurriedly said, "Not about the land, but Jasper."

"Jasper," I echoed.

His face pinched, and his eyes furrowed. "What about me?"

"My visions won't come in clear, which means it directly affects me," she said, shooting me an imploring look.

I nodded and reached my hand out to rub her forearm. "I know, Molly. What's going on?"

"I should have done this earlier, but... but I thought you were going back. I see, saw, your future in Florida. My visions wouldn't come in. I didn't want to create more confusion." She sighed. "Jasper, there is someone I'd like you to meet. Someone I think you know." She reached for his hand holding his ale.

Jasper and I shared a confused look, but he let her take his hand and followed her to two figures standing back from the group. After a double take, I realized it was John, her partner, and Owen.

"Honey," Molly called to the man.

He turned, holding two cups.

Owen turned, his dark gaze taking us in as he settled back on his heels with his arms folded over his chest.

"Jasper, I'd like to introduce you to my partner," Molly said. Her face was ashen and she gave him a watery smile. "John."

Jasper shifted to greet the person, but his body went rigid. His mug dropped to the sand, spilling mead into a dark pool.

"Jasper," I tried, squeezing his side.

Jasper stood fixated on John, his gaze hyper focused and his mouth agape.

Finally, he sputtered, "You're John Garcia."

"What?" I asked, staring between the two of them. "You know him?"

At the same time, John said with brows furrowed, "We know each other?"

Molly's glossy gaze met mine while her lips trembled.

Jasper nodded, unblinking. "Yeah, you're... you're my dad."

Twenty-Four

"So, you're pregnant with Jasper?" Owen asked again. His eyes stared unseeing at Molly.

"How is this possible?" John asked again, cradling Molly against him as his gaze fixated on Jasper. At that moment, I could see the familiar features. The strong jawline, the dark eyes, the same nose, and their mannerisms.

"It's the island," Molly said, rubbing her head, a telltale sign that a vision brewed. Her eyes unfocused and narrowed. "Jasper crossed from his time here, and you came from yours, but you both crossed into our waters now. Your time doesn't matter here. We often have people from different centuries wash up together. You just happen to be related."

John's glossy eyes blinked, staring at his adult son, who was maybe a decade younger than him. He frowned, his breaths staggered and heavy.

Jasper tightened his fingers, holding my hand.

Acid turned in my stomach, bubbling up as uncertainty in my throat. His stories flooded my mind, the facts about his parents slamming into the reality that stood before us. None of this could be possible, but then neither could an island out of time.

Molly rubbed a hand on her rounded belly. "But Jasper is our son. This Jasper is the son I am carrying."

"How..." John started but shook his head. "So how did he end up in my original timeline then? We're here."

Jasper's gaze bounced between Molly and John, his eyes bright with unshed tears. His left hand fidgeted at my side, and his right hand tucked inside of Molly's grasp.

"When you left with Jasper," Molly rubbed her belly again. "You went back to your timeline because it's where you came from. He was with you, in your and his timeline, until he crossed back to the island as an adult."

"What does this mean?" Owen demanded, pacing on the sand. His hands jabbed spikes through his curly blond hair, leaving it strewn on his head. His eyes darted to me before settling back on Molly.

"Molly... Mom," Jasper choked, "dies in my birth."

"Then we have to do something," John demanded. "There are medical healers on the island. Knowing about it can stop it from happening."

Jasper shook his head, rolling his lips between his teeth. "No, no, *you* said she needed a hospital. You said the medical people in the small town couldn't help. She lost too much blood. She needed a blood transfusion."

"A what?" Owen spat, turning his ire to Jasper.

"She loses too much blood. She needs an IV, blood, and a hospital," Jasper said. "You... you said it was your mistake for not acting faster. It ate you alive. You started to drink. I never knew mom. I lost you a couple years ago. I've missed you so much."

Jasper swallowed thickly, his eyes rimmed with tears. Averting his gaze, he sniffed. He wiped at a tear sliding down his cheek.

"Jasper..." John started. His hands flexed, uncertainty twisting his face. When his brows dipped low and his lips pressed into a thin line, there was no mistaking his features in Jasper. Even his mannerism. With a sigh, he stepped forward and wrapped an arm around Jasper.

Jasper's shoulders shook as a sob rocked through him. He leaned into the embrace.

Molly sniffed, tears welling in her eyes. Her trembling lips attempted a watery smile.

After a few moments, Jasper sucked back a breath, an understanding settled between them. John stepped back by Molly and Jasper by me.

"Please, we have to get her to a hospital. Please," his voice cracked. "She will need blood."

"Hold on. You want to put something's blood in her?" Owen interrupted, horror marring his face. He stood between them, a finger pointed at Jasper.

"Does she drink it?" I asked. My stomach twisted at their thoughts of medicine.

Jasper looked to John. His eyes burned with sorrow.

"No," John breathed. "Women dying in birth has decreased drastically over the past hundred years due to advancements in medicine."

A gust of wind raced off the ocean, the briny smell mixed with a sweet undertone. The chill skimmed over my skin and I shivered. A storm was coming. A big one.

"Molly—Mom has to go back," Jasper pleaded, his eyes unseeing as he stared at the darkening ocean. "We have to save her. Save you."

"Next cycle," John said. He rubbed circles on Molly's shoulders. "We'll get everything prepared and make it a safe journey."

"No, Dad!" Jasper yelled.

John flinched.

"You said you waited too long. She's going to have me soon. Sooner than you realized. You have to go this cycle. We can't wait."

"We'd have to start out in just over twenty-four hours," John argued. He shook his head as if it was a final decision. "There's no way we can make a safe passage. There is a storm brewing. We need to plan this out. Set up the boat, life preservers, kits, etc. Molly is about seven months along. We'll go next cycle."

"Dad, no," Jasper said, tears falling from his face. John shifted uncomfortably again at the title but held Molly tighter. "We lost Mom. You grieved every day for her. You blamed yourself for not doing more. You started drinking..." Jasper paused to gulp back the emotion. He continued with a watery voice, "I lost you, too, a couple years ago. You drove drunk and wrapped your car around a light pole. No. No. I can't let that happen if there is something I can do."

"Jasper," John sighed, his expression conflicted. "There's just too much to do for this cycle. The storm is building up to be huge. It's too dangerous. A Washed Up has to go solo past the rocks. The Ferrier can't help after that. Molly's with child and I don't want her to strain herself. I can't help her alone."

"I'll help," he pleaded.

Lead formed in my stomach and my mouth dried. My body shook as reality set into my bones and heart. He could do something. He could take her back, make sure she made it. He could help John cross through the storm. Get her the medical help he claimed she needed.

Jasper's hand clasped mine tighter before he wrapped his arm around me, pulling me close to him. His heart thudded in his chest, the chaotic rhythm matching my own. He rested his cheek against my temple. My vision tunneled. Everything was changing. Everything was unraveling. My mom would be right, after all.

"Mom, you can't believe this," Owen said. He returned to pacing, his long stride consuming the sand before he pivoted back towards the group. "You've had clear visions. You saw a healthy son."

Molly squealed a cry, her frame falling against John, who caught her. He rubbed his hands on her back and rocked with her.

"Nothing is clear," she cried. This was normal with visions about herself. She called them vague shadows. "But I see two paths for Jasper. He will be a healthy... he... John, oh Sirens, I think he's right."

A hush descended on the group. Both Owen and John stared at Jasper anew. John with fear and curiosity, and Owen with raw hatred.

"I don't believe this," Owen thundered. "I'm not helping with this foolishness."

The rain started, no warning sprinkles or looming cracks of thunder, just a downpour of icy water. The wind picked up, slamming the droplets into us and the trees. My body, already numb, didn't process it until Jasper tugged me towards Molly's house.

Thunder sounded in the distance, echoing in my soul. I flinched as a streak of lightning ripped open the sky and bathed us in an ethereal glow as the bright, jagged fingers of the bolt clawed at the sky.

As we stumbled through the trees, following Molly, Jasper clung to me with his gaze fixated on my face. Memorizing it.

I knew at that moment, he wasn't staying. All our plans were done. I'd be a Sea Widow, after all.

Molly's house offered a dry shelter. The four of them packed inside. Wind whipped at the frame and the boards creaked. With trembling hands, she lit the lanterns around the room, bathing the room in orange light.

"Owen has a ship," John started. Guilt darkened his face taking in Owen's expression.

No matter what, Owen was losing his mom if her visions were correct. Either she'd die in childbirth or leave the island. The reality seemed to hit him at the same moment. His eyes widened, getting a far-off look.

"No," Owen breathed. "I'm not Ferrying you this cycle. No."

"She'll die," Jasper screamed.

Owen shook his head. "No, we can prevent it. We know. We can make preparations. Get healers. Send gifts to the Sirens. And if the healers agree, we can prep for the next cycle."

Just as stubbornly as he held on to his mom's vision of us being partners, he set in with his reasons on why Jasper was wrong.

"It won't work! We have to go this cycle!"

"I'm not doing it!" Owen hurled. "You're just confusing her!"

Molly let out a cry, silencing the argument. The three men moved to her side.

I used the diversion to slip out.

A moo sounded, and my gaze darted to the left. The cows I'd traded for the land were sheltered in Molly's barn, protected and safe. My years of hard work stood a few yards away. The goats and pigs should arrive in a few days.

My mind reeled as the events tumbled through my brain. Everything had happened as I originally wanted, yet hollowness ate at my heart. I'd made my trades, brought up a Washed Up, and he was leaving after a cycle.

They didn't need my help to prepare an escape from the island. I'd only be in the way. With Owen's refusal to accept the changes, and with his stubbornness it'd take more than Jasper's words and Molly's blurry visions. They'd need a Ferrier. I pulled a tarp from the hook, covering my head from the downpour, but it did nothing. My body was already soaked and numb.

The lamps that dotted along the path were dark from the winds. Going from memory, I wove through the path, stumbling only on fallen branches. The limbs tore at my flesh, but I pushed on.

Marcus's home was dark and silent, tucked under three oak trees that danced violently in the storm, leaves and sticks lashing around. Rapping loudly on the door, I stood back so he could see me from the window.

The storm deadbolt clicked and the door pulled back, revealing Tara, one of his three partners. Her long auburn tresses were pulled up in a bun and she wore a long t-shirt.

"Rainey," she yawned. "Yuck, it's storming. Step inside."

She backed up to grant me access. A single candle danced on the wall. Easton, another partner, paced behind her with an infant in his arms.

"I'll stay outside. I'll drench your floors," I said, my teeth chattering. "Is Marcus available?"

"Why?" she asked, casting me an odd glance.

"I need to see him about Ferrying someone." A sob racked my form. I swallowed down the repulsion clawing at my throat.

"Oh," she muttered, and then her eyes flew open, and she gasped. Shaking her head, she said, "Oh, Rainey, no. Jasper wants to stay, honey. The way he looks at you…"

I choked back another sob. My body lurched from the effort, but I didn't care about the sight I was before them.

"I need to talk to Marcus," I managed to force out.

"He's at the harbor, checking on his boat," she said. Her eyes were sympathetic as she tilted her head to the side. "You can come in. I'll make an herbal brew, warm you up. We can talk."

"Come in, Rainey," Easton encouraged.

"Thanks, but I can't." I blinked my eyes as they swam in emotion. I had nothing to talk about, anyways. What I had expected and inevitably feared was my reality.

The harbor wasn't a long run, but with the wet ground I tripped and staggered on the familiar path, leaving my knees scraped and my hands raw from catching myself.

I found Marcus's boat with ease, but my voice was ripped from my throat as I called out his name. The storm rocked the boat, trying to tear it out to sea. The heavy line kept it tethered to the dock. It rocked, sloshing water up its side.

Despite the motion, I was able to clamber onboard, hoping he wouldn't react first to a trespasser.

"Marcus," I screamed into the cabin. A *thunk* greeted me. I called to him again, my voice cracking from the strain.

I braced myself on the walls and railing as I ventured down the stairs into the dark cavern of the ship. The lights had been snuffed out. Only thick, damp air clung to the corridor.

"Marcus," I called again. My voice echoed into the darkness.

"Rainey?" His voice shot back. A flicker of light reflected off a mirror before dancing closer, the flame a tiny beacon.

"Yes, it's Rainey." Relief and sadness flooded me.

"There's a storm, you should be at home," he scolded, moving to stand next to me. His tall frame filled the tight space. The flame reflected off his face. The rest of him was cast in deep shadow. "I'm going home as soon as I confirm everything is buttoned down."

"Marcus, everything has changed," I said around a lump in my throat. I swallowed it back and blinked at the tears welling again in my eyes.

"What do you mean?"

"We need a Ferrier for this cycle. Jasper... Molly..."

My voice broke and I couldn't finish the sentence.

"What? No!" Marcus barked. "It'll have to wait. There is a storm brewing. It's too dangerous."

"It'll pass," I said, hoping I was right. "It's... it's a matter of life and death."

"Rainey," Marcus started. 'No' was already forming on his lips while he shook his head.

"I'll up the payment," I begged. My mind scrambled for a bargain. "I have the cart ready. I can add on something for the short notice."

"I don't think so," he said firmly. "There's nothing you got that can help us enough."

Molly's home flashed in my mind. Her life depended on getting her out. Both she and Jasper had confirmed it. Then her yard and the livestock danced into view. Everything I'd worked to accomplish.

"Cows," I said, my stomach twisting and my heart plunging down. My decision was made. "They have milk. You could sell it."

"You have cows for trade?" he asked, the interest evident in his voice. He tilted his head to meet my gaze.

"Yes," I said, closing my eyes.

Twenty-Five

A LIGHT BURNED in the window of my house. The sole beacon in a stormy sea. My mom must have left it on by mistake. Out of her norm, but she wasn't like herself lately since starting a relationship with Bartholomew. Besides, it meant she was home, and I might as well tell her she was right. I should have just partnered with Owen, I shouldn't have gone against Molly's vision, and that I'd be a Sea Widow like she feared.

The door pushed open with a creak, the sound lost in the steady beat of rain. The thunder and lightning had rolled off, the steady thrum of rain and debris-filled yard the only reminders. The storm should pass by morning break. They should have clear skies for their travels.

My eyes, sore and raw, winced at the light. I went to snuff it out when the sound of fabric on fabric rustled from the hearth.

With my back turned to her, I murmured, "Sorry to wake you, Mom."

"Rainey," Jasper breathed, closing our distance. He wrapped his arms around me, burying his face in my hair. Everything felt whole and well. My arms returned the embrace. His heart thudded through his shirt and his breaths came in ragged pants.

For a moment, I clung to him, memorizing his smell, his feel, the way his muscles moved beneath my hands, the way his warmth seeped through and eased my sorrow. I would miss this. With that last sobering thought, I pushed him back.

His hands moved to cup my face, his eyes searching mine.

"Rainey," he choked out.

"Marcus agreed to take you," I said, blinking back my emotion and stilling my face. I needed to focus on facts.

"Marcus?" Jasper asked.

"You need a Ferrier, don't you?" I said, the words harsher than I'd planned. I winced but swallowed back an apology. "And Owen won't do it."

He flinched before his face crumbled, and he sucked back a sob. "Rainey..."

"Don't," I huffed and then sighed, averting my eyes. I rubbed a hand over my forehead. This isn't how I wanted our last time to be together. I didn't want to reject and hurt him to make it easier. But I couldn't have what I wanted.

"Rainey," he started.

A part of me hoped he would ask me to go with him. To his home. But I was foolish. He was a Washed Up. They came and left. They left us behind and moved on.

Still, I had him at this moment. For one more night. I was going to mourn him, anyway.

I wrapped my arms around his neck, pulling him flush against me. His heartbeats increased, music to my own. I swallowed the lump down. This was our last time together. I loved him. Even if whatever we had ended now, I loved him and would continue to.

A truth came to me, burning my soul and directing my heart. It was our last night, and I wanted to know every piece of him. If he was going to break me, I'd take pieces of him and rebuild me. Stronger. More resilient. More numb. I'd use the fragments he left behind as a shield to make sure I wouldn't be hurt again. Ultimately broken, but stronger than before.

Jasper rested his forehead against mine, his eyes closed as he took deep breaths.

I tilted my head to the side, shifting so my lips brushed against his. Soft at first, but as need and sorrow fueled me, I deepened the kiss.

He returned the kiss, urgent and demanding. His hands fisted in my hair, holding me to him. My body molded against his, his heat searing me.

My hands slid under his shirt, resting on his hard torso. With a quick yank, I pushed his shirt over his head, breaking our kiss for a moment.

He quickly pulled me back into his embrace, trailing kisses down my neck. I arched into him and angled my head to the side, giving him more access.

Wind whipped around the house, hissing through the cracks and flickering the single light. Our shadows danced against the stone hearth. My heartbeat thudded in my ears, fueling my brain. With one hand wrapped around the back of his neck and one around his waist, I tugged him along with me as I walked backwards to my bedroom. My back bumped against the door, the wood rough against my skin.

I fumbled for the door handle while my lips found his again.

Jasper pulled back, his breaths in pants. He rested his forehead against mine. He moaned, "Rainey."

"Jasper... I want..." There was so much I wanted, but so little I could have. I wanted him to stay. I wanted to go with him. I wanted to be with him. I wanted him.

"What do you want?" he asked, his voice hopeful. He tilted his head to the side to meet my gaze. Desire and emotion shone back.

I sucked in a breath and settled on the one thing that I could have. I didn't care if I had a tonic or not. "I want to lay with you," I breathed.

He flinched like I'd hit him. His body stiffened. Darkness filled his eyes.

It wasn't what he wanted to hear?

"We'll never..." My voice cracked. I swallowed, my mouth drying. I blinked to clear my eyes, but only spilled the welling tears. I didn't bother trying to wipe them away. More would only follow.

"I can't," he whispered, caressing my chin and placing a gentle kiss on my lips. His jaw worked, holding back more words. Raspy breaths heaved his body.

"I was joking with you when you arrived, and I said you couldn't leave if you laid with a person." Each word was like swallowing fire.

"I know," he whispered. "That's not why."

Stunned, I swallowed and tried to pull back from his grasp. He was already rejecting me. Severing whatever we had. Moving on as we stayed in time. My mind and body screamed. Each battling to be heard. But had nothing to say that I wanted to hear.

I needed space. I needed to leave.

The world came to life around me. The howling wind, the patter of rain on the roof, his rapid heart rate, and his warmth radiating through my shirt that suddenly chilled me. Placing my palms on his torso, I pushed back, but he held on to my back. His fingers curled against me.

"Rainey, please, I want to...but if we do, I won't be able to leave. Dad can't make it alone with the storm," he said, his voice catching. He sucked in an unsteady breath, blinking the tears in his eyes. "Rainey, you could—"

"It's fine," I lied. "I understand."

"Rainey... I love you. I want to stay... I can't," he choked. A sob racked his frame as tears streamed down his face. "Rainey, I love you. I don't want to leave. I can save my mom's life and my dad a life of mourning. I don't know another way. I want to stay. I can't. I love you, Rainey. I know you love this island, but—"

"Stop saying that," I seethed, unable to hear any more. "It's unfair."

"Rainey, I—"

"No!" I screamed, tears streaming down my face. I pointed a finger at him, creating distance. "You're a Washed Up. You're leaving. I knew you would. I understand why."

He didn't stop me when I pushed away from his embrace. Tears wet his face. He licked his lips and trembled.

My body shook as I walked to the door, my vision swimming, a sob lodged in my throat.

"Have a safe journey back, and may the seas carry you home," I muttered before storming out, slamming the door behind me.

THE ANGRY, dark harbor water lashed against the sandy shore. I stood at the edge of town under the canopy where Jasper and I had our second kiss. I touched my lips, but they felt cold.

Numbness dulled the chill against my skin and ebbed at my raw face. The warm and fruitful village and island I loved looked different at that moment. Unforgiving, harsh, and spiteful. The Sirens had taken my gifts but cursed me. My heart foamed with their wrath.

Thick clouds blotted out the moon and stars, but the rain had stopped, leaving the ocean to finish its tantrum. In a few hours, the sun would crest the horizon and start the eve of the moonless night. Even if no Washed Up went back, this was a busy day for the village.

Not knowing what would wash up, the sands were raked and combed for two days to make travel on the shores easier to scavenge through. All the Scavengers would be out, marking the changes in the sands, the crash of the waves, the drift of the wind. None of us owned the beach, nor could we lay claim to sections of it, but we had spots we coveted, and encroaching on another's could lead to future issues if you needed help. It didn't stop sniping, but we avoided overt shows.

My spot would go unclean if I didn't get out there to scrub it, but why wouldn't I go? Jasper was leaving. Molly was leaving. Since he was her only child on the island, Owen would inherit his mom's land. The last of the traded livestock wouldn't arrive for a few days, and he could change the terms after she left since we hadn't updated the village's records yet. He could void any agreement. Besides, I needed the cows to secure Jasper and his family passage past the Sirens. I was further behind than when Jasper washed up.

My body refused to move, my spirit unable to muster the needed strength to push off the building and get my tools. Everything seemed pointless. Years of work, gone. My grandparents' useable land was too small for the workspace I wanted. I really didn't want to leave my village. Maybe I needed to move on from Scavenging and tinkering. Perhaps I could figure out how to make bread and join my mom. Even though every past attempt had ended in burnt or unevenly cooked products. With Molly leaving, I could take up sewing despite having no skill with it. Or I could take up John's role of making rope. They would all provide for me, but nothing sounded right. And I didn't have the skills for them. Nothing sounded like my dreams. I would always want to be a Scavenger.

I rubbed my temples as emotion welled in my throat. I'd done everything needed and still lost. I'd opened my home to a Washed Up, the blessings of the Sirens, and it cursed me. They'd betrayed me. I could only wonder why.

Time slipped by, the sky streaking with glowing light behind the thinning clouds. Even if my heart and mind weren't in it, I needed to start cleaning the beach in preparation. I'd have to build up my tradeable items again in hopes someone would sell a portion of their land. Even if it meant cleaning and leveling land again. I'd have livestock arriving and didn't have the space for them, so I'd either have to try to trade them with other villagers, beg Owen to let me board them in his barn—adding debt on to them—or just send them back and be out everything I'd scrounged together for them.

A whimper escaped my mouth as tears welled again. I blinked them away. Self-pity and wallowing would only put me further behind. I would store the pain away. Let it numb me. Let it dull me from things that could distract me. But keep moving forward.

I saw then why my mom was the way she was. It was so much easier.

But unlike her, I wouldn't have a daily reminder of what I'd lost. I wouldn't have to look at someone with his eyes, his chin, his nose. Other than my hair color, I looked like my father. She had to face that every day. It finally made sense why she hadn't wanted me to lay with Jasper. Why she fought so hard to keep us separated, even if it drove a wedge between her and me. She wanted to protect me from the constant pain that rubbed against the numbness, the desire to forget. So be it. I was a daughter of the Sirens, but I was also Marianna's daughter. Pain and loss would be our common ground.

Taking a last look at the harbor before heading home for my tools, I caught movement stirring on Marcus's ship. My heart clenched seeing Marcus exit it after securing it all night. Instead of going home like he had wanted, he'd stayed and prepped his boat for the passage. He'd risked his life for the prospect of the trades. In a day's time, he'd be taking away everything I'd wanted. His dark form trekked the worn path back to his home, likely to sleep before starting out on the voyage tomorrow morning so he could make it to the rocks in time for the moonless night.

Despite everything they'd done, I sent a wish to the Sirens for Jasper's safe passage. Above all else, I wanted them to be protected. My hand found the chain he'd given me. I ran a finger over the links. It would be my only physical reminder of him, of the time we spent together. Guilt twisted my stomach. I'd have to give it back to him. My heart dropped into my gut, but it had to be done. The sooner I did it, the faster I could get to the beach and start the process over again. The sooner I could return to my old life, this time wiser and more guarded. The sooner I could move on as he was already doing.

Pushing myself off the wall, I cast a look back at the ocean. The churning waves, frothing with foam, slammed harder into the shore, ripping apart the clean sands. The sun-streaked clouds blackened and rumbled. My brow furrowed taking in the change. The storm should have passed. A streak of silent thunder sliced across the sky, the gnarled tentacles clashing against the black clouds.

The few villagers out this early scrambled for cover as a new squall brewed. A few, I recognized as Scavengers. Thunder clapped in the distance, silencing the island. We all seemed to turn towards the sky. With bated breath, we waited as one.

Another streak of flaming-white lightning zigged across the sky. The veins stretched across our horizon. It echoed its visual display and blinked out, casting us into darkness. Then another crack of lightning tore open the sky, the veins piercing at the bulging black clouds, unleashing its content onto our island. The trees bent in the downpour, their leaves streaming in the wind.

I stepped back, pressing my back into the clapboard siding of the shop. Rain danced around, pinging off surfaces and sloshing up. Despite the overhead protection, the wind blew water back at me, drenching me. My already soaked clothes drooped on me, the fresh chill burning my skin.

With the thunder and lightning, even being wet, my spot was the safest until the storm cleared. My gaze scanned the vista. To the horizon was a darkened swirl of angry clouds. The storms, although fierce, would hopefully pass through. The waters would likely be rough, but Ferriers normally dealt with the turbulent ocean. The sands would be a mess and I doubted we could clean them in two days. It would be an even more dangerous cycle than normal.

Another bolt of lightning tore at the sky, the accompanying thunder vibrating through the land and my bones. My teeth chattered and my heart stalled. My eyes darted to the ocean and the boats bobbing on the furious waters.

The waves turned more violent, tossing everything astray. They lashed at the shore and the ships. The ships bucked and swayed, teetering on the enlarging crests. The tether not strong enough for the viciousness, Marcus's boat broke from the dock, tossing in the ferocious waters. With a deafening crash, the waves pushed Marcus's boat into Fredricka's. They both moaned before crashing together again. The sides cracked and crumbled from the force, allowing water in. They surged up with a wave before the dark fingers of the sea started to pull them below.

I stared, my vision tunneled and unfocused. Slipping into the sea was Jasper's chance at rescuing his mom. Saving her life and preventing his father's death. Fear and repulsion bubbled up from my stomach, the acid burning my throat.

"Why?" I screamed at the ocean. Fresh tears welled and spilled from my eyes. The Sirens could be cruel to outsiders, but they were never to us unless we angered them.

"What have I done to you?" I whispered, my voice cracking as a sob ripped through me. Why had they given me everything—the trades, the land, Jasper—only to take it away? Why had they accepted my gifts and then betrayed me?

"Oh Sirens," Beatrice wailed, coming out from the street shop. Her focus was on the tragedy below. Her brown tresses were plastered to her pale forehead and her cotton dress clung to her frame as she scanned the scene.

"Beatrice," I called, sniffing back my tears.

"Oh, Rainey, you scared me," she blurted out, moving her hand to her chest. She jogged the few stores' lengths to join me. She narrowed her brown eyes at me, regarding my messy appearance. "You look the fright. Did you get caught in the storm?"

I sputtered but nodded when no words would come out. I'd been caught in two storms and hadn't slept in almost two days, but that didn't matter.

"This is so odd." She swung a hand towards the ocean.

I just stared at her, unable to find a response.

"A good thing no Washed Up are going back this cycle," she said, her toothy grin on display. She winked at me, not noticing my frozen expression.

A wheezing sound spun in my ears and my vision unfocused. No one knew about Jasper. About Molly. Or anything else because of the storm.

The other villages. Maybe one of them could take them back. It was short notice, and I didn't know if I had time to get to another village, but I had to try. Jasper... Molly... They had to go. I could make it to Bretti's in two days. Maybe they were still at sea. Maybe. Or maybe Sunny would arrive, and I could convince them to let us use their boat.

"Thank the Sirens Owen moved his boat," Beatrice said. She still stared at the sea, oblivious to me. She folded her arms over her chest.

The seas seemed to silence for a moment before they crashed back on the docks and pulled me back to the present.

"What?" I asked, realizing only two of the three Ferrier ships were at harbor. Owen's vessel was missing but wasn't part of the crash. "Where's Owen's ship?" Hope and dread clawed at my stomach.

"He said the storm wasn't done, and moved it," she said. "Guess he was right."

I closed my eyes. A tremble rumbled through me.

"Thank the Sirens, indeed," I said and steeled my nerves for the groveling that would take place. The Sirens still offered Molly, John, and Jasper protection while continuing to punish me.

All my work was for nothing, and I still had the same result. My mom had been right. I fought fate like a fool. And the Sirens had punished me. At least I still had a chance to protect Jasper and his family.

Twenty-Seven

THE STORM CONTINUED to pound our island, but without time to waste, I ignored the risk and tore off towards the cove and the chance of Molly surviving. I wove through the familiar landscape, damp but shielded by the overhangs above. The slippery paved roads gushed with water. The shell-based gravel streets would be worse, so I continued on through the thick of the village.

Around me, confused villagers stumbled out of their shops and homes to stare at the ocean and storm. Sleep and worry tugged on their faces. They murmured about the sunken ships and fierce double storms, the news already making the rounds. It would devastate our village for months, but that wasn't today's issue. We could always trade with another village to use one of their vessels. But Molly couldn't wait.

Outside of the village, the sandy ground, bloated with water, sank around my boots, threatening to trip me. Despite the treacherous ground, I pushed through to the forest, tearing up the street and splashing sticky sand and mud all over me.

The plush forest canopy blocked the ferocity of the rain, but the slick ground, swollen with rainwater and sand, was made worse with fallen leaves and broken branches. My trek was tortuously slow as I passed through the forest, weaving toward the eastern side of the village and the steep cliffs.

From the top of the cliffs, our village, nestled into the side of the hills, was blocked from view by the large trees. A few pinpricks of light at the harbor's edge meant the village was still there. However, the ocean stretched in an inky darkness in all directions. Its dark waves crashed in an angry ballet to the horizon. The tumultuous thunder trembled closer, and lightning streaked the sky in a spiderweb, shaking my core.

Below me was Sirens' Cove, a sacred location. The inlet fed into a towering formation within the walls of the cliffs, providing safety from raging storms. We used it in our yearly offerings to the Sirens. We'd bundle up trinkets and baubles and send them out to the Sirens during the start of the summer before the seas were the worst. The gifts were our pleas for the Sirens to protect us, and they did. Usually. Today was a rare exception. We respected—not feared—our Sirens, but we were never blind to their capabilities.

As I stumbled down the path, my face was left victim to the lashing branches, so I used my hands to pick a careful path. To the right was an offshoot creek from the river that wove through our hills and provided our village with fresh water. Instead of the patient trickle of water over the cliff that plummeted into the cove, the stream rushed in a white river to the frothing sea. I slowed my pace. No matter the urgency, the land deserved respect. A wrong slip and I'd meet my ancestors who were buried at sea.

The stone passage into the cove stood from my ancestors' times. The walls, painted and jeweled in vibrant images of the Sirens and seas, had wall sconces embedded into them that carried torches, each one was set with gemstones and polished rocks to reflect the light in a rainbow of colors that matched our Sirens.

A single flame swooshed in the distance, the yellow bead of light long and slender against the cave's wall. Around it, hues of oranges and purples shimmered, reflecting off the waters in the illusion of gems. Its shadow danced and flickered, but not by the wind's demand. It was tucked far enough back; the wind couldn't reach it. The rest of the cove was cast in darkness, made more menacing by the damp, salty air that stuck to my skin and tickled my nose.

I stood still, listening, waiting for the cave to talk to me. The rhythm came slowly: first the howling wind muted out, then the gushing water above. The squall's thunder rumbled in the distance, moving on after the destruction it had caused. The water sloshed beside me, the cool waves slapping away at the stone. A silent hum filled the air and resonated within me. My breathing calmed in the revered place.

The entrance towered before me, big enough for a sea vessel, but as it petered out towards the back, the sloped roof left room barely high enough for a person to walk. The cave was so vast, my slight footsteps barely sounded above the current and faded into the ambiance of the cove.

Owen's vessel was small enough tucked inside that it didn't come close to the ceiling. Its wooden frame bobbed in the waters, ready to sail into open seas. He sat on his boat, kicked back in a wooden chair on the deck. His feet rested on the wheel, rocking steadily with the motion. Although he appeared relaxed and asleep, he would be prepared to take his ship off when the tides rose.

Seeing him relaxing there was like a faded memory. As young children we'd walked to the cove together, a full day's journey then. As we'd aged, we'd take salvaged boats and pretend to be Washed Up pirates or marooned survivors. Many days of our youth had been spent exploring every inch.

Owen and I also came with our families as the tradition required for honors and celebrations, but it also provided a respite from a day of listening to my mom or the hot summer sun. It was where we solidified our friendship as kids and where it ended when he told me his mom's visions and tried to kiss me. From that day forward, we'd been at odds.

No matter the years that had passed, it was a spot he still used for privacy and respite. I'd forfeited it outside of honoring the Sirens, not wanting to be reminded of that day or his mom's vision. All of her visions had come true, and I guess this one would, too, no matter how much I had tried to change it. Tried to control my destiny. Perhaps that was how I'd angered the Sirens. I had shunned the gift they gave Molly.

And now I had come full circle.

A chilled wind from inside the cave skimmed my shoulders.

"Owen," I called from the entryway. My voice echoed in the cavern. The call back sounded hollow and shrill.

He startled, shifting out of sleep and crashing his feet to the deck. He ran a hand through his disheveled blond hair. His blue eyes, dark in the cave, reflected the flame's light. His head turned as he searched the passage.

"Rainey?" he asked, his voice uncertain. He moved to the edge of the boat to stare down. He still wore the shirt and pants he'd had on last night during the celebration party, which seemed a lifetime ago. The image was a jab to my heart.

"Owen, there was another storm," I said lamely. He'd known it was coming and had moved his ship, protecting it. I ran a hand over my hair and looked to the cool water lapping at the stone wall, separating me from the depths below.

"You don't say," he deadpanned. He rested his hands on the railing, leaning over to stare at me in the shadows.

I rolled my eyes but walked on the trail, skimming the cove and edging towards his ship, using the wooden rail to keep my balance on the slick stones. The trail had been carved hundreds of years ago and worn down further each year. Intricate scenes had been carved into the wood railing lining it. Each time it was replaced, a new design was carved. Centuries of artwork merged into the tale of our island.

He moved to the stern of the boat, closing the distance between us. With the aid of a rope, he silently jumped down to the trail a few feet ahead of me. Even though he was a good head-and-a-half taller than me, he didn't position himself to look down at me. Up close, I could see the exhaustion that tugged on his features and the weariness in his eyes. It'd been a long night for everyone, and his mom was leaving. And yet, he had to take care of his livelihood. Which would be a saving grace for his mom.

I lifted my eyes to meet his gaze. He had a guarded expression, his nose flaring. He folded his arms over his chest. His eyes took in my messy appearance, my water-soaked clothes and dirt-caked skin. Tugging off his t-shirt with a faded sports logo that meant nothing to us, he handed it to me. His bare chest was suntanned like the rest of him.

I used his shirt to wipe the nature off my face and clean my hands.

Uncertainty curled in my stomach. I'd made my opinion known for years, as he had. Yet now I was going to beg for his help and offer the only thing he said he wanted. Hopefully I wasn't too late.

"Why are you here?" he finally asked, looking behind me. His face scrunched, and his voice changed. "Are you alone?"

"Yeah," I said, blowing out a long breath. I blinked to clear the emotion bubbling up. I sucked in a breath and squared my shoulders. There wasn't time for pride. "I came looking for you."

His eyes widened. "Why are you looking for me?"

I let out a humorless laugh, but it didn't loosen any stress. "Marcus and Fredricka's boats were destroyed."

"Whoa," he said, running a hand over his mouth. His focus flicked back to his capable and unharmed boat. His gaze slowly tracked back to me, understanding darkening them. His body straightened, ready for an argument.

"Owen, you have to ferry them," I blurted out before I thought better and cringed. I took a step towards him, the crunch of shells sounding in the cave. "Owen..."

"What? No," Owen said, shaking his head. He screwed his face up like something smelled foul. His hands moved to his hips and he shot me a glare.

"Owen, there is no one else. I know... I know everything is hard and changing, but..." I licked my lips and averted my eyes. "Owen..."

"No," he reaffirmed. His body stiffened and he sucked in a breath. With a disgusted sigh, he turned to jump back on his boat.

Panic clogged my throat and blurred my vision. He had to see reason.

On instinct, I reached out and grabbed his arm. His sinewy arm rippled under my touch. Years of sailing had tuned his body.

He stilled, and slowly tracked his gaze to stare at where my hand held him. Then his hard gaze moved to meet mine. His muscles tightened, but he didn't try to wrench free of my grip. He turned to me, his face a hardened wall.

I swallowed thickly. Fear and disbelief curled in my stomach, bubbling up in nausea.

"Owen, your mom will die. You have to help them," I pleaded, my fingers tightening on his arm.

His jaw ticked as he stared at me for a beat.

I held my breath, waiting, hoping he'd understand. That he'd agree and race back to the island. Another part of me wanted him to say no and refuse, which would leave Jasper here. But that'd destroy Jasper. He'd then have to watch his mom perish, continuing his hopeless loop.

"I believe her visions, I always have, but the storms will destroy anything out there," he said. "It'll kill us all. Her vision must be for the next cycle. There's no way it is for now. Anything that deals with her life directly is vague at best. We need to wait." His eyes flashed with concern in the dim light, as if he was trying to convince himself. His body tensed. "The storm is a warning. We can't cross the Sirens."

Of course, he had to argue. Even if his points were valid and logical, they were wrong.

"Jasper said..." I started. Seeing his face darken, I grimaced, realizing using Jasper's name wouldn't help convince Owen to help out.

"Jasper said he didn't want me to Ferry him," Owen spat back. "Said I'd push him overboard."

My eyes fluttered shut. Images of the beach and Jasper flooded my mind, stealing my breath. My heart panged and my body caved forward in a whimper. It was a few short weeks ago, and yet it felt like a different time. My voice cracked, but I managed, "Owen, please."

Before I could continue, Owen snarled and shook his head. Raising his other hand, palm out to pause me without unsettling my grip on his arm, he said, "Mom didn't confirm that. Yes, she says she's pregnant with him. She confirmed they needed to go. But since we're not going back this one, it'll be the next one. Mom's vision will still come true. They always do."

My heart clenched at the comment. It was natural for him to say that, but standing there, knowing everything I'd lost going against her vision, my heart splintered. The sharp shards stole my breath for a moment. Now I was there trying to convince him of the truth of his mom's visions.

"Molly believes him," I choked out. "Jasper believed it too much to deny him. He says they have to go back now." I squeezed his arm tighter, trying to make him understand the urgency.

"No, Rainey, no," Owen said and finally slid his hand next to mine to remove my grasp. His calloused fingers were rough on my skin. Tightening my fingers around his arm, I stepped closer. His blue eyes widened, following my movement. His breath caught as I stood, almost touching him with my chest. It was the closest I'd been to him since we were kids. We stood for a moment in silence, each staring at the other.

There was so much history and resentment between us, and yet we'd be each other's future.

My stomach flipped. Nothing was going right. Owen and I were just going to argue again until one of us stormed off. Molly and Jasper had to leave to save everyone. Owen had to see reason. But the only reason he believed in was his mom's vision.

I closed my eyes and let out a shaky breath, hoping he still believed enough in the original vision. The crux of our separation. My last chance to convince him. He'd be forever right, as would his mom's visions. It'd be my final gift to Jasper, Molly and John.

Opening my eyes and steeling my resolve, I looked him in the eyes.

"I'll partner with you," I whispered, the words bitter on my tongue. The words carried on the wind, chilly and full of promise. The cove waters lapped beside us, the slosh the only sound as my promise hung between us. My stomach churned, but I didn't take the words back. "If you still want to, we will partner."

He stalled, his body rigid, as if waiting for me to take it back or attack him. Instead, I slid my hand on his arm to his hand. Our fingers intertwined. His strong embrace was warm but chilled my nerves. Although it wasn't what I desired, it was what the Sirens had determined was to be mine. I couldn't turn from them again. Not if I wanted everyone to be safe.

His fingers curled around my own, rubbing softly against my hand. His touch was soft in the dank cave, but it sent thousands of reminders through my nerves that he wasn't what I wanted.

His gaze tracked to our hands. He licked his lips and swallowed hard. His glossy eyes found mine again. He blinked, his body lurching back as if realizing this wasn't a dream and he needed to respond.

"What?" he stammered, the word echoing around the cavern. "What did you say?"

"Owen, if you still want to, I will partner with you. We can make it official the day after you get back from taking them." I placed my free hand on his fingers clutching my hand.

His eyes fell to my touch. His face warred with disbelief and hope. A shaky breath racked his frame.

"Rainey," he murmured, his voice cracked. He blinked, emotion welling behind his eyes. He croaked, "Don't joke with me."

"I'm not," I yelled. My voice bounced back, making me flinch at the shrillness of it. Softer, I said, "I'm not. I wouldn't joke about partnering with anyone."

"Are you sure?" he asked measuredly.

"Yes, if you ferry them back this cycle, I will partner with you," I said more confidently than I felt. "I understand your reservations, I do. I would normally go with your experience, but...but he talked about his mom, Molly's, death in his birth. If there is a chance to save her—them —we have to try. We need to save your mom. When you return from the trek, we'll partner."

"Rainey." He ran his free hand over my shoulder and rested it on my neck. "You'd do this for him?"

"Him and Molly, yes," I said. My shoulders stiffened behind his touch, but I didn't pull away. "I spitefully went against the vision. I didn't like my future planned for me. I wanted my own path. Not the Sirens'. I was wrong to do so." The words were acid on my tongue. My heart screamed that it was a lie, but the proof lay lapping at our feet.

He stared at me, his face belying his internal war. Finally, he nodded.

My body numbed, realizing my fate.

"Rainey, I will be good and loving to you," he whispered. His gaze flickered to our hands before returning to me. Hope and fear shone back.

Despite his agreement, I couldn't let him believe it was more than it was. It wasn't fair to him to risk everything for a lie. The Sirens would likely punish me more if I wasn't honest.

"I know you will be good and loving to me, but I don't believe you are in love with me. You call me a land Siren. A Siren can only snare you away if you don't know what you want. You're of the sea. You just can't see it. I, or the vision, keeps snaring you because you can't see what you want. The vision has been your life. Making it reality. Proving your mom right. I understand and respect the importance of it. I don't love you as a romantic partner. We were once friends. We will be again. We will build a life together. We will partner. Keep up the image. I will not tell anyone about what we discussed today, the agreement we made. We are partnering as the Sirens led us to do. I will honor you." My eyes fixed on his blue ones, so much like his mom's. My stomach twisted as I said, "And any children we have."

A smile curved his lips and his fingers tightened around me. Then his gaze tracked down, catching at the gold chain on my neck.

"I'm giving it back," I whispered, my voice thick with emotion. I stilled, waiting for his reaction.

He straightened, swallowing. His eyes hardened as they met my gaze again. "Do I need to pretend I'm the father of his baby?"

My breath hitched. I looked away. Heat clawed at my face. It was something everyone would expect. This wasn't a conversation I wanted to have, but as my to-be partner, he was owed the truth. I muttered, "No, it isn't possible. We never laid together."

He didn't need to know it was because we didn't have the tonic with us, nor how to make it, otherwise we would have. Or that I hadn't care the night before but it had been Jasper who stopped us.

He shifted, his hands rubbing my arms. He tilted his head to meet my eyes.

"I'm sorry, Rainey," he whispered. "I know this is hard. A lot is changing. I know you..." He blew a breath out, his eyes searched my face. "Honestly, I don't know anymore. I thought..." He sighed and squeezed my hands. "I do know we will be good together."

I nodded, pulling my lips between my teeth and averting my eyes. Uncertainty tugged at my heart, but I forced a smile.

"We will be," I murmured, trying to convince myself.

"Rainey," he whispered, his voice gentle.

I looked up.

He leaned in, his eyes dilated as he closed the small gap between us and brushed his lips against mine. My body screamed to pull away, to push him away, but I stayed, trying to force Jasper's image and that I was betraying him from my mind. Owen was my future. Jasper was my past. I'd be a Sea Widow in private. Jasper would get safe passage back home with his mom.

When I didn't protest the kiss, he deepened the embrace. Despite my heart's protest, I returned his kiss while numbness frayed at my nerves. I had to honor my promise. According to the vision, we would have multiple children together. We would do more than kiss. He was my future, but despite his many declarations of the vision in the past, Owen had never taken anything from me. He never tried to sneak a kiss or a touch other than the day he told me about the vision. He always asked to court me. Now, I was asking him to risk his life to Ferry the man I loved, and their mom and partner.

His tongue traced against my lips, and I parted them. He swept his tongue inside my mouth. Taking slow, luxurious caresses, he tasted me. I didn't return the intimate touch. Instead, I closed my eyes to it and tried to blank my mind, let the numbness consume me.

Owen pulled back, his eyes hooded. He smiled sweetly at me and pulled me against his chest. His strong arms wrapped around me. The beat of his heart thudded in my ears, drowning out my own.

I stood there, my heart in my throat and tears rimming my eyes. My body and heart ached to feel Jasper, to hold him. But that would never happen again. I had betrayed him in order to help him.

Owen leaned his cheek against my hair. He murmured, "I'll be good to you. I'll do all I can to make you happy. I'll give you all the children you want or none if that's what you want. I care about you. You are my destiny."

He was so focused on the vision. On fulfilling his mom's vision. He didn't care about the reality of it.

"We'll be okay," I said, my voice cracking.

"We will be," he agreed, nodding. His face turned somber. "I'm not him, but I love you."

Twenty-Eight

After waiting for the storm to pass and the waters to calm, Owen and I returned when the sky was painted black, and the last sliver of the moon glowed like a beacon in the sky. The stars in their display provided the astrological navigation sailors had used for millennia. Tomorrow the sky would be moonless, the Sirens' song silent, and the stars would help Jasper leave my life forever.

When we arrived the harbor was empty, the wise villagers at home already. The night hung around us, the buzz of insects breaking the still air. The angry waters of the late evening now reflected glistening moonlight and lapped lazily at the shore, their destruction done.

Owen walked beside me, our arms occasionally brushing together and his lips dancing in a smile. His arm hovered towards me but before he'd touch me, he'd yank it back. I kept my hands tucked at my sides, fisted against my legs. My expression was blank as I allowed the numbness to set in. There was too much on my mind, and instead of focusing on it, I just counted the rocks on the path.

When we crested the hill to enter town, a few glowing lanterns hung in the windows. Some merchants were working on orders through the night and the bakers were getting an early start. The town continued on despite the heartache unsettling my life and the destruction at the pier. Life always carried on.

"Do you think we should head to my house?" he whispered, cutting his gaze to mine. "Let everyone know I'm ferrying them?"

"That's probably where they're all at," I said. Lead settled in my stomach. If I went with him to his house, I'd have to see Jasper again. My heart shattered at the thought, stealing my breath. Taking a steadying gulp, I cast a glance back at the ocean to still my reaction, and then towards Owen. "I'm going to head home. I'll let my mom know our plans so we can prepare for the celebration. I'll help round up needed supplies." Numbness settled like a mist on my skin and heart.

Owen's lips curved into a large smile. He nodded. "We'll head out in the next few hours. You should consider saying goodbye to my mom." His face fell at the thought. "She'll want to say bye."

I nodded and looked away. Tears rimmed my eyes and I didn't bother to wipe them away. Sucking in a breath, I reached my hand for his arm. "Thank you, Owen," I said.

He covered my hand with his, the warmth of his hand odd against my cold flesh.

My feet felt like sludge walking the familiar path back. Molly and John didn't need a goodbye from me. I didn't want to hear her heartfelt thank you for understanding, or her well wishes with Owen. She wouldn't rub it in that her vision was correct and I'd partner with Owen, but it'd feel all the same.

The chilly post-storm air stung my skin and whipped my hair. Rubbing a hand through my tresses, it snarled on the dried bits from my trek through the woods. Despite the frigid temperature, I dunked my head in the water bin I used for my welding. I breathed into the water, letting the bubbles rise and splash against me. After wringing my hair out, I walked to the front.

The house was eerily still, the doors and window shuttered closed, but it felt awake and tense. I furrowed my brow, scanning around, but nothing felt off about the perimeter. Nothing rustled and nothing peered back. Something or someone was waiting for me inside.

My breath stuck in my throat and my heart sounded in my ears.

Silently, I pushed the door open. A sole lamp burned on the wall by the hearth. The warm glow cast shadows along the wall and counter. A loaf of bread had been left out for me and my stomach rumbled.

A sob stuck in my throat and my eyes watered. I'd been hoping Jasper was waiting for me. That he'd snuck away, unable to part without one more goodbye or bearing a magical solution that would allow him to stay.

But he was a Washed Up. And the Sirens had spoken.

I scoffed at my foolishness and left the bread on the counter, no longer hungry. There'd be time to eat later.

I tugged off my mud-caked boots and dirtied clothes. The chill of the room settled over my damp skin. A shiver stole through me and my teeth chattered.

"What's going on?" Mom asked from the doorway. Her rumpled clothes and hair spoke of her inability to sleep. She had an old wool blanket draped over her shoulders.

I started to speak, but only a watery whine came out. My face crumbled, and hot tears rolled down my cheeks.

She came to me in a flash, wrapping her arms around me, like the countless times as a child when I'd been scared, her warmth a comfort.

"He's going back," I choked out.

"I know, sweetie, Molly told me everything," she murmured into my hair. She rocked me like she did when I was young and had had a nightmare, only this time, her soft words and warmth wouldn't change anything.

"Owen," I said, my mouth drying. I stuck my tongue to the roof of my mouth to get moisture. "The other ships were destroyed. Owen... Owen's taking them. He'll Ferry them past the Sirens."

Mom stilled, her hand resting against my temple. Her frame stiffened and she didn't breathe. Waiting for the rest.

"Owen and I..." I let out the sob that was lodged in my throat. "We're going to partner. I told him we could make it official the day after he returns."

"Oh, Rainey," Mom murmured. Her body deflated, and her arms tightened around me, pressing me closer.

I shifted against her to rest my head on her shoulder and the chain caught against my skin, the cold metal a burning reminder. My fingers rubbed against the twisted links, and my stomach curdled.

"I need to give this back to him," I whispered, lifting it up for my mom to see. The candlelight glinted off it.

"He gave it to you. It's yours."

"It was different then," I sniffed. "I don't want the reminder. I don't..."

My voice broke.

"Do you want me to take it to him?" Mom offered. Her unspoken understanding sent splinters through my heart. I could send my reminder away. She sat cuddling hers.

"You'd do that?" I asked, blinking back tears and sniffing.

"Of course," she cooed. "Of course."

She could help me, protect me from more heart ache, where she couldn't have been.

"He was early twenties, and so handsome and sweet. You look so much like him but are his exact opposite."

My mind stalled. She'd just told me more about my father in those sentences than in all my years. "Mom?" I croaked.

A gentle hand smoothed my hair back. "It's time we talked about this, about Thomas. I should have told you years ago."

She'd never spoken his name before. The emission seemed to release something in her. Instead of costing her to tell it, it was like a lock had opened and the pain could escape.

"He washed up after the storm season. He started out with Molly and Jeremiah, Owen's father."

She took a heavy breath, but continued, "They'd just partnered, and Molly was pregnant with Owen. Molly wanted to honor the Sirens for bringing Jeremiah into her life. Thomas was strong and helpful, at first. As an expert sailor, he talked about being a Ferrier."

"He wanted to stay?" I asked before realizing it.

Mom shrugged. A swallow bobbed her body. "He helped your grandpa with Ferrying a Washed Up back on the next cycle. Grandpa wouldn't let him go with him out in the sea, said it was too risky, but they went through the prep work. I don't know if it was wanderlust, greed, or he thought it was the easiest job to have, but he decided he *needed* to be a Ferrier, and the best way to make it happen was to get in close with a Ferrier. My dad was and is one of the kindest people. He hung around the property more and more. Each day felt like a gift. I craved to see him, touch him. My parents told me to stay away from him."

I hadn't heard that version before. I'd always been told her parents had been welcoming.

"But since he was helping my dad, I'd sneak out to talk with him when my dad was distracted. One night he showed up at my window."

Heavy silence crowded us in the room.

After what felt like hours, she spoke again. Her pained voice startling me. "He came by every night. I looked forward to his visits, and when he started to skip nights, it destroyed me. I'd cry, seek him out during the day. He'd promise he had been tired and would come by that night. Not able to get enough, I started meeting him anywhere and at any time."

Her voice broke. Her breaths shook, but no tears welled in her eyes. She met my gaze, the fierceness burning bright, but also love. She was ripping this wound open to help me.

"Mom, you don't have—"

"Yes, I do," she growled. "I should have already told you. This is just as much your story as mine."

I nestled back down on her. Her thudding heart was the only sound for a few moments.

"As the villagers have told you, I caught him with others. I thought I could make him love me. If I just was more persistent. If I didn't whine about him not coming around at night. If I was more."

My heart panged for her. She'd been so young. So naïve.

"When I realized I was pregnant, something changed in me." She stroked my hair. Her eyes got a hazy look. "I never told him about you. I had choices to make, but I knew with certainty he wouldn't change. The village could bully him into being a father, helping to provide for you. But the last thing I wanted was for him to shun you. For you to ever feel like you weren't enough. You are enough, Rainey. You are everything. You're amazing."

My mind couldn't grasp everything she was saying, there was too much, it overflowed. But my heart thudded in response, filling me with love and sorrow for my mom. For her loss, but for her strength and bravery, too.

"I sent him away."

"What?" Everything stilled. Even the flickering candle seemed to hover in place.

"He wasn't enough for *us*."

"Who Ferried him?" I sputtered, one of the only mysteries on the island burning in my mind.

"He did. I told him if he wanted my dad to take him seriously as a Ferrier, he'd have to prove he could do it. The fool used an old rowboat. And I let him."

"You mean..."

"The Sirens dealt their justice."

The knock came two hours later. After washing my entire body with warm water and changing into fresh clothes, I'd curled up against my mom and fallen asleep on the chair, wrapped in her arms and blankets.

"Who could that be?" Mom hissed. She rubbed a hand over her face and sleep from her eyes but got up to check the door, pulling a blanket around her shoulders.

I glanced towards the window where a weak stream of sunlight poked through the cracks in the shutters. Most would expect me to be at the beach cleaning my area by now. Mom should be in the middle of baking, but it was too early for sales.

"Jasper?" My mom gasped, standing up straighter and blocking the door frame.

My eyes darted to the door before I could think better of it. I could see his mussed hair, messy and weaved from him running his hands through it countless times. Thankfully, I couldn't see his face. Instead of moving to get a better look, I forced my eyes to stare at the old, faded fabric of the chair.

"Marianna," he murmured.

My stomach turned, warming at the sound of his voice. My brain kicked in, and my nerves singed. I slumped further down in the seat so he couldn't see me.

"What do you want? Aren't you leaving, Washed Up?" Mom snapped. She gripped the door to close it.

A sad smile skidded across my face. From telling me not to bring in a Washed Up, to trying to make it so he wouldn't go on the transport with me, she'd been trying to protect me. And, after I defied her, she still was trying to be my last line of defense. To give the protection she'd ignored, too. Perhaps we were more similar than I realized. We both had Washed Ups, and although different in all aspects, both of us sent them away.

"Molly... Mom," Jasper started and stopped. I could imagine him running his hand through his hair again. His voice cracked when he asked, "Is Rainey here?"

"It doesn't matter where she is," Mom said, starting to close the door. "You won't see her again. Safe travels."

A tense moment passed. I couldn't hear what he whispered, but Mom sighed in response.

"Wait, hold on! Wait outside, I have something I need to give you," Mom said, her voice soft. The door clicked closed and she padded over towards me.

I leaned back to look up at her over my shoulder. He was just beyond the door. If I called to him, he'd probably open it. But what good would that do? One last goodbye would only further destroy me.

"I'll give him the chain." She softly smiled and her eyes were glossy. "Sit up and I'll unfasten it."

I blinked repeatedly as I leaned forward. I pulled my hair back so she could access it.

Her hands were soft, but I missed the weight of the chain and my fingers traced where it had been around my neck.

Mom opened the door. A warm breeze skittered into the house, carrying the scent of lemons and salt.

"This is yours," Mom whispered. "She wants you to have it back."

"No," Jasper boomed. I jumped at the ferocity of his voice.

"It's yours, Jasper," Mom said. She shifted closer to him, blocking the doorway.

"No, I gave it to Rainey," he said, his voice cracking. "It's hers now."

A sniff sounded.

"Jasper," Mom murmured.

"We're going to leave soon," he said, not hiding the emotion in his voice.

My own emotion welled in my eyes and lodged in my throat.

"I wanted..." Jasper said.

His sob filled the air.

"Oh Jasper," Mom whispered. She opened the door wider, fabric rustling.

I turned in the seat so I could look over the armrest but stay below.

Mom had Jasper wrapped in a hug as his body shook.

My heart shattered, the pieces fracturing and scattering on the floor. The numbness in my chest turned into an unbearable weight and made me gasp.

My brain lost control of my self-preservation. Before I realized it, I had started moving off the chair, but Owen's voice paralyzed me.

"What's taking so long?" he shouted. He stomped down the path.

"Owen," Mom spat, her voice cold. She shifted to keep her arm around Jasper and face Owen. "What are you doing here?"

My mouth fell open. She'd never used that tone with him before.

I whirled around to stare at her like Jasper and Owen did.

Owen stammered, staring at Mom in confusion.

Jasper caught sight of me, his dark eyes bulging in surprise.

"Rainey," he cried, stepping towards me.

"No," Owen bellowed and grabbed Jasper's shoulder. His fingers dug in, grabbing fabric and skin. "Leave her alone."

"What the hell, man?" Jasper shoved Owen back. Owen stumbled, smacking his shoulder into the frame but righting himself. Instead of continuing, Jasper turned to me. "Rainey, can we talk? Please?"

Owen's eyes darkened and a smirk curved his lips.

"You have no more business here." Owen rubbed his shoulder. He stepped next to Jasper, but his focus was on me. "Right, Rainey?"

They all turned to stare at me. My face slackened and hatred burned through my veins. I didn't want to be any of their businesses.

"What do you two need?" I gritted out, not caring what my face showed. "Why are you here? Shouldn't you be heading out?"

Jasper frowned. His mouth opened to say something, but Mom shook her head at him.

"Owen, I'll have everything prepared for when you return," Mom said, casting me a sad glance.

"Thank you, but that's not why I am here," Owen said.

"Prepared?" Jasper asked. His gaze shot momentarily to Mom before returning to me.

"What else do you need?" Mom barked, ignoring Jasper's question.

Owen grimaced and rubbed his forehead. He sighed. "I was coming to see if we can have Rainey's boat. My emergency vessel is too small for three to fit safely."

I nodded dully. I waved my hand to its location outside.

Jasper shot me a confused look. "You need your boat," he sputtered.

"She'll get another one, don't worry about her," Owen said, cocking an eyebrow at him. He stood taller to look down at him. "She's not your concern anymore."

Jasper's face darkened and he furled his fist. "Rainey, can we talk?" he murmured.

"No," I whispered.

"The boat's right there." Mom nodded to the door and outside. A snarl curled on her face. "If that's all, have a safe trip. We need to tend things here."

Jasper's face fell, and he looked imploringly to me.

My heart yearned to talk to him. To take back the last goodbye we had. But regardless of how it went, it was goodbye.

"Also," Owen said, drawing my attention back to him.

Mom tilted her head at him and cocked an eyebrow. "What else do you need? Aren't you already getting your way?" Her words were clipped and harsh.

Owen swallowed and shot me an apologetic look. "Mom says Rainey has to come. According to her vision, the only way we survive is if Rainey is there."

"What?" Mom, Jasper, and I shouted at once.

"No," Mom barked. "Absolutely not. Your *family* has already done enough to my daughter. She will not risk her life out on the ocean by the Sirens."

Jasper nodded.

"Why?" I asked, drawing the ire of both Mom and Jasper. "Why do I have to go?"

Owen shrugged. "She freaked out when Jasper left. It wasn't a big guess where he went," he said, rolling his eyes. "I told her he'd come back when Rainey turned him away. But she insisted Rainey has to come. John and I both tried...But she says her vision is clear on it."

"I can't, though," I sputtered. My gaze jumped to Jasper and my heart twisted. "I'll just be in the way."

"Mom's visions... they're always right..." Owen started, his voice droning on again while I tuned him out.

Mom looked to me, her green eyes full of fear and anger. She already knew what I was going to do.

Even if it destroyed my heart to have to see Jasper, I couldn't anger the Sirens more. I couldn't ignore their request through Molly's vision. I had to finish their punishment. No matter how cruel it was.

Twenty-Nine

OWEN STEERED us through the surf and into the dark blue ocean. The farther we sailed from shore, the angrier the currents turned. The normally-clear bottom churned with fierce froths, slapping our boat. The waves threatened to toss us, but Owen kept us on a smooth course.

Below deck, he had a small cabin set up for cots and chairs. He also kept some goods and water barrels down there. A few oil lamps were attached to the walls, but he kept them unlit.

The space was big enough for the four of us to rest while Owen steered, but the room was thick with unspoken truths and failed promises. After helping Molly and John into the cabin, I made a quick exit before Jasper could say anything to me. My chest tightened, but not from the sea. His watchful gaze followed me up the stairs and I refused to look back.

The wind beat at my face, whipping my hair from its braid. Pulling a long brown strand from across my face, I walked to the stern and stared across the sea, watching our island grow fainter. Instead of fresh air, the breeze fluttered with salt and storm.

My eyes cast to the horizon, searching for the storm on the wind. Bloated gray clouds blotted out the sun, but none appeared to be thunderheads.

My stomach rolled on a wave, and I licked my lips. I'd never been this far away from my land. The ocean didn't scare me, but I didn't cross it. It was a constant presence, protecting us and providing for us. As the island grew small in the distance, the majesty and overwhelmingness of the ocean swallowed me. Endless blue expanse encompassed the island, but being on the boat was like being an ant in a river. One day, the ocean would be my grave, like all my ancestors. But I hoped it wasn't today.

"You might be better in the cabin," Owen called. His blue eyes fixed on me. His blond hair tangled in the wind. He nodded towards the stairwell, encouraging me to go down.

"No." I turned back to the sea. I could face the ocean, unlike Jasper, who waited below.

A spray of cold water splashed over the rail, hitting my face. I rubbed my cheek with the sleeve of my shirt as I felt the air shift. Jasper had to have joined us. I closed my eyes and rested my hands on the railing. Staring across the sea, I forced my eyes to stay forward.

"Everyone settled?" Owen asked, his voice tight.

"Yeah," Jasper called.

My heart thudded in my chest. He was so close and yet, he was untouchable.

"Rainey," Jasper whispered.

My body tensed. He stood a few yards behind me but was unreachable.

Instead of responding, I pushed off from the rail, making sure my gaze wouldn't align with his, and moved to the bow.

"How long will it take?" I called to Owen, ignoring Jasper. Settling on the railing, I allowed my eyes to find Owen.

He watched me, his expression unreadable. After a moment, he turned his attention back to the ocean.

"We have hours to go," Owen said. "You may want to rest."

"Do you rest when you ferry people?" I asked. A frown twisted my lips.

"I'm the Ferrier, you're a... passenger," he finished awkwardly. He cast his eyes to the stairwell and back to me.

I understood what he wanted, but as that would put me in tight quarters if Jasper followed, it was one of the last things I wanted to do. I anchored my feet to the deck.

"Well, this is the only time I'll ever see this part of the ocean, so I'll stay up here," I said, folding my arms as I tried to look natural on the deck.

His jaw ticked, but he didn't argue.

"So is this what it's like to ferry them? You stare at waves upon waves and watch out for storms?"

He narrowed his eyes at me, annoyance flittering across them.

Out of the corner of my eye, I noticed Jasper move to the railing, his strong hands steadying him. Even though I didn't look up, I felt his heated gaze on me.

A lump bobbed in my throat. Pinpricks raced up my nerves, and the desire to watch Jasper gnawed at me.

"This is the easy part. When we get to the rocks, things will get tense." Owen watched me from the wheel, his expression hardening.

"Shouldn't you watch the ocean?" I asked, fanning my arm out to encompass the world.

"I am," Owen chuckled.

"So, if I remember the tale correctly, Ferriers take the Washed Up to the green rock, lured by the song of the Sirens. From there, it is the blue rock where Ferriers are never to cross, for if their eyes fall on the beauty of the Sirens, even without the song on the moonless night, they will be snared to the bottom of the sea."

"No, it's much worse than that. The saying is to help Ferriers keep hope."

"Why? The Ferriers come back."

A sad smile skidded across Owen's face. "The Sirens are always out there. They try to lure Washed Up and Ferriers to them. You must have blind faith you'll return home when the Washed Up exits the vessel. Our heart's want leads us home or to the Sirens."

"So, then is it true the Sirens can see your heart's desire and unless you know it, they'll use it to lure you to them?" I asked, cocking an eyebrow.

Owen bobbed his head back and forth, screwing his mouth into a thin line. Finally, he said, "You must know what your heart wants. When they sing, you chant to yourself, reminding you of your love. When you are close enough to see them on the blue rock, you close your eyes and let your heart's want lead you back home."

I stared at him a beat, wondering what he focused on when ferrying others. He stared back, his jaw tight.

A thought occurred to me, and I asked, "How do the Washed Up make it through them, then? They are songless, but you said their beauty will snare you, too."

Owen looked away, licking his lips.

"Owen," I asked louder. Fear clawed at my throat.

His gaze cut to me, hard and unyielding. Finally, he said, "Most don't."

"What?" I yelled, momentarily letting my eyes cut to Jasper. Instead of the unnoticed glimpse I'd hoped for, my eyes caught his gaze. His brown eyes focused on me, emotion burning bright in them. My heart dropped to my stomach. I gulped and looked away, lead filling my veins.

"We don't talk about it much to anyone but other Ferriers." Owen averted his gaze.

"Then why take them?" I screamed. What would happen to Molly, John, and Jasper?

"They want to go back," he yelled back. His palm smacked against the wheel and he snarled. "They know it is a risk."

"We make them believe it is possible!"

"It is," Owen said, swinging a hand toward Jasper. "His dad made it out with him. It is possible!"

I blinked instead of following his gaze. My eyes unfocused as I stared at the ground. "How many? How many make it past them?"

Owen shrugged in defeat. "I'd say a quarter of those who I bring out. Your grandpa had a higher rate. Marcus and Fredricka's are on par with mine."

"Then why are you risking your mom's life?" I asked, emotion burning in my eyes.

"She says it is the only way!" Owen yelled, his own emotions fracking his carefree façade. Fear and anger darkened his face and his eyes narrowed in dark slits. "I'd rather not be doing this! But I can't stop her! She'd take a rowboat."

I ran a hand through my hair. She knew the dangers, and yet was willing to risk it. Her vision…

"It's possible," Owen muttered.

I slumped against the railing. The hard wood pressed into my back. Our island offered a lie to the Washed Up. We aided the Sirens in luring them back to them. Maybe that's why the Sirens didn't punish us for letting them go back.

We spoke of the risks to the Washed Up, but I had believed it was completely possible and most had made it. The water always carried risks and demanded respect, but our Ferriers returned to us. But only about a quarter of the Washed Up successfully crossed through. Yet Molly was certain they would succeed. And John had once before succeeded with an infant.

"Rainey," Jasper whispered, shattering my thoughts. His voice was close.

I jolted. My gaze instinctively jumped to him. My heart reached for him, but I remained rooted to the spot. I wanted to talk to him. Tell him I love him. Hear him say it back. But it wouldn't help and only fracture me more.

"What in the seas are you doing?" Owen hissed, stomping away from the wheel. He balled his hands into fists as his long strides ate the distance.

"Knock it off, man," Jasper gritted out. He stepped in front of me. His arm almost brushed against me, and I sucked in a shaky breath.

I used the diversion to step back. Gather space. Gather my thoughts.

"You're leaving." Owen got in Jasper's face. He stood glaring down at Jasper.

Jasper cursed and fisted his hands. His brown eyes darkened, and his lip quavered.

"You wanna hit me? Go for it!" Owen yelled, spittle flying. He crowded Jasper's space. "This'll be your last chance."

"I don't care about fighting you," Jasper yelled back, shoving Owen out of his space. He didn't pursue him. "I care about…"

Jasper stopped himself but his gaze flicked momentarily to me.

Owen reared back and squared his shoulders. Lurching forward, he shoved Jasper back a few steps.

Jasper's face reddened as he snarled and he moved to punch Owen.

I screamed, "Enough!"

The wind tore my scream.

They both jumped, their attention swinging to me.

"Enough," I said, my voice watery. They both blinked, their faces softening. I figured I was crying by their sudden worried expressions, but I didn't care. "Jasper, go back to your parents."

"Rainey, can we talk?" he pleaded, taking a step towards me, hand outstretched. He tilted his head, his eyes beseeching as he tried to snag my gaze.

"She already said no." Owen moved to stand between us. "Back off."

"This isn't your business," Jasper spat.

Owen laughed, his shoulders rippling.

"What?" Jasper demanded.

Owen stood straighter, cocking his head to the side. "It is my business," he sneered.

Jasper shot him a confused dark look.

"Didn't Rainey tell you?" he asked, posturing.

"Tell me what?" Jasper's gaze settled on me.

I averted my eyes. Sighing, I rubbed my temples.

"Tell me what?" Jasper repeated, his voice shrilling. His body stiffened as his face reddened.

Owen glanced over his shoulder at me, a triumphant smile on his lips. He frowned, taking in my appearance, but turned back to Jasper.

"Rainey?" Jasper pleaded. "Please talk to me."

Stuck on a boat in the ocean made hiding impossible, but I went back to the rail. Refusing to look at either of them, I closed my eyes, letting the wind cool my face. Goodbye was hard enough, but I didn't want Owen witnessing it. I didn't want to witness it or live it, either.

"What is going on?" Jasper yelled, but he didn't move closer to me.

"When we return, Rainey and I are partnering," Owen crowed. He folded his arms over his chest and smirked. "Just as we knew we would."

"What?" Jasper stammered. I felt his gaze bore into me. "Rainey?"

"It's true," I called over my shoulder. Numbness thawed in my heart, dulling the rapid beating and chilling my nerves.

"What? Why?" Jasper demanded, emotion thick in his words.

"What do you care?" Owen countered. "You're leaving. You're just another Washed Up that left. It's none of your business. Did you expect her to be a Sea Widow... for you?"

Tears rimmed my eyes but didn't fall. From a chill or something else, my body shuddered. My lungs burned for breath, but the sob lodged in my throat wouldn't let air past.

"Rainey?" Jasper whispered, his voice cracking. The air shifted, and I knew he'd moved closer. If I turned around, he'd probably be in arm's reach.

"Go back with your parents," I choked out, not leaving my spot on the rail. If I touched him, I may never let him go.

The moment he went down, I knew. The deck felt colder. Void. Numb.

"Rainey." Owen stepped up behind me. His warm hand rested on my shoulders. I bristled under his touch, and he removed it. He hovered. Before finally shifting away, he said, "There is some food in the galley. We need to keep nourished."

My gaze drifted to the stairs leading to the cabin, where Jasper waited with his parents.

The passage blurred as my eyes unfocused. My feet were rooted to the floor, unwilling to move.

"I can grab it," Owen said. He averted his gaze, his mouth a thin line. "You can watch the sea."

Taking in the low gray clouds and steady waves, I nodded in agreement.

He gave me a nod before heading down into the cabin.

The sun shimmered behind the clouds as they drifted across it, the haziness creating glowing billows. A rumble caught my attention, and I turned back to the cabin. Another rumble above started, followed by a crack in the sky. Echoes sounded in the distance.

I cursed and turned back to face the direction we were heading. Looming ahead was a massive forming thunderhead, the bulbous features dark and heavy but illuminated by pulses of lightning behind it. The waves responded, pounding the boat faster. The boat bucked.

"Owen," I screamed, but the uptick in wind ripped the words from my mouth. A gust of sea mist slapped my face, distorting my vision.

My knuckles tightened around the wheel, forcing it on course. I blinked, but the salt burned my eyes.

"Rainey," Owen yelled behind me. He rushed to stand next to me.

"A storm popped up," I yelled back.

Waves smashed into the boat's side, showering us in salty gusts.

"The seas," he cursed, taking in the monstrosity. "Rainey, we can't survive that. We have to turn back."

"Owen, your mom," I screamed.

"Rainey, we'll all die!" he yelled. His mouth trembled as he cast a look below deck. His face paled and he grimaced. He moved to take the wheel. "We'll... we'll have to wait for the next cycle."

"No!" I yelled, shoving him back.

His feet slid on the wet deck, but he remained upright.

"Rainey," he groused. He regained the distance and pulled at my fingers clutching the wheel.

"Owen," Jasper screamed, joining us on deck.

Owen didn't release his grip but twisted to look at Jasper. He snarled, his blue eyes flashing with hate.

"Shit," Jasper swore, seeing the brewing storm.

"We have to go back," Owen called out, still digging at my hands. "It's too dangerous."

"No," Jasper cried. "Mom... she's in labor. Her contractions started."

"What?" Owen bellowed. He dropped his pursuit of my grasp on the wheel as he ran back towards the steps.

Jasper watched him go and turned his gaze to me. Sorrow pooled in them.

"Rainey." Jasper bowed his head.

"Jasper, go help your mom," I gritted out, straining to keep my grip.

"Why, Rainey?" he said, stepping closer. His aroma tickled my nose. Ash and cinnamon. His nearness warmed me, and I shuddered. "Why are you partnering with him?" The last sentence sounded pained as he spat it out.

"It doesn't matter," I said, not meeting his gaze. I blinked away the welling tears. He didn't need to know it was for his ferrying. "Our paths separate here."

He nodded and sniffed. He rested his hand on my shoulder, his fingers gently rubbing circles before withdrawing them. I missed his touch the instant he removed his hand.

Thirty

THE STORM DISSIPATED AFTER AN HOUR, but the waters continued their angry dance. With the break in the weather as Owen steered, I set up the other boats. Even if I didn't want him to leave, I needed to make sure he was safe. Instead of allowing my brain to focus on Jasper leaving, I slipped into the familiarity of prepping to travel.

My boat was bigger than Owen's emergency one and would fit the three more comfortably. I put in blankets, some flasks of water, and containers of meat and bread. Without knowing what would happen when they crossed, I wanted to make sure they had necessities if they spent a few days at sea. I put a tarp over the items as an additional protection, and they could also use it for protection from the weather.

Owen's emergency boat would take us back to the island if anything happened to his ship. The tiny vessel wouldn't fare well. With the Sirens' blessings, we wouldn't need to use it. As an afterthought, I tossed in a few canteens and a tarp.

The rain started again, the soft pattering dampening the deck in large splashes. Then it turned into cold pelts, welting my skin and burning my face. A shiver stole through me and I rubbed my arms.

Storms would likely follow them, at least through the Sirens' reach. I tethered three life jackets to it. Washed Up weren't usually sent with them, unless they scrounged them up or traded, but Owen had brought them from his private stash for his family.

The fourth and last life jacket, I tossed into Owen's and my boat. My stomach curled thinking about it, but the decision had been made and I would honor my promise.

"Rainey," Owen called to me from the helm. His wet blond hair was plastered to his face.

"What?" I barked back, checking over my work again to make sure everything was secured.

"Go below deck, it's not safe," he yelled. He nodded towards the steps.

"No," I shot back.

A crack of thunder sounded, followed by the silver threads of lightning.

"Rainey," he growled, straining to keep the vessel in the right direction.

The Sirens had to punish me more.

"Fine," I spat. Not wanting to add to his worries, I moved to the steps. The dark passage bobbed and weaved with shadows, the only light the lamp they had lit below.

"Rainey," Molly called out. Her voice sounded tired.

"Yes, Molly?" I stared into the long shadows.

"Please, come sit with me," she said and grunted. Her cot squeaked as she shifted.

Sucking back a breath, I eased down the steps. The space was warmer than above and dry. Salt and the briny smell of ocean clung to the wooden walls. Molly sat with John on a cot tucked in the corner. Jasper leaned against the far wall, arms folded over his chest, head tilted back, staring at the ceiling.

A gold chain peeked beneath her shirt. The original to Jasper's. Her good luck charm for a voyage. It'd helped Jasper as an infant get safely through. I wanted to see if he wore his, the one I returned, but at the same time I didn't want to see it. See the finality of what we'd been.

"Are you okay?" I asked, hovering in the doorway. My feet hesitated to enter. I could still turn and run back up.

She patted the spot next to her. "Some contractions," she said, easing as it passed. "Come sit by me, please."

"Contractions? That means... the storm.... Will you be able to make it?" I stammered as I moved to sit by her. The mattress and springs bowed as I gingerly rested next to her.

"We have time," Molly assured.

"We have to try," John said. His gaze bounced between us and Jasper. Fear and sorrow burned behind his gaze. His dark eyes were much like Jasper's, and my stomach twisted.

"John, you made it before," I said, forcing a watery smile. "You made it with an infant, according to Jasper. Now you... now you have Jasper to help you." My voice strained towards the end.

"Rainey," John started but swallowed. His focus turned to Jasper again, and regret darkened his face.

"John, you will save your family," I said, swallowing down the emotion. "The boat is all set. I put in provisions in case you need them."

"I'm sorry, Rainey," Molly said, not hiding her sadness and letting tears stream down her face. She ran a hand over my knee. "This doesn't seem..."

"Molly, we all knew your vision. I was the one that was fighting it." I clasped her hand in mine. I went to speak again, but my mouth wouldn't open, and I sniffed.

"This doesn't feel right, at all," Molly said, bowing her head to catch my eyes. Her blue eyes scrunched in confusion. She blinked and flinched; likely another vision was developing.

"It's because it's all happening so fast," I said. "The truth. The voyage. The storm. Goodbyes." My gaze fell to the wooden floor. A faded, threadbare red-and-white rug covered most of it. My gaze unfocused on the pattern as I tried to stop my mind from running.

"Rainey, you've been like a daughter to me," Molly said. "I was honored to trade the land to you. You cared about it as much as my family has. Will continue to. You are remarkable. Driven. Caring. Loyal."

I nodded and ran my tongue over my teeth. My so-called loyalty had me partnering with Owen. I'd told Jasper I loved him and within a few hours, I was partnering with another man.

Molly wrapped an arm around my shoulders and pulled me into a hug.

She leaned in close to my ear, her voice more air than a whisper. "I know what you did to help Jasper. Don't ever question your loyalty. If I would have known sooner, I would have intervened. It shouldn't have happened like this."

I pulled back from her, tears blurring my vision. It wouldn't have happened this way had I not gone against the vision the Sirens gave to Molly.

"Rainey, it wasn't supposed to be that way," she mouthed to me, keeping her face from both John and Jasper. "This is wrong."

I swallowed but it didn't help the emotion in my throat. "We have to save you," I mouthed back to her. My eyes fell to her swollen belly and then returned to meet her blue stare.

She hummed in her throat as she peered at me for a moment.

"I think you and Jasper should talk," Molly said, taking me by surprise.

My eyes darted up first to Molly and then to him. His intense gaze was focused on me, almost pleading. My heart twisted and my mouth trembled. I blinked and looked back to the rug.

"There's nothing to say," I said and shook my head.

"There's always something to say," Molly said. She sighed and rubbed her belly. She leaned in again. "There is so much between you two. It may have only been a short time, but time means nothing on our island. Rainey. We can all see the feelings you two have for each other."

I sucked back a sob and rubbed my forehead. "It'll only cause more pain," I choked out. "I'm tired of pain."

"Numbness is a poison," Molly whispered. "It steals our life with a promise of taking the pain, but it takes our joy, too."

I snorted a laugh. My life wouldn't be numb. I had the island. My family was there, too. I would have the land I'd worked so hard for by partnering. Through all my efforts, I'd ended up where I started. Years of trying, working endlessly, and fate still won. I had my scavenging, and based on Molly's predictions, I'd have children. "The numbness will pass."

She shook her head. "Not unless you actively fight against it."

I nodded even though I didn't agree. I didn't want this conversation to be our last one.

"Molly, thank you," I choked. "You showed me love. You helped me live my dream. You gave me a choice. I just want one more thing."

She furrowed her brow. "Rainey, I'd give you anything, but…" She lifted her palms. "I don't know what I could give you. What is it, Rainey? What can I help you with?"

"Just make sure you all make it?" I choked out. "Get everyone past the Sirens."

She pulled me into her embrace, rocking me like a child. The aroma of cinnamon and oranges swarmed around us. Her warmth and love seeped through. Memories from my childhood filtered through my mind. She'd always been there to offer me a hug when I fought with my mom. The look of joy when I asked to purchase the land. Molly had even helped me scope the best spot for a house.

"Rainey, you have my word," Molly said. She rubbed my back as we swayed. "My vision was clear. If you came, I would see my son grow up. John and I will be with him. We'll make it."

My vision swam, pixelating into rainbow drops. I smiled at her. Jasper would grow up with his mom. His childhood would be changed. I didn't know what would happen with the adult Jasper once they crossed over. If he would go to John's time or back to his own. That was the part we knew nothing about. Either way, he'd have his family. Unless the Sirens saw to it to stop him, and he became part of the seventy-five percent that didn't make it and only his younger self did. The thought caught in my throat, and I sucked back a watery sob.

She shifted so her lips were next to my ear, her voice barely a breath. "Talk to Jasper."

"I can't," I mouthed back, salty tears streaming down my face.

Her hands cupped my face, forcing me to look at her. She waited until my gaze locked on hers, and said, "You can."

Gently, she turned my chin to face Jasper. He pulled his bottom lip into his mouth and his fingers curled against the wall.

"Rainey?" he whispered. His voice was cracked and raw.

"Jasper," I said. My heart twisted and stole my next breath.

Molly eased back so that only space and emotion hung between Jasper and me.

He took a step towards me. His chest heaved up as uncertainty warred on his face.

I stood up from the cot, my legs swaying with the boat before I found my footing.

His hand reached for me, slicing through the distance. My brain screamed to not touch him, not cross the line. If I did, I may never heal.

With a shaky breath, I lifted my hand to meet his.

A thunderous crack rocketed through the air, rattling the walls and unseating the cot. The ship lurched to the side. Jasper and I toppled back. The moment shattered.

"What happened?" I yelled, jumping to my feet.

John helped Molly back into the cot, running his hands over, her checking for injuries.

I turned back towards the hall.

Jasper had already raced up the stairs by the time I made it to the staircase. I darted up, flinching from a gust of chilly wind that misted my face with water.

John followed behind me.

The deck was soaked. Water lapped over the rails. The tied-down items rattled in their holds. Both boats remained in place, the tarps repelling water.

Jasper pulled to a stop, his body rigid.

In front of our vessel was a green rock. The mammoth structure pierced the ocean, dwarfing our boat. The ragged edges clawing heavenwards. The emerald surface reflected the crashing waves and rippling thunder. With it, our futures would be divided. There was no going back. For the first time in my life, I would see our Siren mothers; witness their awesomeness and cruelty as Jasper and I would part ways. Jasper to save his family, and me to fulfill their fate for me as Owen's partner.

Thirty-One

OWEN STEERED us directly toward the green rock. The boat bucked on the waves, spraying foam over the bow. The wind howled, tearing at our breath and words. Another gust bashed against the vessel and my feet slipped. I stumbled on the slick surface, sliding into a barrel. My hand scraped against it, rubbing raw. Scrambling up, I ran towards him.

"Owen," I screamed, joining him and Jasper at the wheel.

"Rainey," he swore. His eyes flashed for a second, settling back to their normal blue. He gritted his teeth, holding the boat at course, set on colliding with the rock.

"What are you doing?" I yelled, tugging on the wheel to avoid a collision.

"Let go!" he screamed. His eyes pulsed again in shimmering blue.

"Dude," Jasper yelled and shoved Owen. "You're going to crash us!"

Owen's feet slid on the rain-drenched deck. Losing his footing, he let go of the wheel to catch himself from falling.

"What the seas?" Owen shouted, shaking his head. His focus turned to the looming rock and his eyes bulged. He joined me at the wheel, pulling hard to the right.

"What happened to you?" I spat. My breath came in ragged pants and a shiver stole down my spine.

He shrugged, his eyes clouded in confusion. "I don't know," he said, but his eyes cut to the rock and his jaw ticked.

My heart pounded in my ears. What were the Sirens doing? They could be toying with him. But then why weren't we all affected?

"I thought there was supposed to be a song. Lured to the green rock by their song?" I said, trying to piece together the tales. The wind whipped around, whistling, cold and charged. But there was no song. Even the ocean, frothing around us, seemed muted.

"You don't hear it?" Owen stammered. His eyes darted to Jasper. "It's so loud. It's never this loud!"

Jasper shook his head, his gaze landing to me.

We both shrugged in confusion.

"Gah," Owen growled. He grabbed his ears and grimaced. His knees hobbled. With a jolt, he squared his body and his vacant eyes flicked to the emerald boulder.

Before he could move, I grabbed his arm, warm and strong. He startled and shot me a confused gaze.

"Owen, how can you hear their singing? And your eyes," I said, flicking my fingers toward his face. "What's going on with them?"

"What about my eyes?" he hissed.

"They glowed," Jasper said. "Multiple times."

"It's their song," Owen said, running a hand through his hair. "When the Washed Up hear it, their eyes glow, too."

"Then what happens?" I asked.

Owen averted his gaze and ran a hand over his mouth.

"Owen," I yelled. "What in the seas happens?"

"Some of them jump," he whispered. His head bowed and pointed to the rock. "They try to swim for it."

I could guess what happened next. The Sirens claimed them.

"Do all the Washed Up get entranced by the song?" Jasper asked.

"No," Owen said, swallowing hard. "About half make it past. Ear plugs don't work. Loudness doesn't work. Only willpower works once you hear it. Today is so much worse than any other trip."

"Why? What's different?" I asked.

Jasper cut his dark gaze to me. He blinked at me and sighed.

"Am I distracting you?" I yelled at Owen. I didn't want to be there, anyway.

He flinched and mumbled, "I don't think so. Besides, Mom said you had to be here in order for us to survive."

My stomach twisted and uncertainty pooled in my veins.

John joined us at the helm, his hair tousled and his face long with weariness. His dark eyes scanned the horizon. He let out a large breath, his body deflating as he took in the vastness around us.

"John, do you hear singing?" I asked.

John furrowed his brow and his eyes darted around, unseeing. He shook his head. "No, I only hear the storm and the water."

"Why can't we hear it?" I asked, waving my hands between the three of us. "But you can?"

"I... I don't know." Owen shook his head. Confusion and annoyance flittered across his face. "I always have. It's been a whisper until tonight. Your grandpa said he never heard it, either."

"Because their heart belongs to someone else," Molly said behind us. She braced herself against the wall, a grimace on her face. Her long, damp brown tresses whipped around her in the wind.

"What are you doing?" I screeched, moving to help support her.

John beat me to her side. His arms wrapped around her.

"Our journey is coming to an end," Molly said, tears building in her eyes. She rubbed a hand over her belly. "We are going to say goodbye soon. We need to start moving."

She gripped my arms, letting her tears fall. "Rainey, I love you like a daughter. I always have. I always will. You made this possible for us. Take good care of my son."

I swallowed and looked down. Dread pooled in my stomach, acid burning up through my throat. My body screamed not to let Jasper leave. Not to go with Owen. To find a solution. Everything felt so wrong. But instead, I pursed my lips and nodded. Meeting her gaze, I whispered, "I promise."

Owen cocked his head to the side, rubbing his ears. He flinched and grasped his head. His eyes flashed again. "It's so loud," he hissed. "We need to move."

"The sun will set in an hour," Molly said. She scanned the horizon.

Her brow furrowed, taking in the clouds. She sucked in a breath, staring at Owen. Her face scrunched. "The clouds are masking the sun. It's a trap. We need to wait until then."

"No, the storm's getting worse," Owen argued. His knuckles whitened on the wheel. "We need to clear the blue rock before it's impassable."

"No," Molly said firmly. "You can barely control yourself now. You can't control the boat if you see them. Wait until their song stops. You will survive this."

"I've done this before," he sneered. "I'm the only one here who has. Don't tell me how to do my job."

"You're right, but the Sirens are all our ancestors and you're under-estimating them," Molly countered.

A snarl rippled over Owen's face and his hard gaze bore into Molly. She met his rage with calm assurance and a cocked eyebrow.

"Is it always this hard?" I asked, moving to stand next to him. Distracted from Molly, his eyes shot to me, blue and bright, but they didn't seem like him. They felt different. Cold. Distant. His muscles tightened and he stood straighter. I laid a hand on his bare arm. It was cold and clammy from the storm.

He yanked it away, screeching, "Don't touch me."

My eyes flew open wide, and I stepped back, hand still hovering in the air.

Mist and something else hung between us.

He shook his head, and his eyes beseeched me. "Rainey, I'm... sorry."

"Your mom's right," I said, glancing back at Molly. "We need to wait until the sun goes down to go any further."

Owen scowled, his eyes darkening, the change instant. I stepped back.

He seethed, "You're not in charge here. This is my ship!"

"Owen," Molly snapped. She grimaced and clutched her stomach as she stumbled back, hand reaching for the wall. She whimpered and squeezed her eyes tight as her face pinched in pain.

John caught her back, helping to support her. He rubbed her shoulders and whispered to her. Jasper darted to her other side and helped ease her down in my rowboat.

Fate was going to happen. There was nothing I could do to stop the Sirens' plans.

In the few seconds when our attention was diverted, Owen grabbed the wheel. He shifted the sail, catching a gust from the storm, and sent us cascading across the water.

"Owen," I bellowed.

But it was too late.

The shining blue beacon, larger than the green, sprouted from the ocean's waters. The waves slapped against it in foamy bursts. The towering rock was ringed in layers, each layer a lighter shade of blue until it pierced the sky. There seemed no separation between it and the heavens.

With his reckless approach, the ship moaned and bucked on the water, slapping down hard, sending spray flying over our heads. The dock sloshed with salty sea water, soaking the floor and racing down into the cabin below.

When a wave bashed into the side of the boat, my feet slipped on the deck and I cascaded forward. I braced my hands out to protect my face.

Jasper's strong arms wrapped around my waist. His heart pounded, the rhythm familiar and soothing. A sound I could always listen to. Despite his soaked clothing, his warmth reached me. For a moment I paused, allowing myself to feel safe and protected in his embrace.

Owen growled, breaking the moment. The world tumbled down around me. The wind sliced at my face. The waters gusted against us. The ship bounced unyieldingly on the choppy waves.

"Get your hands off of her," he roared, his face red and blotchy.

"Turn us back to the green rock until the sun sets." Jasper rubbed small circles into my back with his thumbs. My body eased against him, snuggling against his torso and my head resting on his shoulder. A pang built in my heart, seizing my breath. I was going to miss him.

"You're not in control here," Owen roared again. Leaving the wheel to spin uncontrolled, he leaped towards Jasper, his hands grabbing for purchase.

Jasper turned us so his back took the blunt of Owen's assault. I slipped out of his embrace, racing towards the wheel as Owen and Jasper threw blows at each other. Skidding on the deck, I came to a hard stop when I barreled into the railing by the wheel.

The wheel spun so fast I couldn't touch the handles without getting hurt. Looming ahead was the blue rock, drawing nearer and nearer. The rocky surface would tear apart the boat and us. With a grimace and groan, I grabbed for the wheel, screaming as the handle bashed my arm. My hand throbbed, the red sting welting around my palm. On the second attempt, I grabbed a knob and held on. The weight crushed against me, straining my muscles. My legs screamed and buckled as I anchored onto the deck, trying to change course.

Before I could get us out of the path, a wave crashed against the side of the boat, spilling chilly water across the deck and knocking us off course.

My breaths came as pants. My body ached from the chill and force, but I continued to turn the wheel, directing us back to the green rock. Another rogue wave slammed into our other side, tilting us the other way. Our ship listed to the side. But another wave righted us. A third wave stole my footing, and I slammed into the deck. Metallic blood spilled in my mouth. I blinked, but stars popped in my view as my vision swam.

Wood grinding on metal droned out the storm and water. The ship smashed against the rock again. As the ship splintered into two, a thunderous boom sounded in all directions.

"Get the boats on the rock!" Owen screamed. His face was bloodied, his hands mangled and bruised, and his eye purplish as the lid started to swell. Jasper hadn't fared better, but he ran to help Owen and John move the row boats to the blue rock.

The blue rock had ledges and lips running along the dozens of feet of above the ocean surface. Pools of caught water glinted back the setting sun, the gleaming, gem-like light a promise and lure of treasures.

I stilled and looked up. The storm parted, the black clouds rolling off and evaporating under the intensity of the sun. We were too early. Molly was right. The storm was a trap.

"What's going on?" I yelled. I knelt to help Molly up and off the boat deck. John raced back, taking her other side.

Molly shook her head, her eyes squinting as she groaned. "My visions are all merging together. I'm seeing... too much."

"Get her seated," I ordered, scrambling to grab the canteens tossed around the deck before the ship slipped into its watery grave.

Jasper and Owen each offered a hand to Molly. John stayed close by. Despite the ripple of a contraction, Molly joined them on the rock. She knelt to the ground, a grimace twisting her face. She bit back the pain, and when it eased, she sucked in a raspy breath.

"Mom, I thought you said if Rainey came, we'd survive," Owen said, shooting me a bewildered look. He ran a hand through his tangled blond hair and stilled to watch his ship slip below the waves. Owen blinked and swallowed, his eyes red-rimmed and glossy. His livelihood and family were both gone today. He growled. "I never would have risked her coming—"

"Owen," Molly snapped. We all froze. Her piercing blue eyes shot to Owen's, her face dark with annoyance. "We are still alive. We have vessels and the sky has cleared."

"But..." Owen started.

"No, Owen, no buts. You didn't listen. You let their song pull you. If Rainey hadn't been here, we'd be with our Siren mothers."

His eyes jumped to mine. Redness clawed at his cheeks, and he swallowed.

Maybe I was his land Siren. But then, what did that mean? What was I luring him from?

Thirty-Two

THE SUN TOUCHED THE HORIZON, its dazzling light reflecting off the calm waters in a display of shimmering fire. Reds, oranges, and purples rippled across the waves. The sky was painted red, the peacefulness a lure.

"How long do we wait?" John asked, rubbing Molly's shoulders.

"Until night fall," Molly said.

I hunkered down a row above them on the tiered ringed edges of the rock, away from both Jasper and Owen. Shivers stole through me as a gust of air skimmed across my skin. My damp clothes stuck to my body, chilling me further. Around us, the ocean current calmed, the lazy waves dancing in the fading sunlight.

In a matter of minutes, if Molly's vision was correct, Jasper, Molly, and John would sail across the Sirens' perimeter, disappearing from our lives forever. No matter the pain tearing apart my chest, I wished Molly's vision to be true again and for them to make it safely past and not to a watery grave. Then Owen and I would return to our island, if the waters allowed us to in the small boat. Numbness wanted to settle in, ease my pain and my mind. But Jasper sat a few feet away, and my heart clenched, shattering the peace. The sharp shards sliced at me, and tears rimmed my eyes.

Jasper sat behind his mom, his sad gaze focused on me.

Owen sat on the other side of Molly. His blond curls had dried in the wind, tousled on the breeze. Worry sharpened his face. His mom was only partway through a difficult journey.

Molly grimaced as another contraction started. She said they were still far apart. John's concern darkened his face and he grimaced helplessly at each one.

A flash of golden light pooled below the surface. At first it was a small point of light, like a star beneath the currents, but it expanded, rippling in the waves.

"What is that?" I hissed. My muscles tightened, ready to flee but with nowhere to go.

"Close your eyes," Owen said, smashing his shut. "Keep them shut, too."

"What? Why?" Jasper asked, standing to stare at Owen. His fists tightened at his side.

"It's the blue rock," Owen said. "If the song doesn't lure you, their beauty will. They are coming."

Jasper shot a glance my way. My face heated when I met his gaze. Something flickered behind his eyes.

"If you know what your heart wants, it won't matter," Molly said, rubbing her stomach.

John kissed her forehead, pulling her towards him.

Jasper opened his mouth but closed it. He shook his head and moved towards me. Picking his path through the shallow pools, he took careful steps. I edged away, scooting with each step he took, trying to be discrete.

"Rainey," Jasper said, noticing. His jaw ticked, and he looked away before turning back to me with mournful eyes. "Can we talk?"

"There's nothing to talk about," I muttered. I picked at the salt drying on my pants. The material stiffened against my leg.

He sighed, his entire body deflating. "Rainey, this isn't—"

I held up my hand. "It doesn't matter, Jasper. Talking will only hurt more. Your family will be safe and that's what is important."

"You are, too," he barked.

"I'll be fine," I said, the words acidic as the lie rolled off my tongue.

One day I would be, when the numbness had edged off the pain and the routine of life filled my time and rubbed away at the rawness. I'd fit back in my routine... but with Owen. My stomach curdled.

"Rainey..." he started. He took in an unsteady breath and looked towards the sky like he was asking for help. "Rainey, I know you love the island and your land..." He ran a hand through his dark hair, his mouth twitching as he warred with himself. "Rainey, what if you—"

"Look what we have here," a velvety voice slithered from the ocean, the words lyrical as they carried on the wind.

"This is why we should have stayed at the green rock until sunset," Molly said. Her jaw ticked. She resettled herself and stared at her hands.

"What's going on?" John asked. He wrapped his arms around Molly.

She smiled and patted his arm like a child. "That's sweet, honey, but you're at a deficit here."

Golden silky strands pooled on top of the water, swirling and dancing in the current, and then bowing down and up as a head breached the water. The most beautiful woman I'd seen stared back at me. Her skin was the color of fresh grass. Dark purple eyes tracked us above pert red lips.

"Is that a... a..." Jasper started.

"A Siren." I nodded. My eyes drew to her.

Jasper covered the distance between us, startling me when his hand traced down my arm until our fingers interlocked. His warm touch sent a shock through me. Without thought, I tightened my fingers around his.

"Jasper," I whispered, my mouth dry. We shouldn't do it, but I wanted to. His hand felt right in mine.

He tugged me back, pulling me farther up the blue rock with him. Closer to him.

I yanked my hand away, unable to bear to keep the connection knowing he was leaving. Searing pain jolted through my nerves.

The Siren smirked at him, sun glinting off her razor-sharp teeth. Her ruby-red lips curled into a smile.

"My sisters have been watching you." She cocked her head to the side as her gaze bounced between all of us. "You've been fun."

Heat burned my face, and my fingers furled. The Sirens had been playing with us.

Her smile grew watching my reaction.

"Owen, no," Molly hissed. She yanked on Owen's arm and pulled him back from the ocean where his fingers traced the water.

His head lulled. His blue eyes glowed as he gazed upon the Siren. At his mom's words, he flinched and blinked repeatedly. Then his eyes returned to normal.

Molly pulled him into a hug. He took in a shaky breath, his body trembling.

"What is going on with you?" I yelled at him. He winced and swung his head to me. "How are you a Ferrier and this affected by them?"

Owen shot me a dark look. "This hasn't happened before. I always stop at the green rock, focus on..." He averted his eyes but met mine again. His lips pressed into a thin line and he swallowed, regathering himself. "Focus on you, on the vision, on our destiny. Then when the sun sets, we move to the blue rock."

"Why isn't that working now?" John asked. "The sun is almost set. She's here, now, with him. Shouldn't it be easier?"

He had a point.

Molly gave John a sad smile. Her eyes drifted to me and Jasper.

"His heart no longer yearns for her," a new Siren cooed, emerging from the water followed by three more. Golden hair shimmered over her bronze skin. Her eyes glowed like topaz. She laughed, the melodic chimes a beacon to a broken heart. They sounded of hope and joy.

"Yes, it does," Owen snapped. "My heart still yearns for her!"

The shrillness in his voice echoed off the ocean.

They laughed, music on the sea.

"Leave my son alone." Molly pushed Owen behind her. She sat up straighter, pushing her shoulders back. Her blue eyes hardened.

"Hm," a red one in the back murmured. Her red-scaled body shimmered like rubies on the water. "Our daughter, Molly."

Molly's face slackened, her color draining.

"How do they know?" Jasper whispered. He stood only a few paces behind me.

"We know all our children, son Jasper," a blue one called, joining her sisters. Her light blue skin glittered like an opal.

"She," a silver Siren with black hair said, looking at me, "is Rainey, daughter of Marianna, daughter of Isla, daughter of Evangeline, daughter of—"

"Oh, stop boring us with your family history," the red one spat and flicked water that turned into diamonds at the silver Siren.

The silver Siren snarled, baring her teeth and lashing her long tail, the fins fluttering in the air before sending a cascade of water back.

"Sisters," the blue one sang. "Enough."

Molly cast a glance towards the horizon, the last rays of the sun edging out. "The moonless night is almost upon us," she said. "Bear with it for a few more minutes."

"Then let's not waste time," the silver one hissed. "Our Daughter wishes to leave us?" Her yellow eyes narrowed in on Molly. She slithered onto the rock near John and Molly, her body smoothly trailing over the weathered edges, leaving beads of silver water on the surface.

"What an ungrateful brat," the red one spat. Her hair pooled in a fiery glow around her in the water.

"What sacrifice do you have for us?" The blue one emerged from the water to join the silver Siren on the rocks. Her gold eyes flashed and shone as lights welcoming a ship home to dry land.

Owen squared up next to his mom, trying to block her from the Sirens.

Jasper stepped closer to his mom. His gaze locked onto Molly and John.

"I sent my gifts ahead of our travels," Molly stated.

"Yes, and now you are on our rock. Safe and sound. You wish to leave our island. One we built and protect. What sacrifice do you have to offer for our love that you shun? One worthy of our lost blood. One to show our land kin not to betray us."

"I have none." Molly wrapped her hands around her belly as a wave of contractions rippled through her stomach and she cried out.

I had nothing either. Everything we had except the rowboats went down in Owen's ship, but what would be worthy of their lost child?

"Me," Jasper yelled, sloshing water in a shallow pool as he moved towards his mom.

"No!" I screamed before I could stop myself.

The green Siren smiled at him. Her green-and-yellow hair flowed in streams behind her, and her yellow tail flicked out of the water, spraying us with glittering droplets.

Jasper dodged around Owen. He headed to the water to offer himself.

"He's a Washed Up," Molly shrilled. She lurched forward and grabbed Jasper by his t-shirt. John stood and helped pull Jasper from the edge.

"It's okay," Jasper murmured to Molly. He clasped her hands in his. "It's okay. You need to go."

"It is not okay," Molly shrilled. She turned her heated gaze to the Sirens. Their faces lit in amusement watching her. "He cannot stand in my place. He's a Washed Up."

The Sirens all turned their heads to him, synchronized either by their thoughts or shared intent, and then sneered as their gazes turned to me. My veins singed from the scrutiny.

"He's a Washed Up," I choked out. I swallowed, stepping away from the edge, hoping to draw them my way and from Jasper. But more splashed behind me, offering no reprieve. At least another dozen bobbed around the blue rock.

"No, he's not," the silver Siren challenged, slipping back into the water, moving to watch him. A wicked smile danced on her lips. "Why is he not enraptured with our beauty? Even our diluted children should be affected."

"He knows his heart's desire," the red Siren spat, her eyes boring into me. Pride glinted behind them.

A large grin split across the silver Siren's face as she glanced at Jasper and Owen. "A true Siren's daughter, snaring so many hearts that don't belong to her."

Jasper turned to stare at me, his brown eyes pleading. "I love you," he whimpered.

My breath caught in my throat. Had I been a land Siren to him? Spikes speared in my heart, refusing to believe the lie. Even if he wasn't my destiny, the one the Sirens had shown Molly, I still loved him, and only him.

He licked his lips and turned back to the Sirens. "Then a trade. Let the four of them leave safely and I'll stay with you. I will be the sacrifice. The lesson for the island."

"Jasper, no," I screamed. My heart rammed against my chest. Why were our Siren mothers being so cruel?

"Rainey," he murmured, my name like a prayer on his lips. "I love you."

I wanted to call out to him. Wanted to tell him I loved him. To stay. But what good would any of it do? The Sirens would get a show and still destroy my heart.

He looked around helplessly at the Sirens that had first joined us. Serrated teeth gleamed in faded light. More dots bobbed in the distance. More Sirens coming to taunt the prey. Jasper edged closer to the ocean, picking his way over the loose rocks. "Do you accept my trade?"

The Sirens bobbed in the waves. Their glittering eyes fixed on Jasper. The silver Siren turned to the red one. "Well, sister?"

"Molly's our blood," the red Siren said, a smirk lighting her face. "My blood."

"So... so am I, then," Jasper stammered.

"We know." The red Siren snarled. "I know my own blood."

"Jasper, honey, no," Molly said. Despite everything, Molly bolted to the edge where Jasper stood. One hand grasped her stomach and with the other she wrapped her fingers around his arm. "No, baby, you can't do this."

"Yes, he can," the red Siren encouraged. "He can offer himself. He is of our blood. A sacrifice in measure. We'll consider it."

"No," I said, my feet finding ground as I leapt over the ridge to the lower level. Rocks slid with me, biting at my skin.

Jasper swallowed and nodded at the Siren. He pulled Molly into a hug. She sniffled and a new wave of tears fell.

"Please, take Mom and go," Jasper said to John over Molly's shoulder and nodded towards the boat. He turned to Owen, a pained look on his face. "Owen, take—" His voice cracked and he swallowed.

He parted his trembling lips, took a long, ragged breath, and clenched his fists. "Take Rainey and go."

"Jasper," I yelled, my shrill scream carried off in the wind. Moving one row lower, I crept past two Sirens lurking in the waters below the surface.

He glanced back at me over his shoulder, his eyes red and bright.

I managed, "I love you, too." I sniffled and repeated, louder and stronger, "I love you."

He bounded over the rocks and was by my side in an instant. His arms wrapped around me. Warm and strong and right. Sobs rocked his body as he clung to me, repeating, "I love you, I love you, I love you..."

It would be the last time I held him. The last time I felt him. The last time loving someone would feel right.

"Mom," Owen said, his voice strained and cold. His face twisted in agony watching us.

Guilt should have coursed through me. I promised to partner with him. I'd honor my promise. But I'd also been clear I didn't love him. Maybe after years together, the guilt would come.

"You always saw Rainey as the mother of your grandchildren. We always said I was... I was the father. But was I the father in your visions?" Owen's words carried heavy on the wind.

Everything seemed to stop. My heart stilled. My breath stopped. Even the ocean seemed to go silent.

A Siren's laugh pierced the silence. A cruel, sharp burst.

I blinked, and the world moved again. Jasper's fingers pressed lightly into my back, pulling me closer to him.

My eyes tracked up to meet his. Despite his glossy eyes, he smiled at me. My heart warmed and pumped through my body. I returned the expression and wrapped my arms tightly around him.

Molly stilled, her eyes searching the rocks unseeing. Her fingers trembled as she pressed them to her temples. "Of course. You—" Molly let out a shriek. She shook her head. "I... I always thought it was you. You're my only son. I'd seen the vision for over a decade. Who else could it be?"

She stilled. Her eyes bulged and her hands fell to her stomach. Slowly, her gaze lifted to stare at Jasper.

"But I *saw* your future in Florida. I've *only* seen your future in Florida."

The Sirens cackled, their sounds like thunder cracking, deafening.

Did that mean...? My heart pumped as hope filled me. Was her vision wrong? Had I been right that Owen wasn't my future?

"Mom?" Owen asked again, his voice raw.

But did it matter? Promises were already made.

Molly shrieked, grabbing her head, falling to her knees. Blood trickled from her nose. John stumbled over the rocks to get to her.

"Mom," Owen and Jasper screamed. Owen knelt beside Molly.

"Do you enjoy our gifts to you?" The red Siren slithered closer to her.

Molly groaned, her head lolling to the side.

Owen's gaze turned to the Siren. He growled and leapt up.

John pulled Owen back before the Siren could touch him, but she lunged forward and instead grabbed onto Molly. John screamed but Owen returned the favor and held him back.

"Daughter," the Siren purred. She stroked a hand over Molly's head. Glimmering light trailed her hand, dissipating into the night. "See clearly now."

Molly gasped, her voice raspy and raw. "Jasper, I misunderstood my vision. I saw your life in Florida. Still the same handsome man, but older. It didn't occur to me it wasn't you. But you have... you have two life paths. The Jasper I carry now is the one I see in my visions. I am with him, as is your father. He has the future I see. You are the reason that this Jasper gets to be. You're the reason he'll grow to know I am his mother. But he will not be you. He'll grow with the same loving father, but not in grief.

"Jasper," she gasped, sucking in a breath, her eyes rolling back. "No, Jasper, no. I'm sorry. I was so wrong."

I wanted to scream, "Wrong about which vision?" But it seemed moot.

"It's okay," Jasper whispered. His grasp tightened on me for a moment. His body shook against mine. His heart raced. "I'll go with them so you can go freely. I am the sacrifice needed."

Thirty-Three

EVERYTHING WHIRLED AROUND ME. Jasper wouldn't survive the trip. Molly confirmed it. She'd been wrong about the vision. The Jasper she saw was the son she carried, not the man standing next me.

And he was offering himself as a sacrifice to save his mom.

Thoughts slammed in my brain. Words rolled on my tongue, but what could I do? Molly was going to make it. Owen and I would partner, and her vision come true, even if it wasn't the correct way. And Jasper would save them. By sacrificing himself to the Sirens.

My fingers dug into his arm, holding him to me as my mind raced for a way. A path. Something to protect him.

"We haven't agreed to that," the blue Siren scolded.

"Haven't *yet*," Jasper gritted out.

She smiled at his determination, but he just frowned back.

"He needs a lesson," she said. Her eyes shimmered and changed as she batted them at him.

He snorted at her. "I'm a son of your daughter, your son, Washed Up or not. I can stand in her place as a sacrifice. I am her blood. Your blood."

I stilled a second. He was. He wasn't a Washed Up of the outside world. He was a returned child of the Sirens. He was Molly's blood. He was the Sirens' blood.

The Sirens seemed to agree as their faces contorted into a sneer.

"I don't like this," the blue Siren spat. Her silver eyes turned to Owen. A wicked smile curled her plum-colored lips. "He's more fun."

The red Siren continued to pet Molly's hair, softly humming. Molly licked her lips, her eyes clouded over. "Jasper, you're an anomaly. You changed the past. You shouldn't have been able to cross the border. You shouldn't have washed up. You changed everything. You were meant to change everything."

"Was I in the visions before Jasper washed up?" Owen asked. His expression darkened as he stared across the vast ocean.

My heart stalled. Was he? But it did it matter now?

Molly rubbed her temples. "I don't know. I'm sorry, Owen. I don't know."

"But..." Owen sputtered, staring between them. His gaze tracked to me and something shifted behind his eyes. He blinked and his eyes rimmed with tears. "Your visions... you always said me and Rainey..."

"I know," Molly whispered. Tears streamed down her face. She grimaced again, her body trembling. "Owen, I don't think I saw the father. I just assumed. Owen, I'm so sorry. You were my only son. I didn't know. I was wrong."

Numbness oozed into my pores, slithered down my spine, and wrapped around my heart. The vision that had led so much of our past was incomplete.

Jasper rested his head against mine, taking ragged breaths.

But Jasper... Jasper was taking his mom back. I promised Owen I would partner with him.. But the real vision...

My mind spun, unable to grasp onto any thought too long.

Owen snorted. "It's been a lie. I followed a lie," he sputtered. His gaze bounced between Jasper and me. His eyes, burning with blue fire, met mine. "Rainey was right. I..."

Owen bellowed, his fists clawing at the air. His agony carried across the ocean on the wind. An angry breath heaved his frame, flaring his nostrils and rippling over his muscles.

The Sirens' laughter filled the air and Owen crumpled to the ground. Angry waves trembled through his body.

"We'll take him as a trade," the blue Siren sang, her arms reaching for Owen. The red Siren hissed excitedly at her sister and laid Molly on the rocks. The other Sirens, the silver, green, and countless others that prowled in the waters, stretched their arms towards him.

"NO!" I screamed.

Tears streamed down his face as he gasped for breath. He scrambled back from the edge. His wild blue eyes scanned around at the waiting Sirens.

"Do you come willingly?" the blue Siren slithered. Her silver eyes flashed like stars.

Owen gulped and looked around at all of us. John and Molly stood together. Jasper and I held each other. He swallowed, looking to the ground, alone.

"Owen," I screamed, but he waved me away.

Jasper and I scrambled to him.

"Leave me alone," he spat. He squared his shoulders and sucked in a breath, leveling the Sirens with his gaze. "You were right all along."

"Owen, you have love that is strong enough to protect you from the Sirens. You always came home," I said.

"Now he'll go to his real home, with us," the red Siren said. A large smile cut her face. She raised her arms out to him for an embrace. "He'll be a lesson for the island."

Owen's head tilted, his eyes glowing in golden splendor. His face stilled as he stood before the Sirens.

"Home," he said, his voice flat and echoed. He moved to the edge, the ocean's water lapping at his feet.

"No," I screamed, tugging him back. "No, Owen, no. You have so much more in your heart."

Without looking away from the Sirens, he shoved my hand aside.

"You've been a Ferrier since you could sail," I started. "You've always wondered what was beyond. I always wanted the island. You wanted more. You always came back to the island because of the vision. Because you believed it, but you believed it because you believed your mom. Your family is your connection. I've never been your connection. You've never had issues with the Sirens before because your heart lay back on the island with your family, and you knew it. It's why you fought so hard for your mom's vision to be right. Now your family is leaving to where you're not following, and your broken heart has no anchor anymore."

His step faltered and his head twitched to the side. His fingers curled against his side.

"Owen, you always thought your heart desire was to partner with me, but it wasn't. You've always wanted the adventure to explore and return home. Return to your family. When you leave on an expedition, is it me you see or the depths? Your goal has been to honor your mother. Following her visions. Your mom is going. What is your heart's want?"

"My heart's want?" he strained out. His blue eyes flinched, the golden light dulling.

"Owen," I said, taking his hands. He cringed from my touch but didn't pull away. "Owen, this is your chance. What is it that you want? Do you want me, or do you want adventure and to return to your family with tales?"

"He wants us," the Sirens roared, their words filling my thoughts and clouding out reason.

My mind screamed against the assault. White lights popped in my vision.

"He's ours, young daughter," they taunted.

A hundred glowing eyes bobbed in the water around me, each as a precious gem offering riches and treasures. Each offering a permanent home and grave beneath the waves.

"He's not!" I yelled back.

Jasper rested a hand on my waist, his warmth an anchor.

"Owen," I cried. "I will honor my promise. I gave my word to you. By our Siren mothers, I will honor it if you want to partner with me. Do you still want to?"

The wind skimmed my arm, chilling my heated flesh. On the wind hung our future, our promises, and hope.

"It is your choice," I whispered, my fingers squeezing his arm.

"No," he squeaked as Jasper took his other hand. His eyes flickered to him, dark and stormy. "No, I don't want you."

"What do you want?" Jasper asked.

The Sirens smiled at Owen, inching closer. Their hands rested on the rock, ready to claim him. More circled around us. Eager claws twitched for the fresh prey.

But they were only giving us the illusion of choice. They could have us all now. We only served as entertainment to them.

"Owen, what do you want?" I echoed Jasper's question.

"I want adventure," Owen said. "I want tales to tell. I want my family. I want more."

"It exists out there. More than an island you've traversed and know every foot of."

"He is ours," the Sirens sang, bobbing closer.

"We've accepted him as the sacrifice," the red Siren said. Embers sparked from the tips of her hair. "One of my daughters wants to leave. I'll take one of her children as payment. As the sacrifice and warning. He is ours."

"No, he's not," I growled.

"Daughter," the silver Siren warned. "We could take you all."

I stilled. I had angered the Sirens already and they had destroyed our Ferriers' boats. Now, I was fighting them on the rocks with their ocean surrounding me.

"Better," the silver Siren said, taking in my silence.

"You need a trade to take one of our children," the blue Siren said. "A worthy one. Not baubles and fleshy fruits."

Molly cleared her throat, drawing the attention of us and the Sirens. A determined expression hardened her face.

"You let Jasper go before," she said. "He's one of your children."

"But we knew he would return," the green one said. "We knew his destiny. No other children you bear will return. Their blood will be lost."

My mind reeled. An idea blossomed.

"Molly has two sons," I said, grasping at the fragments. "One will return with me, and one you plan to make an example for all those who want to leave. That an equal sacrifice is required to lose your blood. You said no other children of hers will be on the island."

Molly nodded, her gaze turning to the Sirens. "She's correct, and you just showed me I will die bearing any child on the island as an example to others."

The Sirens around the red one hissed at her, baring their sharpened teeth.

The red Siren cocked a haughty eyebrow and shrugged.

"Owen," I said, grabbing his shoulder.

He flinched but turned to look at me.

"You don't want me. You don't want the island," I said. "Right?"

Guilt twisted his face and he looked away. His body heaved with a breath.

"It's okay. The Siren mothers enjoyed watching it unfold for the decade. Their own private show. They knew it was misinterpreted."

His glossy eyes tracked back to me, hope brightening them.

"Owen, get your mom and John into the boat," I said.

"What?" His attention jumped to the Sirens.

"Get them ready," I said. Sucking in a breath, I added, "Get in the boat. You've sent Washed Up across the border before. Just this time, you're going with them. Owen, we aren't meant for each other. We both feel it. Your heart is out there. Your real future waits for you. Be safe. Find love. Be happy."

He smiled but his eyes were sad as he scanned my face one last time. He nodded. Looking between Jasper and me, he said, "Be safe. May the sea carry you home."

"Rainey?" Jasper asked. His brows dipped in confusion, and he ran a hand over his cheek.

"I love you, Jasper," I said, moving to stand next to him.

He took my hand, rubbing his thumb over my palm. "I love you, too."

Molly turned towards Jasper, her arms outstretched. She pulled him into a tight embrace before releasing him. "Jasper, you can't come with us."

Hope skittered over Jasper's face, but he said, "What's going on?"

"Jasper, I was wrong in my interpretation of the visions. The Sirens... the Sirens were right not to let me know the full future. I shouldn't have burdened my first son with knowledge he couldn't handle. But you are an anomaly. The Siren mothers have blessed me with clear visions. If you come with us, you'll enter John's timeline. With him..." She rubbed her hands over her belly. "...you'll cease to exist. You have to stay. Or exit on your own to go back to the time you left. But you love Rainey. You wanted to stay. You planned to stay with her. By the Sirens' blessing, you get to."

"We've done no such thing," the blue Siren spat. With a wicked smile, she added, "You're finally just understanding the gift we gave you. Finally embracing your Siren. We still need a sacrifice. Our children cannot freely leave."

Despite everything going on, Jasper leaned over and brushed his lips against mine. A large smile spread across his face.

Briefly, I returned it before turning to face the Sirens.

"You've said Molly won't bear you any more children on the island," I said, my eyes bouncing around the gathered Sirens. "Right?"

They snarled at me, and I took it as a sign they agreed.

The last of the sun was snuffed out. Night was upon us. Molly and her family needed to start. Urgency singed my nerves.

"I see two paths forward," I said, raising two fingers in the air. "One, you let the three of them pass safely through and Jasper and I go back home. Molly's visions will come true... and we'll have many children on the island." My face reddened as Jasper sucked in a breath and shot me a wild look.

Molly beamed at him and nodded.

Jasper's arm tightened around me. His heart raced.

The silver one laughed. "Daughter, I don't see how we benefit. That is not a trade or a sacrifice. We already know this future."

"The second option," I said, steeling my resolve and nerves, "is one of her sons is your sacrifice and lesson to the island while the other leaves the barrier. And then this rock becomes my grave and you receive no more children from Molly's line. They end with her."

The silver Siren stared at me a moment, her smirk growing and her eyes assessing me with satisfaction. "Rainey is truly our daughter."

Thirty-Four

"You must earn passage," the green one hissed. Her voice was shriller than a song, and her eyes glowed like emeralds as she launched from the water. Her long, serpent-scaled body tapered into a point. Citrine and peridot fins danced along her shimmering body.

Although I saw her coming, I didn't notice the two next to me leap from the water. The three together twisted and turned, a kaleidoscope of colors, their arms slithering around and pulling Jasper into the water with them.

His mouth opened, but no sound came out. His arms reached skywards. He disappeared beneath the inky surface with a splash, the dark waters consuming him.

Everything seemed to stop for a moment. The ocean's current, the wind, my heart. We were so close to our wants. I'd fought years against the vision. I wouldn't stand idle, even if it meant my death.

I dove into the waters, the icy chill racing up my spine and numbing my thoughts.

The angry waters, dark and turbulent, whipped around me. I gulped in air, my eyes and lungs straining for oxygen. Somehow, without light from the moon or the sun, the inky world came slowly into focus. The layered waters rippled with life and promise.

Glittering gems dotted the waters following the Sirens' descent. More Sirens had joined the three, racing Jasper to his grave. Their brilliance was the beacon allowing me to see in the void.

With each push of my legs, I slid farther into their lair. The world above blinked out. Only darkness loomed above. My mind and spirit warred. Below me was an illuminated paradise. Towering rocks twisted into an ocean palace, their long tendrils creating the towering blue rock. A natural formation was dwarfed by the mass below. Gems and baubles were draped over every surface. The treasures amassed reached beyond view likely to the ocean floor. Hundreds of Sirens gathered around the mammoth structure, each their own shining colorful promise of unlimited treasure of happiness. Each offering ecstasy and your heart's desires.

My lungs screamed the deeper I swam. Black dots darkened my view, dimming the treasures.

"Our daughter is weak," I heard in my mind. I whipped my head around, and my eyes bulged seeing more Sirens in the distant currents. Their eyes glowed in a rainbow of jewels, all promising false treasures. All mocking my weakness. "Prove you are our daughter. Prove you are worthy to carry on our lines."

Turning back towards Jasper, my eyes focused through the haze for a brief moment. Beyond the treasure, mixed in and glinting white, were bones, tossed about after a feast was finished. The water picked at whatever bits had remained, leaving them barren and polished.

That would be Jasper's fate if I didn't save him. Except he'd be displayed for the village to see.

It could be mine, too.

My heart thudded in my chest and pulsed life through my veins. I was alive. Life was still possible. I was their daughter. Born from their sea and blood. Their strength swam in the veins pumping through my body.

I was a Siren's daughter.

The water pulsed around me, cold and with warning. I may be a Siren's daughter, but I wasn't acting like one. Instead, fear drove me. Not the confidence and assurance they'd granted us.

I stilled my muscles, letting the fight drain from me. The ocean sounded around me. Songs of the whales drifted on the current. The calamity of it settled my heart. Beating as one. The rhythmic pulse of the ocean throbbed through my veins. Calming. Reassuring. Protective.

Jasper sank faster, his legs and arms dragged down now by half a dozen Sirens. Beads of his ruby blood floated to the surface. He struggled against their grasp, but it only encouraged their hunger and lust.

My heart screamed. The waters thrashed around me in response.

He was mine. I was his. If I couldn't rescue him, we'd share a watery grave at the bottom of the blue rock like so many before us. But we were Sirens' children. We were made of the sea. It ran through our veins and the Sirens' strength beat in our chests.

He'd Washed Up, back at his home. Through the Sirens' trickery, using Molly's visions and my stubborn pride, they led me to him. Now, they wanted me to earn him. A gift I originally shunned and was willing to cast back to them. One that broke and strengthened my heart. To prove I had the strength to bear the promised Sirens' children. Ones worthy of losing a strong daughter. Ones that bore their blood.

I was Rainey, daughter of Marianna, daughter of Isla, daughter of Evangeline, long-removed daughter of the Sirens. I was one of them. My foremothers would not take what was mine.

"Jasper," I screamed in my mind. The word, red hot, burned the pain away and pulsated through the currents of the water.

To my surprise, he turned to me, his eyes wide in the depths, visible from the glow of the Sirens.

Before thinking more on it, I bellowed, "Come to me!" My hands reached toward him.

As if strengthened by an army, or because I was one of them, as was he, he ripped his limbs from the Sirens. Long gashes ran along his arms, weeping blood into the ocean. Undeterred, his arms stretched towards me as his legs kicked behind him.

His body and lungs were weak from the lack of oxygen and slowed his progression. Determination strained his face and he fought a losing battle against the currents.

"Jasper," I called again, pushing against the muscle fatigue and the dizzying dots popping in my view to swim deeper.

His body pushed harder.

One Siren reached for his foot with her orange hand and black claws. A wicked smirk curved her lips and her eyes flashed with fire. I thought she meant to yank him back into their clutches. Claim him and me permanently. But she pushed his shoe, boosting him farther through the waters. The waves rippled around him in aid.

"Hurry, daughter," she sang in my mind.

My hands clawed at his arms, securing a grasp on him. Without hesitation, I pushed for the sky, pulling him with me, calling to the ocean for help. It answered. The strong waters hummed around me, encouraging me towards the darkness above. My lungs ached, but we breached the surface. Searing hot air burned my lungs, pushing life painfully through me. My body racked against the sensation, and I gulped again. Blinking, the dots faded. The inky night surrounding us, the splendor of the stars drenching us in ethereal light. The paralleled promise of the treasures below.

"Our daughter," echoed in my mind. "In blood and heart. You are safe for now."

In the distance, Owen had John and Molly in my old rowboat, slipping through the Sirens' protection. They all wore life jackets as he and John paddled their way across the calm water.

"Jasper! Rainey!" Molly called upon seeing us, her face shrouded in darkness. "I love you!"

"I love you, too," we both called back in unison, clinging to each other.

"Take care of each other. Love each other. I am so proud of you both," she said.

"Thank you," John called. "You gave us our future."

Jasper's hold tightened around me. Two futures had been provided tonight.

Owen called out with a wave, "May the seas carry you home!"

I called back, "And may they deliver you where you want to be!"

"Hurry, little daughter," the silver Siren called, bobbing in the distance, her hair glittering like black diamonds despite no moonlight.

My gaze jumped to her and the Sirens beyond. They'd cleared off the rock but circled around it, giving us a large diameter but watching us with their glowing eyes.

The warm night air whipped around us. Clean and salty, the promise of a happy future carried on it.

We scrambled up the rockface to Owen's emergency boat. The vessel was just a speck on the ocean. After pushing it into the water, I hopped in. I held my hand out to help Jasper in. He let go of the edge he had held to keep the boat anchored to the rock.

When he stepped in, the boat shook, lapping in a few splashes of chilly water. The motion matched my stomach. So much had happened. Loss. Gain. Sacrifice and love.

Not releasing my hand, Jasper pulled me to him, wrapping his arms around me. His heart thudded through his shirt, his heat a familiar comfort. My body melded against him. Relief warmed my flesh. He was with me and safe. A Sirens' blessing was granted.

"Rainey, I love you," he said into my hair. His arms tightened around me.

"I love you, too," I murmured against his chest.

He tilted his head against mine. He furrowed his brow, staring across the ocean as Owen and crew grew smaller. "Rainey, it's weird. I see two childhoods. I see two different lives. They both feel like mine."

"You changed your history. You changed Molly, John, and likely Owen's futures. You physically lived the one without your mom. Those memories are yours. The Jasper crossing with Molly is living the one you see your mom in."

"So, they're both my memories now?"

"I guess," I said, shrugging. "The Sirens gifted you with sight of both."

"What does this all mean?" he asked with a chuckle. "What happens now?"

"It means if you want to stay, you can," I said, steeling my voice. "If you want to go home, you can. Your future is your choice."

"Let's go home. To our home." He smiled against my temple before placing a kiss on it. "We can figure out everything there. Together."

Together.

A thought halted me.

"One question. With everything happening, why didn't you ask me to go with you?" I asked, pulling back to look him in the eyes.

"What?" he sputtered. "I tried, multiple times. You either cut me off or something catastrophic happened. I figured you wanted to stay on the island you loved and fought for. Or the Sirens were intervening. But wait... why didn't you ask to go with?"

"It was your journey. You had the chance to leave and not look back. If you wanted me to join you, I thought you'd ask. I don't know what your world holds or the troubles you'd take on out of guilt if I asked. Then the storms happened, and to get a Ferrier I had to promise Owen..."

Jasper pulled me tight against him. He shuddered as he took in a large breath. "We'll talk about that someday. All of it. We'll make sure there aren't any lingering doubts, fears of guilt, and why the hell you promised Owen what you did. Not today, though. I don't want to fight today. We can fight and make up after we get home, eat, and sleep."

I eased back to look him in the eyes again. Despite the weariness and fatigue clinging to his face, his eyes were bright with love and hope. He leaned over, brushing his lips against mine before deepening the kiss.

Unable to get enough, I wrapped my arms around him, pulling him to me. He was mine. And I was his.

A gust of icy water splashed us, ending the moment too soon. We startled back, his dark eyes hooded and hazy. My fingers curled around him.

"Daughter," the silver Siren warned. Her voice hinted at the earlier melody.

I blinked and turned to face her and her sisters hovering close by.

"Just because you're our daughter and could see the error with the vision others couldn't does not mean it protects you," the silver Siren said. "We granted you him underwater for your cleverness and will, and our continued amusement. Our song starts in just a few hours when the sun rises, and our treaty will end. My daughter, go home while you can."

Thirty-Five

We rowed through the night, watching the stars dim and fade in the brilliant streaks of the sun, the familiar constellations my compass home. Yellows, oranges, and pinks warmed the sky, bringing with them the start of the first day of the new moon cycle. The start of Jasper's second cycle on the island and the first one with our new future.

My island had always been a part of me, the ground that had birthed me of the sea. Seeing it on the horizon filled my heart and soul with hope. The Siren mothers had granted us passage. They'd taken our sacrifices.

The sun was high, bathing the island in its heat when we washed up. Owen's boat kept us from falling into the ocean, but our clothes were waterlogged and hung in heavy clumps on us. My tongue and mouth were parched from the long journey back home. My skin, protected from the sun by my shirt and pants, itched and ached from the continual paddling and salty coating.

But we were home.

A dozen or so Scavengers littered the beach on their second round of scrounging for the large items that had made it ashore. They watched with wary eyes as we dragged our boat behind us. Had I been there with them as planned, I would already be home with my treasures. Jasper would be lost in the sea if Molly's vision was correct. And they always were. Even if they were misinterpreted.

Waving, I called to them, my voice harsh and scratching.

They waved back when they realized who we were, but quickly returned to finding treasures and ignoring us since we were not Washed Up. Not their treasures.

Jasper linked his fingers with mine. His skin was hot and chapped from the sun and ocean. I wrapped my arms around his neck, pulling him close. His heart thudded in his chest. Despite the salty dryness, I pulled his head down and met his lips.

His hands moved to cup my face, tangling in my wind-blown hair. The kiss deepened. We held each other for a few minutes before a long and taunting whistle cut our reprieve.

"Let's go home," he said, a smile lighting his face.

The short hike to our house felt like forever, the sand clumping to us and dragging at our tread. We dragged the boat home, each with one side, and let the back skim on the sandy path.

A twirl of smoke tumbled from my house's chimney. My heart swelled seeing it. I didn't know what would happen: if the house was mine or not. What the council would decide with Owen gone, too. But that would be figured out. Even if we had to move back to my grandparents' house, we were together and would figure out another plan.

I shoved the door open. Yeasty bread and bacon wafted in the air, mixing with the smell of the ocean. My stomach rumbled.

Mom startled back, brandishing her spoon like a weapon. Relief washed over her face upon seeing me. She tossed her spoon and ran to pull me into her embrace, tears streaming down her face.

"You made it," she sniffed. She rocked me back and forth, clutching me to her. "I was so concerned."

"We did," I said. Emotion welled in my throat. "The Sirens granted us passage."

"But Jasper," she said, a smile spreading across her face as she pulled him into the embrace. "You came back?"

"Yes, ma'am." He smiled and returned the hug.

"I'm so glad you did. I should be sorry for not believing you loved my daughter. But I'm not sorry. She's mine to protect. I am very happy you love her, though, and have shown it. We will work on our trust of each other."

He nodded.

"But Owen..." she gasped, releasing Jasper. "You promised..."

"Owen went with Molly and John," I said. A relieved breath escaped me. Regardless of the pain, I would have honored my promise. "He's not coming back."

"Huh," my mom said, rocking back on her heels. Relief filled her face. She clicked her tongue against her teeth. "Then what Molly did makes sense."

"What did she do?" I asked, my stomach tightening.

"She left written notices that you are to receive the plot of land you bought and keep the animals, regardless of if you partnered with her son or not. She also left the rest of her property to her son, but she didn't specifically say Owen. She said, 'My returning son." Mom raised an eyebrow at Jasper. "Somehow she thought you might come back."

"So that means..." I asked, hope blooming in my chest.

"It's yours, Rainey. The land is yours." Mom beamed. She clapped her hands together. "You did it!"

I pumped my fist in the air, the victory unleashing something inside of me.

"So, I guess that means you have a house," Mom said, shooting Jasper a cheeky grin. "No more earning your keep here. John left quite a bit of rope behind to trade. You have land, a house, and some items to initiate trades with. Your parents provided a generous future for you."

"She's right," I said. "You have your own home now to do with what you want."

Jasper slung an arm around my shoulder, tugging me to him. "I kind of like it here," he said.

"Would be kind of crowded, though," Mom said, rubbing her chin. Her eyes skipped to the bedrooms.

"What if you take up my mom's—Molly's house?" Jasper said to my mom. "That way you and Bartholomew can have alone time."

Mom's face reddened and her jaw dropped.

I chuckled. "Mom, there are no secrets."

She pursed her lips, but a smile still tugged on them.

My eyes took in the counters heaping with ingredients. Dozens of breads cooled on the table. "Mom, why do you have so many ingredients? You can't sell that many breads before they spoil."

She cast me a dubious look. "In case you forgot, tomorrow we were supposed to be honoring an ill-advised partnering."

My mouth tightened into a thin line, and my eyes narrowed. Pointing a finger at her, I said, "Ill-advised? You pushed! You yelled. You tried to create dates for us. For a decade, you wanted me to partner with him up until I told you I was!"

"Well, things change," Mom said, patting my arm and shooting Jasper a look. "Sometimes we can't see past our own pain. Fortunately, the Sirens helped you."

That they had. At this cycle's festival, I would need to send them a generous offering—and not just baubles or fruit.

"Oh," Mom said, her face brightening. "Willis wants you to stop by to talk about the land."

"I will, tomorrow." I rubbed my face as the days and nights finally caught up to me, tugging at my eyes and stiffening my muscles. "It can wait."

She cocked an eyebrow at me, a smirk flittered on her face. "Already sloughing off your duties? You get the land and think you can stop working?"

"Ha, ha," I said.

"He doesn't expect you today, Rainey," Mom said. "See him before the festival." Her face darkened, and she put her hands on her hips. Her eyes flicked to the window and then to me. "What are you planning to do today? It better not be Scavenging. You need rest."

"The first thing I'm going to do today is strip out of these wet clothes, clean up, then, if he's willing, I'm going to lay with Jasper, and then I'm going to sleep for a solid day. Maybe two. Then I'll talk to Willis about the land and figure out everything about the animals."

"That sounds like a good plan," Jasper said, rubbing my shoulder and resting his head against mine.

Mom smiled. "Leave your clothes in the hall. I'll wash them. The pot on the hook is ready if you want to clean up."

"Thanks, Mom." I wrapped my arms around her again. She patted my arm and hugged me back.

"I love you," she murmured into my hair. "I'm so glad you're home."

"Me, too," I said.

"One thing." Mom gave me a watery smile as she pulled something out of a drawer. Jasper's chain dangled from her fingers. "I promised him I would hold on to it for you, since it is *yours*."

Had things turned out differently... No. The Sirens had blessed us, and I wouldn't consider the alternative.

Before heading down the hall, Jasper helped me clasp the chain back on.

Jasper lugged the heavy pot to our room. I smiled, realizing it was ours. My clothes littered the hallway in soggy messes as I trudged to our room. Nothing but the chain remained on my body. Jasper tossed his clothes out with mine. They skidded on the floor, leaving a wet trail.

I closed the door. Leaning against it, I let out a breath. He stood before me, naked and watching me. Finally, we were together. No visions in the way. No more ocean. I threw my arms around his neck, burying my face into his chest. "I love you."

"I love you, too," he said, returning the embrace.

With gentle hands, we cleaned each other up, the slow, meticulous process teasingly delightful.

Tossing my rag into the water, I met Jasper's gaze and said, "I want to spend the night laying with you."

He cracked a smile, pulling me towards him.

And that's what we did.

RAINEY SNUGGLED AGAINST ME, her rhythmic breathing soft and gentle. Her dark brown hair spilled across her pillow and onto mine. Her nose scrunched and she groaned as a thump hit her stomach. She was pregnant with our fifth child. If the island elders were correct, and they always were, she'd birth our second son in a few days.

Most islanders had one to three children. Mom's vision said the Sirens would bless Rainey with many children, and they had. Each one was a reminder that they had let a child past them, knowing they would have many more in return.

Rainey and I had been together for fifteen years, give or take a moon cycle. I was no longer considered a transient Washed Up. I was a returned child of the Sirens, as far as the village was concerned. Whatever the truth, I had two sets of memories. Ones I lived that had shaped me, and ones given to me like dreams. Gifts of the Sirens. The memories were of the version of me that made it back with Molly... er, Mom. He grew up with both parents, and if I see it correctly, we have two younger siblings.

Rainey mumbled something. I ran my hand over her hair, tucking a lock behind her ear.

Her leg draped over me, and her nose pressed into my neck. I shifted to adjust myself. Her calloused fingers curled on my bare torso. I stopped myself from kissing her awake. She needed rest.

Two nights ago was a moonless night, and like all the ones before it, we were out Scavenging washed-up treasures even when I thought she should rest. Our two eldest had joined us for the first time to help. Each found a jeweled treasure, gifts from their Siren foremothers. Rainey and I hauled in an old seventies' refrigerator. With the metal mostly good, it was a huge—if not odd—score.

A clatter rang from the bedrooms across the house. A smile tugged on my lips. Rainey and I had built a room onto the house after our first two children were born. A large bedroom with our own ensuite—well, a wash basin and piping to remove our waste. The kids now had our old rooms and restroom.

A door squeaked before it slammed shut. Molly was up. She'd wake her siblings up for reinforcements before ambushing us.

Our eldest, Molly, named after my mom, was born several years after we washed up together. The Sirens had granted us safe passage and, as promised, Rainey birthed multiple children. Our daughter Molly had visions like my mom, but Rainey said they were stronger and more precise. Her favorites were always of her Uncle Owen, who her brother was named after. When she was old enough, she'd follow in his footsteps and explore the world beyond the Sirens.

Molly said one day she'd set sail and cross the barrier. She'd find her uncle, have great adventures, and return him to the island with us. I didn't know how it would happen, but I believed her.

Marianna, our second daughter who went by Anna, took after her other grandmother with her gift of baking. Our youngest, Luna, who turned three last moon cycle, had her uncle's adventurous heart, but her love was the island and knowing everything about it. She was always trying to venture into the forests and ocean.

After each of their births, a villager would bring us a note from my mom. She'd seen our children and, in the letters, promised of their amazing futures. Even without knowing at the time that I was the father, she knew them all. A part of me believed Mom knew Owen wasn't the father but didn't understand how that was possible. She was a kind woman by the stories the island told, from the echo of memories

I saw, and the few short days I spent with her. She offered Rainey a path that didn't include partnering with her son, and what she thought her visions showed. I didn't know why the Sirens let me pass through, be it I was their child or because it entertained them, but I found myself thankful each day that I was returned to the island. Thankful for the journey I had growing up despite the pain.

My daughter Molly told us we'd have seven children, and I looked forward to the days leading up to and beyond with them.

She also told us of days when Rainey and I would cross the barrier and visit my parents, but we would return. And one day, my parents would come back to the island to stay. I didn't know how any of it would be possible, but I believed her.

"Sh, they're sleeping," Molly's voice called out, her harsh whisper as loud as thunder.

I rubbed a hand down Rainey's back, massaging in circles. She groaned and pressed into my side, sending heat and need through me. Her arms wrapped around my torso as she buried her face into my side. Her hot breath sent tingles across my skin. Soft kisses traced my muscles as she woke up.

Maybe if we were quiet, we could have private time before joining the kids. My body thrummed at the prospect.

I kissed the top of her head and whispered, "I love you."

"I love you, too," she said, not lifting her face. In between kisses, she murmured, "The kids are up."

"Mhm," I agreed, trailing kisses down her cheek and then jaw. She shifted so her lips met mine.

"We can pretend to be asleep," she said against my mouth. Her hand slid down to grab me.

I groaned and ran my fingers through her hair and down her back.

She had read my mind.

Someone knocked and then opened the front door.

A familiar whisper, warm and loving, filled the room.

"Grandma!" Owen cheered. His siblings joined in the excited chant.

Marianna whispered a response, trying to spare us a few minutes. She murmured promises of the beach and collecting fruit for breakfast.

Bartholomew's deep voice murmured something about spoiling the kids. He laughed when Marianna scolded him. Serena, their only child together, and Rainey's half-sister, preferred the farm life to village life. She often stayed out there any chance she got, while Marianna split her time between the island sides. With Rainey due soon, Marianna had come back to help out. As she was doing then.

"Do we just let her take them?" Rainey asked, watching our bedroom door but not getting up.

"She'll bring them back," I assured her, running my hands down Rainey's side and resting them on our growing child.

Rainey smiled, looping her leg over my hips so she straddled me.

"Then we have some time to practice for number six."

Afterword

A year after the pandemic started, I was stuck. I was querying books, entering mentorship contests, and spinning my wheels. I wrote three books in a year, but I couldn't focus anymore. Instead of revising or drafting, I took to seed writing— something I had my students do when I taught fourth grade. Each day I'd sit down and just start typing. During this time, I was also watching a show about unknown mysteries around the world. One episode included many debunked tales of the Bermuda Triangle and some still unexplained. What happened if an island existed inside this mysterious swatch of ocean?

Washed Up was not meant to be a Fantasy Romance. When I sat down to write it, I was in a bitter mood and ready to write my first story with an unhappy ending. I had PLANNED that Jasper would go back, willingly and without remorse. He obviously had other plans. I didn't realize it was my first Romance book until I started revisions and went to map the pacing that I knew was off for a fantasy. It was during that time I also realized I wrote New Adult and not Young Adult. I also realized When Shadows Bleed was NA/A. It was a big time for self-discovery.

Perhaps the original version, with a Washed Up who freely goes back without a second glance or care about a possible Sea Widow, waits to be written. Siren Island has many stories to tell. Some may be more Fantasy than Romance, but this is Jasper and Rainey's story, the one they fought to be told while I tried to tell another. They won not only their ending, but how the story was told.

Acknowledgments

The idea came when we were still in the "safer at home" part of the pandemic. The vaccine was just becoming available. Bethany listened to me vent about... everything. Then this idea started to form, and she encouraged me to keep writing while I waited. I ended up putting it to the side after a week with five query rejections for a different project.

When I started my annual August Fast Draft, Madelyn kept asking to read it. I had never allowed a reader to read while I drafted. My first drafts are called Draft 0 for a reason. Still, I sent it to her to break out of the fear. The first draft came in just below 60K. It obviously grew. Madelyn championed the book when I was ready to just let it live on a shelf— I mean, who would want to read about an island out of time with Sirens? I had no idea how to query it. With Madelyn's encouragement (yelling and nagging), I sent queries out. Despite agent interest and requests, I realized shortly after sending queries out that I was meant for Indie publishing.

As with every story, they would not exist without the foundation my mom and sister built. My mom's endless support of whatever hobby I was interested in and the countless hours my sister and I spent building worlds and characters will forever inspire me. Miss you, sis. Also, my partner's complete and odd support is crucial. He can't really explain what I am doing (he gets the writing story part, just not why I would want to or how much work goes into drafting, revising, and everything else) but he'll nod and say, "go for it!" As always, he'll self-lessly play video games for hours upon hours so I can write in peace. My four-legged kiddos also played a big part in it. My pup helped me resolve a major plot hole. She insisted she needed to go out (she didn't) but while I paced and grumbled for being pulled away from the part I was stuck on, the resolution came to me. She can sense when I'm frustrated and seems to always know how to help. My cat made sure to sit on my ankles so I couldn't move and would keep writing.

I also wanted to thank you, my readers. Your engagement and interest in my work both baffles and excites me. Thank you for going along for the ride!

About the Author

Amelia J. Rivers is a bitter cinnamon roll who lives in the Midwest with her husband, a legion of demonic cats, and a pampered dog. Data diver by day, writer by night. She also spends as much time with her nieces as she can. She is an emerging author of paranormal fantasies. This is Amelia's second book.

https://www.ameliarivers.com/
    https://linktr.ee/ameliarivers

Also by Amelia J. Rivers

When Shadows Bleed